"A DARKNESS IS COMING." The girl's voice spoke doom. "There are shadows on Easter Hill. That is why it is happening. That is why Fluter is dying."

Jessica cried out these words though Maud realized with a spasm of fear that the child was no longer talking to her, but staring wide-eyed through the open window, talking to something out beyond the treetops of the open park. No longer delicate and polite, Jessica seemed charged with a visible power...

THE SEEING

A novel of psychic horror, a vision of undying evil...

THE
SEEING

**William P. McGivern
and
Maureen McGivern**

TOWER BOOKS NEW YORK CITY

A TOWER BOOK

Published by

Tower Publications, Inc.
Two Park Avenue
New York, NY 10016

Chapter One —————————————————

It was just after two o'clock in the morning when the little girl sat upright in bed, eyes wide and staring, and began to scream.

Ellie Groves, the child's baby-sitter, scrambled from the big chair where she had been dozing in front of the flickering, sign-off pattern of the television set.

As the sharp screams from the bedroom subsided into a series of desperate sobs, Ellie stumbled across the shadowed living room, calling the child's name in a voice that revealed her own fear and confusion.

Jessica Mallory, four years and five months old, sat erect on her narrow bed in a tangle of sheets and blankets, an expression of tension and dread on her pale face. A thin, whimpering sound came from her throat and tears filled her staring eyes.

"Jessica! Jessica, what is it?" Ellie said, sitting

beside the child and pulling her into her arms.

"They are *dead*! They're both dead! My mommy and daddy are dead!"

It was then that Ellie Groves noticed the time, ten minutes past two, the illuminated hands of the bedside clock glowing through the darkness of the room.

In the light spilling from the hallway, Ellie could see Jessica's clothes on a chair, laid out for the morning—red corduroy overalls, a white T-shirt, socks and a small pair of red tennis shoes. She was comforted by the friendly look of the room—red-and-white checked curtains with fringed tie-backs, a small brass replica of the Liberty Bell, a Snoopy poster thumb-tacked to the wall and curling at the edges, and a row of picture books on the window sill.

Ellie Groves felt her own heartbeat slowing down. With a sigh of relief, she said, "Jessica, it's all right. You just had a bad dream. I'll do what my mother used to do when I was little. She'd blow in one ear and that bad old dream would go out the other, and I wouldn't even remember it when I woke up the next morning."

"It wasn't a dream—I saw it happen," Jessica said. She had begun crying again, hopelessly and helplessly, and Ellie could feel the child's heart pounding like a tiny hammer against her body.

"Mommy was so frightened that she woke me up," Jessica said, the words muffled by her sobs. "Hold me, please hold me, please!"

"Of course, I will, Jessica. Of course I will!" Ellie said, feeling the shudders coursing in spasms through the little girl's body. "It was just a bad dream—"

6

"No, they're *dead*. My mommy was calling me. My mommy was afraid," she said, her hysteria rising to an ominous intensity.

Ellie Groves was seventeen years old, a junior in high school, and intelligent enough to know she was facing a situation she couldn't handle alone. The Mallorys had lived in this suburb of Philadelphia for only a few months and had left no phone numbers for her to call in case of an emergency. No friends, no doctor, no minister. Just a note on their flight plans. Because they needed a baby-sitter for this one weekend, the couple had called the student placement bureau at Ellie Groves' high school. Daniel Mallory had business in Detroit, and he and his wife Monica had flown there yesterday and were returning early this morning.

The baby-sitter thought of phoning her own father, but she guessed he would say something such as, "Just hang on, honey. I'll be right there." It would take him at least a half hour to reach the Mallory apartment, and Ellie knew she shouldn't wait that long because Jessica was fighting her now, struggling and shaking her small head frantically, dangerously close to shock or convulsions.

Gathering the child in her arms, Ellie hurried to the phone in the front room and asked the operator to connect her with the police. Within seconds, she was speaking to a dispatcher and within minutes after that a squad car with its dome-light flashing pulled into the dark, quiet street and parked near the three-story apartment building.

The two men seemed to fill the small living room with their cheerful, reassuring bulk—a gray-haired sergeant with a gentle voice and a young patrolman

7

who made notes and who, it seemed to Ellie, would prefer to face an armed mugger in a dark alley than this strangely distraught child.

Sergeant Kelly talked as seriously to Jessica Mallory as he might have to a deputy chief at City Hall.

"Just let me ask you a question or two, if I may," he said. "First of all, if I've got it right, you went to bed about the usual time. Around nine o'clock?"

The child's agitation had subsided. Now she lay across Ellie's lap, limp and slack in her arms. Her face seemed empty of emotion. Even her enormous, dark eyes, polished with tears, were absent and withdrawn, as if she were staring at something other than the familiar objects around her—commonplace furnishings given a lightness and gaiety by a scattering of tasseled pillows, brightly framed travel posters and a window of green, hanging plants.

After hesitating, the little girl nodded.

The sergeant then asked her what time she'd had her supper, whether or not she'd taken a doll to bed with her and other gentle, amusing questions, which Ellie realized had no special significance but were the big sergeant's way of gaining the child's confidence.

"All right, I'll tell you what I'm going to do," the sergeant said. He glanced at Ellie. "Now what time was it you said Jessie woke up?"

"It was just a little after two o'clock, about ten minutes after," she said.

"Then the best thing we can do is call the airport and make sure this little lady's mother and father are having a nice, quiet trip."

He asked if the Mallorys had left their flight plans, and when Ellie Groves gave him the information—

Central Airlines, Flight 61, leaving Detroit at twelve-fifteen—the sergeant went to the phone and asked the operator for Central's information counter at the Philadelphia airport.

"I don't blame you for feeling frightened," he said, after dialing the number. "I've had some pretty bad dreams myself and I can tell you I was plenty scared."

Then he spoke into the phone, a harder edge to his voice. "This is Sergeant Kelly, Philadelphia police, Sixteenth District. Who'm I talking to?"

"Jim Taylor, Central Airlines, Sergeant. What can I do for you?"

"Well, Mr. Taylor, this is no emergency, you understand. But I'd appreciate it if you could give me the present status and whereabouts of your Flight 61 out of Detroit."

"I'll check on that, sir. Just hold on a minute." After a brief delay, the airlines clerk came back on the line. "That flight is on schedule, Sergeant. Should be landing in Philadelphia in about one hour and fifteen minutes. The aircraft has just been handed over to the radar control facilities at Pittsburgh."

"So everything's going smooth and easy," the sergeant said and smiled at Jessica Mallory, who watched him intently with tear-bright eyes.

"Everything is routine, Sergeant," the clerk said. "Weather and visibility excellent, there's no turbulence, no electrical storms in the area. You got someone coming in on Flight 61, Sergeant?"

"Well, not exactly. I was checking for a friend . . ."

"Tell your friend that everyone on 61 will be in Philadelphia right on schedule."

"Thank you, Mr. Taylor." Sergeant Kelly replaced the phone and smiled again at Jessica. "You heard that, I guess. Your mother and father are just fine, so's everybody else on that plane. Now you'd better hop back to bed so you'll be..."

The sergeant's smile suddenly felt stiff on his lips. There was something in the girl's eyes, a concentration that made his casual words of reassurance sound like pointless echoes in the now silent room. "—You'll see, dearie," he went on, making a clumsy gesture with his hands. "You'll be having breakfast with them in the morning."

"Mallory, that's an Irish name, isn't it?" Patrolman Ross asked Sergeant Kelly. The two policemen were walking along the quiet street toward their black and white squad car at the curb about a half block from the Mallory apartment.

"Sure it is," the Sergeant said. "A good old Irish name which probably accounts for that kid's imagination." He shook his head. "But those weren't imaginary tears."

As the two men reached the car, they saw the light above the dashboard phone blinking. The sergeant lifted the receiver, pulled it through the open window on the driver's side and said, "Sergeant Kelly, Car 219."

"Sergeant, I've got a call for you on a civilian loop," a police dispatcher said, "I'll patch it through." The connection was made and the voice said, "We've located Sergeant Kelly. Go ahead, Central..."

"Sergeant, this is Jim Taylor at the Philadelphia airport."

Sergeant Kelly frowned at the phone, startled by the tension in the clerk's voice. "Yes, what is it, Mr.—"

"Goddamn it, Sergeant, did you have some information that we didn't? Did you know something about that—"

"Now hold on," Sergeant Kelly said. "Just settle down. What are you trying to tell me?" He heard people shouting in the background, the sound almost drowning out Taylor's voice. "Speak up, man! Speak up!"

"It's down, I tell you. Almost before I hung up talking to you, we got the flash. Flight 61 disappeared from the Pittsburgh radar screen..."

"What does that mean, Taylor?"

"Flight 61 from Detroit to Philadelphia crashed about a minute later, ten miles north of Harrisburg." Taylor's voice suddenly rose sharply. "It broke up and burned, with everybody dead. While we were talking about it..."

Sergeant Kelly felt the sudden, uneven stroke of his heart. "Jesus, Mary and Joseph!" he said softly, and looked up through the autumn-bare trees to the lighted windows of the Mallory apartment.

Chapter Two ——————————————

When it was subsequently confirmed that Daniel and Monica Mallory had died in the crash of Philadelphia-bound Flight 61—along with crew members and sixty-seven other passengers including a senior United States congressman and a team of Japanese trade experts—the judicial and welfare systems of Pennsylvania moved into action, speedily and humanely, to provide for the Mallorys' only child, four-year-old Jessica.

She was taken that same morning by a juvenile court departmental car to a living facility, where she was given breakfast and a brief medical examination. Then she was mildly sedated and put to bed in a ward with a dozen other youngsters waiting to be processed and assigned to foster homes throughout the city.

A social worker by the name of Elizabeth Scobey

was assigned to prepare a case history on Jessica Mallory and her parents. Miss Scobey was a practical, no-nonsense person in her early forties, with short, shiny brown hair, a stocky figure that was nonetheless firm and quick and active. As a rule she wore pants suits of durable double-knit in subdued colors, and her bustling, nervous energy complimented her customary expression, which was one of amiable severity. Miss Scobey's eyes were by far her best feature, warm and dark and lively, glinting on occasion with humor. She had never married. The one young man who had shown attention to her some years ago (he had been a clerk in the city amusement tax office) was drafted in the early days of the Vietnam War and married a Southern girl he'd met during his basic training in Georgia.

Perhaps because of this lack of a family outlet for her warm-hearted emotions (her black cat, Morticia, could only absorb a fraction of it), Miss Scobey had a limitless reservoir of love and sympathy for the orphans and the neglected children assigned to her custodial files.

Elizabeth Scobey worked in an office in the center of the city. From her desk she looked out on Philadelphia's ornate and gingerbread City Hall with the figure of Benjamin Franklin perched on top. Past that gray and intricately structured edifice, she could see—on good days—the green expanse of Fairmount Park, and on superb days, with the wind coming off the river like sparkling wine, the black drives twisting through the park all the way to the great white and columned art museum.

On this crisp, late fall day, Miss Scobey sat at her

desk studying the information she had obtained by a routine court order on Jessica Mallory and her parents. The couple had had a joint checking account at the Penn Central Bank, with a current balance of four hundred and sixty-seven dollars. In the Mallory apartment there were modest wardrobes of clothing, as well as toilet articles, toys, and children's books, and a neat stack of unpaid bills which Miss Scobey found in a kitchen drawer—the usual dry cleaning, market and drugstore bills, and last month's phone bill for fifty-odd dollars.

Miss Scobey had been impressed and touched by the bright travel posters. It seemed such a brave attempt to provide a sense of color and space in the modest apartment.

In the child's room, a plank of unpainted wood had been placed across two filing cabinets to form a desk. On this makeshift desk were sheets of ruled notepaper covered with what she assumed to be the late Daniel Mallory's handwriting, some sort of scientific work apparently, symbols and equations which meant nothing to Miss Scobey.

In one of the filing cabinets were two framed diplomas. Daniel Mallory had earned a degree in physics from the University of Pennsylvania, and his wife, Monica, née Griffith, a bachelor's in classics studies from Bryn Mawr. Daniel had been twenty-eight at the time of his death, and Monica, twenty-six.

In the same drawer she found Jessica Mallory's birth certificate. Clipped to it was a handwritten promissory note, dated five years earlier. It was an IOU made out to Monica Griffith in the amount of two thousand dollars and signed in a bold, flourishing script: Boniface.

The IOU was not notarized, so Boniface, whoever she or he might be, Miss Scobey reasoned, was someone Monica Griffith must have known and trusted—possibly a relative.

Miss Scobey tapped her pencil against the top of her desk, a rhythmic gesture of frustration. The puzzling thing about the case of Jessica Mallory was that there had been no response so far from friends or next of kin. Usually the exact opposite was true. A tragedy of this sort (and, of course, the crash had been covered by the newspapers and networks) usually lent a spurious but therapeutic celebrity status to children orphaned so cruelly and suddenly. In most cases the phone calls with offers of succor and support would start immediately. A grandparent in the Midwest. An aunt and uncle in Toledo. A cousin in the armed services. Bonds of blood were stronger than steel, Miss Scobey believed, and they were strongest in just such emergencies.

But not in the case, it would seem, of little Jessica. Two weeks had passed since the death of her parents, and she was now living with a foster family—fine, solid people named the Farrs. Yet in that two weeks, no one had called to inquire about Jessica. No one on the face of the earth seemed to care what might have happened to the little girl. And this not only puzzled Miss Scobey; it angered her. Because somebody *should* care.

What was fueling Miss Scobey's impatience and exasperation in this particular case was her conviction that Jessica Mallory wasn't alone in the world.

On one of Miss Scobey's visits to the Farr foster home, Jessica had indicated as much. Standing at the windows of her small, pretty bedroom, she had pointed out into the shadowy street. "I am waiting for him," she had said quite clearly, but Miss Scobey's practiced, tactful questions couldn't elicit any more than this single, unexpected statement. "I am waiting for him..."

Miss Scobey, however, was not about to give up. Pouring herself a fresh cup of coffee from the office Silex, she placed a note pad and a sharpened pencil on her desk and picked up the telephone to try to find some conduit to the child's past.

First she called the churches in the neighborhood where the Mallorys had lived—St. Andrew's Catholic, St. Mark's Lutheran, and the Second Presbyterian. She drew only blanks. Next she got out the Philadelphia telephone directory and began dialing the Mallorys and Griffiths listed in the city. Scobey made a good start that day, but the job was so seemingly endless that she asked her supervisor for assistance. With the help of two efficient young clerks assigned to her, she completed the check the following afternoon. Yet the result was the same— nothing but blanks.

Each set-back served only to strengthen Miss Scobey's resolve. She cabbed across the city to Thirtieth and Market Streets where, on producing credentials, she was allowed access to the morgue of the *Philadelphia Evening Bulletin*.

Settled comfortably in a reading room under bright overhead lights, she began an examination of the obituaries that had been collected for the past ten years under the name Mallory. It gave her a pang to see the most recent entry, Daniel and Monica, survived by daughter Jessica.

Nothing in the Mallory file was of any help, and it wasn't until, hours later, deep in the Griffith file, that she stumbled on her first clue. Her eyes were so tired by then that some of the words had begun to blur together and, as a result, she'd almost flipped past the significant information on a clipping dated five years earlier.

"Mrs. Mary Griffith, widow of Eric Griffith, Sr., survived by son, Eric B. Griffith, and daughter, Monica Griffith Mallory..."

Miss Scobey felt a pleasurable thrill of elation. This was the link. Mrs. Mary Griffith was Jessica's deceased maternal grandmother. And Eric B. Griffith was the child's uncle.

Removing her glasses, Miss Scobey massaged her eyes with her fingertips, her weariness more than counter-balanced by the gratitude she felt at having found the little orphan's next of kin. As she collected the obits to return them to the files, she saw through the window that the darkness was laced with the season's first thin streaks of snow. Miss Scobey then decided that she would have a Stouffer's TV dinner tonight to celebrate her victory. A special on beef stroganoff with au gratin potatoes and new peas had caught her eye in the frozen-food section earlier that day. She'd treat herself to that with a glass of red wine and pick up a quarter pound of chicken livers for Morticia. Then she'd get on the track of Eric B. Griffith bright and early in the morning.

By the time she'd stopped for lunch the following day, some of her enthusiasm had diminished. She could find no Eric B. Griffith listed in the phone books for Philadelphia or its suburbs—Germantown, Darby, Cynwyd, St. David's, Bryn Mawr, and Chestnut Hill. After an avocado and alfalfa-sprout sandwich and a cup of tea, Miss Scobey continued her dogged pursuit at the public library, casting her nets wide and covering New Jersey from Camden to the seashore, south through Media and Chadds Ford to Delaware. With her tired and reddened eyes, she probed the agate-type directory listings in Atlantic City and communities south of it. And from there scoured the phone books of Doylestown, Coatesville, Newcastle, Marcus Hook, and Wilmington.

Once again, Miss Scobey's overworked eyes nearly betrayed her. In the township of London-grove, Pennsylvania, located in Chester County thirty miles southwest of Philadelphia, she found what she had been looking for—the name of Eric B. Griffith, as clear as daylight. She realized she had missed it the first time she had turned the page and only the sheerest good luck—an omen, you might say—had prompted her to turn back and recheck the names.

Tightening her scarf against the cold evening winds that would be coming off the river, Miss Scobey left the library and started home with the pleasant conviction that she had at last achieved a breakthrough in the Jessica Mallory case.

The following morning she dispatched a letter on official stationery to Mr. Eric B. Griffith, R.D. #1, Black Velvet Lane, Londongrove, PA 19130, advising him of Jessica's present address and circumstances, and requesting a meeting with him to discuss certain arrangements and considerations in regard to his niece's future.

When that letter failed to elicit a reply, Miss Scobey—one week later—sent off a second letter by registered mail to the same address. Somewhat to her surprise, a receipt for this letter was returned promptly with a carelessly scrawled signature requiring a bit of guesswork on her part to identify it not as "Eric Griffith" but as "Maudie Griffith."

Miss Scobey surmised that the couple had been out of town and had missed her first letter. However, since another week went by with no further response from either Eric or Maud Griffith, Miss Scobey was forced to conclude that they had no intention of answering her letters.

Attempts to contact the Griffiths by telephone were equally fruitless. On two occasions the receiver was definitely lifted, but no one replied to her queries. Her "hellos" fell into a windy silence. On both occasions the connection was broken abruptly. On her third attempt, a man answered but mumbled his replies in a chuckling, deep-South drawl which she was almost certain he put on to deceive her.

The line hummed and grunted with responses such as "They'se not at this place no-how . . . I thank you-all got da wrong numbah."

Simmering with exasperation, Scobey put down the receiver, more determined than ever to get to the bottom of this nonsense. Tomorrow was her day off and Elizabeth Scobey had a gratifying notion about how she would spend her free time.

By nine the next morning her blue Volkswagen was pointed south on the Industrial Highway, traveling past stands of frost-blackened trees and snow-patched fields enroute to the tiny village of Londongrove.

Chapter Three —————————————————

Once she was beyond the iron and stone growth of the city, the countryside was lovely—low, rolling meadows, rugged Quaker meeting houses, church steeples white against the gray skies, and horses and big-horned Santa Gertrudis cattle standing like woolly cut-outs on distant hills. This was horse country—pony clubs, point-to-point races, horse shows, and fox hunting with well-schooled hunters and hounds coursing over a challenging terrain of stone hedges and split-rail fences.

The estate homes in the country dated back to the Revolutionary War, with double chimneys, immaculately tuck-pointed fieldstone walls, kennel runs, and schooling rings.

Eric B. Griffith's name was on a mailbox in front of a two-story red brick rowhouse, which stood, inside a white picket fence, at the intersection of an unpaved country road and Black Velvet Lane.

Aware that she was being watched from the upper window of the house, Miss Scobey went up a rough flagstone walk and rapped loudly with a brass knocker shaped like a grinning fox-head. The door was opened by a tall man whom Miss Scobey judged to be in his early or middle thirties.

"Yes? May I help you?" the man said.

"Are you Mr. Eric B. Griffith?"

"Now look, if you're selling something—"

"My name is Elizabeth Scobey. I'm a Social Service worker assigned to juvenile court in Philadelphia. May I come in, Mr. Griffith?"

"Yes, I believe we did receive some correspondence from you, Miss Scobey," Eric Griffith said. "Actually, my wife Maud takes care of the mail. I find it a bloody bore. Also, we travel a great deal, Miss—Scobey, was it?"

As she nodded, Griffith flexed his hands in front of him and went on talking, a tension in his voice that struck Miss Scobey as being at variance with his casual smile.

"My wife and I are in the stock business, you see. Not bonds and shares but horse-flesh, which requires that we visit tracks, attend the yearling sales, send reports back to our clients, and so forth. Since we've been on the move, we didn't get to your letters until just a few days ago."

They sat in the living room of the Griffiths' small home, Miss Scobey on a settee covered with stained rose damask, her hat and gloves beside her. Griffith had not asked her to remove her coat.

The case worker was curious about Eric Griffith—about his nervousness, his quick smiles,

21

his seemingly careless but, in fact, erratic gestures.

He stood by the fireplace, an elbow resting on the mantlepiece in a practiced manner, fingering a black briar pipe he had taken from his tweed jacket. Under the jacket he wore a yellow vest. The collar of his tattersall shirt was spread by the bulky knot of a red wool-knit tie. He was tall and strongly built with large powerful hands, which he kept twisting in front of him in what seemed to Miss Scobey an oddly defensive gesture, considering his muscular bulk and his easy, patronizing manner. He seemed to have taken out the pipe to control his restless hands. His head was narrow, with high cheekbones reddened by weather. The eyes were blue, pale and arresting, but he was losing his fine, blond hair. A widow's peak was pronounced and sharp, defined by expanses of pink scalp on either side of it. He was not wearing riding boots or even stout walking shoes, she noticed, but laced brown street shoes that were wrong, she thought, with the bulky tweed coat and yellow vest.

Miss Scobey also noticed that she had lost Eric Griffith's full attention. He continued to smile at her, but every now and then his eyes went past her to a row of bottles on a table in the corner of the room.

"I called your home several times, Mr. Griffith. The first two times I was cut off. The third time I talked to someone at this number, but I'm afraid I didn't understand him. And he certainly didn't understand me."

Griffith smiled and said, "That was probably Jimmy. He cleans up after parties here, puts a good shine on boots, but I'm afraid he's not at his best with twentieth-century gadgets like the telephone. However, for what he does, he's a good old boy."

Griffith put his pipe on the mantle, went to the table that served as a bar and poured himself a splash of whiskey in a squat glass decorated with daisies.

"Would you like a touch of something? I think there's sherry . . ."

"No, thank you. Nothing at all."

"Perhaps we'd better get down to the point." Mr. Griffith was still smiling, and nothing in his manner or tone indicated a transition in subject. "I didn't get in touch with you, Miss Scobey, because there was no point in it. I was shocked by my sister's death, but my wife and I have nothing to offer the child, nothing at all. We've never seen Jessica and she probably doesn't even know who we are. So I thought it best to just leave it that way."

Although her professional and personal opinions were not important here, a surge of loyalty to Jessica Mallory compelled Miss Scobey to say, "I think that's unfortunate, Mr. Griffith. Jessica is a most affectionate and intelligent little girl."

"That's quite irrelevant," Griffith said. "The fact of the matter is, if my sister and Daniel Mallory were so keen to bring a child into this world, then they should have made provisions to take care of it."

Question, Miss Scobey thought: How did he know they *hadn't*?

"I advised them to make sure they could handle things before they—" Griffith shook his head and took a sip of whiskey. "Well, that's beside the point, too. What is important, Miss Scobey, is that Maud and I refuse to be saddled with responsibilities not of our choosing. Is that clear enough for you?"

"Yes, of course, Mr. Griffith." Opening her

handbag, Miss Scobey took out a leather-bound notebook and unscrewed the top of an old-fashioned fountain pen. Griffith watched warily as she dated and initialed a page of her notebook.

"Mr. Griffith, juvenile court has no authority to suggest who may be responsible for Jessica Mallory's welfare. The court's only function is to find a suitable home for children such as Jessica, where they will have a chance to grow up in an atmosphere that is loving and stable and permanent."

Griffith raised his eyebrows skeptically and said, "Well, if that's true, Miss Scobey, why did you get in touch with me in the first place?"

"Because there *is* a way you can help, Mr. Griffith."

"Oh? What's that?"

"Well, simply by telling us about your own family background, your sister's education, for instance, medical history, where you grew up, your hobbies, just general historical background that will help us to establish and evaluate a profile of Jessica."

Griffith, she suspected, was making an effort to control his relief. "Well, along those lines, I'd be glad to help."

He smoothed his fine, carefully combed hair, the pressure of his hands sharpening for an instant the widow's peak that furled like a blond flag above his forehead. "I'll ask Mrs. Griffith to join us," he said.

As he went to the stairs to call up, Miss Scobey decided he was like a child released from school on a fine spring day. The sullenness was gone from his lips, the defensive anger from his gestures. And there was a buoyant expression on his face as he repeated

24

his wife's name saying, "Maud? Maudie, would you care to join us?"

At the same instant, Miss Scobey heard the click of high heels on the uncarpeted stairs that led down to the small entrance hall. Griffith poured himself another whiskey and raised the glass to the tall, blond woman who joined them, her eyes narrowing in a near-sighted inspection of Miss Scobey.

"Darling, this nice lady is helping to find a suitable home for Jessica. Miss Scobey, my wife—Mrs. Griffith."

"How nice of her." Maud Griffith sat gracefully on a spool-backed chair beside the few glowing coals in the fireplace. "Would you bring me something to drink, Eric? And wouldn't Mrs. Scopey like something?"

"It's Miss *Scobey*, Mrs. Griffith. And thank you, no."

"Probably all for the best, not drinking on duty. Might drop some of the little dearies on the wrong doorstep," Maud Griffith said.

"We don't deliver them like newspapers, Mrs. Griffith. We're very careful that—"

"Thank you, Eric." Maud Griffith accepted a drink from her husband and ignored Miss Scobey's statement.

A fine pair, Miss Scobey thought. Maud Griffith, in her early thirties probably, but dressed a good bit younger than that in a tight red turtleneck sweater and swirling black skirt that revealed her slim but muscular legs. Her hair was blond, her cheeks round and shiny and her lips full but tight over a row of fine, white teeth. Her blue eyes were quite lovely— clear, healthy whites dramatizing the darker

25

pupils—but there was nothing innocent about them. They were so watchful and unemotional that they looked like shiny globes of colored glass.

And Eric Griffith. For all the carefully tucked-in stomach and the shoulders held back like a cadet *and* the fastidiously arranged hair, the country tweeds and plummy weskit, Griffith's knees gave him away, Miss Scobey decided, indulging herself in an uncharacteristic but nonetheless gratifying prejudice. They weren't the knees of a young gentleman or horseman. They were an unsteady base for his tall, large frame; essential joints unstrengthened by exercise, walking or hard work; the knees—in fact—of a spectator striving always to wear the colors of a participant, a man more accustomed to the bleachers than the arena.

Miss Scobey raised her pen as a cue, and cleared her throat.

Eric Griffith seemed to savor the role he was playing, pacing slowly in front of the fireplace, pausing occasionally to deliberate over his choice of expression. He spoke with practiced skill, the words and sentences flowing as easily as if he were reading from a script. But while some of his comments were droll and caustically amusing, Miss Scobey had the impression that a corrosive anger may have been simmering just below the surface of his statements.

The facts that emerged from his rambling and discursive account became more and more rambling as he made a third trip to the bar.

His sister Monica, he explained, was ten years younger than he. They had been raised in a small town on the eastern shore of Maryland. After high school, Eric had attended the University of Virginia.

26

He dropped out after two years because, as he put it, "I couldn't stand the boredom of classrooms, professors drilling facts into us."

Miss Scobey noticed an animation in Griffith's voice and features when he digressed from linear biographical details and veered to a discussion of theatre classes he'd taken at the university and his work with local drama clubs. He had played Marchbanks in *The Doctor's Dilemma* and Professor Higgins in *Pygmalion*, and read the weather reports on the campus radio station.

Yes, Miss Scobey thought, appraising his obvious but rueful pleasure at these reminiscences. He was an actor all right, using practiced dramatic pauses, and his hands and body to compliment them. It was all a performance, except for the anger, and that emotion seemed like a ground swell supporting everything else, powerful currents independent of external circumstances.

"Actually, a Broadway director—his name was Ira Washburn, you may have heard of him—he also worked with Guthrie in Minneapolis—he was kind enough to say that what I lacked in dedication I might make up for with the odd trick or two, or, who knows, with a bit of natural talent."

Maud Griffith yawned lightly, then frowned as if an unpleasant thought had occurred to her. She began to massage her knee with the tips of her fingers.

"I think I'm in a draft, Eric."

"A fat lot Washburn knew—" Griffith went to the bar and refreshed his drink. Then he stared at his wife, and it seemed to Miss Scobey he was returning with some reluctance to present pressures and irritations. "Well, it's always something, isn't it, luv?"

With an edge to her voice, his wife said, "I haven't felt well all morning."

"Oh, good God!" Eric said. Obviously exasperated, he stared about the room, focused on a small knit afghan on the sofa, scooped it up and dropped it without ceremony across his wife's slender legs. "I trust that will do until we can helicopter in a team of specialists from Johns Hopkins."

The narrative continued. Griffith and his sister, Monica, hadn't been close. After marrying Maud Mercer Saxe, Griffith had moved to Chester County while his sister was in her last year at Bryn Mawr.

"Saxe was, *is* the name of my first husband," Maud said with a small smile. "Don't you think Miss Scobey should know all about that, dear?"

"No, I don't think that's necessary," Griffith said with a curious intensity.

"But shouldn't an adoption agency want all those gossipy details?"

Without glancing up from her notebook, Miss Scobey said, "Please go on, Mr. Griffith."

"Of course, Mallory knew a good thing when he saw it. My sister had an adequate job, took care of everything, finances, the house, the child, which left Mallory, the boy genius, free to invent God-knows-what-kind-of mouse-trap to bring the world to his door. Monica came into a few thousand dollars on her twenty-first birthday and that went down the drain, too. Mallory was one of your wild Irish dreamers, head in the clouds, hitching his fortune to any star or crystal ball that came down the pike."

Maud tucked the afghan about her knees and

said, "So naturally, they left nothing for little Jessica."

Miss Scobey made a question mark in her notebook. How had Maud Griffith known *that*?

"The least they could have done is take out flight insurance," Griffith said, and to that comment Miss Scobey added another question mark.

Something occurred to Miss Scobey then—the unpaid loan Monica Griffith had made to someone around her twenty-first birthday.

Miss Scobey had a shrewd idea what particular drain that money had gone down. "It's not important, but I'm curious, Mr. Griffith. What does your middle initial stand for?"

"Boniface. B for Boniface. I was christened Eric Boniface Griffith."

"It was his father's notion," Maud said with a little laugh. "The original Boniface was the first of the big spenders."

Miss Scobey closed her notebook. "Thank you, Mr. Griffith. I won't bother you any further."

"Tell me, Miss Scobey. Why were you interested in my middle initial?"

"I was just curious," Miss Scobey said, rising and turning toward the door.

"I don't believe you," Eric Griffith said, and his anger was closer to the surface now, raw and ugly in his eyes. "I know why you're here. You can't fool me with your talk of Jessica's welfare." He mimicked Miss Scobey's words in a hard, unpleasant voice. "'We just want something loving and stable and permanent—'"

"That happens to be the truth, Mr. Griffith."

"You're snooping around here for money," Eric

pointed a long, bony finger at Miss Scobey. "Trying to put the squeeze on good old Boniface. Sure, I borrowed two thousand dollars from my sister but only to cut them in on a Daily Double at Belmont Park that would have made us all *tens* of thousands."

"Mr. Griffith, believe me. The juvenile court isn't interested in these details."

"I did everything I could to help them. She was my sister, practically my baby sister." There was a sudden glint of tears in his eyes, something lost and forlorn in the sag of his shoulders. Turning, he braced himself with a hand against the mantle, a gesture so mannered that Miss Scobey couldn't guess whether the tears and emotions were genuine. "I taught her to dance when she went to her first cotillion . . . she wore little white gloves. But I won't be pressured this way, I won't be made responsible for things that don't concern me!"

Maud Griffith followed Miss Scobey out the front door and down the flagstone walk to her car.

When Miss Scobey was behind the wheel, Maud Griffith said, "Let's make sure this doesn't happen again." Her hands held the car door open and her bright eyes stared coldly down into Miss Scobey's. "If I wanted a child, I'd make one of my own. Just remember that. So don't you ever try again to unload Jessica Mallory on this doorstep. Find another warm, stable home for the little dear."

Miss Scobey hardened her jaw and looked at Maud Griffith with sharp disapproval. "That will be my pleasure, Mrs. Griffith."

"Good," Maud said and slammed the door shut.

Miss Scobey put her car in gear and drove with

unaccustomed speed down the narrow dirt road that would take her out to the Philadelphia Pike. She was thinking with angry anticipation of Monday morning when she would have the satisfaction of typing out her notes and appraisal of these strange creatures who lived on Black Velvet Lane.

Maud Griffith stood watching the Volkswagen with its "*I Found Jesus!*" sticker centered on the rear bumper below the license plate. When the car disappeared at the first intersection, she turned and walked briskly up the path to the house.

Her husband stood smiling in the open door looking to where the small blue car had turned out of sight behind a screen of bare poplar trees.

Chapter Four —————————————————————

Jessica Mallory collected her belongings from the bedroom in Mrs. Farr's home and began to pack them neatly in a red vinyl suitcase. Sweaters and socks and nightgowns, a pair of patent leather shoes with straps, a Raggedy Ann from her bed, a gray flannel coat with a black felt collar—she carried these to the table where the suitcase rested and stacked them beside it, wondering how she could fit them all into one small piece of luggage. Perhaps *he* could carry the doll and the box with the tea set.

Jessica was humming as she went back and forth from suitcase to closet and chest of drawers, content and secure because the colors she had learned to trust were comforting now—a gentle blue suffused with yellows that spread warmly in the area located directly behind her smooth forehead and bright eyes.

The colors had long been companions to the little

girl, many of them bright and cheering, some that made her somber and thoughtful, while others frightened her—the brilliantly radiant ones with edges like flashing diamonds, searing illuminations that warned her of coming dangers—the colors she had seen the night of the crash that took her parents' lives.

The packing finished, she went to the window and pulled back the curtain, looking up and down the street, watching. The Farrs lived in an old section of Philadelphia, a suburb called Jenkintown, an area of red brick houses with white wooden porches and sidewalks lined with dogwood trees, whose branches arched so close to second-floor windows that young Jessica often watched for minutes at a time while the birds hopped within arm-reach from twig to twig and pecked at black, wintered bark.

The child still thought sometimes of her father and mother, but in a fond, almost dream-like fashion. They were like pictures in her story-books, familiar faces she could now recognize and study for as long as she wanted to without feeling any hurt at all.

She could remember the white coconut cakes her mother had baked and one of her father's dress-up ties, the one with red hearts. She remembered being quiet and patient in the afternoon when her mother was at work and her father was at his big desk in the corner of the bedroom. These were the times when she played writing games at the windowsill, using the graph paper and big felt-tipped pens he gave her, drawing moons and suns and faraway stars she had just begun to know.

He had never minded if she'd interrupted him

with questions. In fact, she couldn't remember that he had ever been cross with her, even on that dreadful afternoon that she had begun to cry, sad and helpless, as faint patterns had begun to form in her colors.

Standing at the window now in Mrs. Farr's home, she thought back to that time (another winter when she had been smaller) when her mother came home with snowflakes on her coat collar, a shine of cold winds in her hair. They had played together that afternoon a favorite game called "Guess what I saw today."

"You saw ladies," Jessica might say, vague pictures of her mother's experiences forming in her mind. "You saw taxis, you saw a kitten, children and a little red wagon with a wheel off."

But she had brought a terrible stillness to her mother's face that day when she said, "You saw the old man hit by the big car and the policeman running. You saw all that!"

Just then Mrs. Farr stopped in the open doorway of Jessica's room and looked with a mild frown at the open suitcase on Jessica's bedside table.

"Now what's all this?" she said.

"I thought I'd get ready," Jessica said.

As a foster parent, Mrs. Farr was accustomed to the frequently moody and confused behavior of lonely, disoriented children, and so she nodded and said matter-of-factly, "Well, that makes sense, I guess, Jessica. In the meantime, I just took gingerbread out of the oven. Would you like a piece and a glass of milk in the kitchen with me?"

"Could I have them up here, Mrs. Farr?"

"All right."

Later, Jessica placed the tray on the table beside her suitcase, closed the bedroom door and lifted tea things from their grooved box—tiny cups and saucers and spoons which she set out in a service for two, carefully breaking the gingerbread into halves, placing the sections neatly on the gilt-flecked saucers. Then the girl went to the window again to look down into the street where the thin sunlight slanted through the trees to brighten the old sidewalks.

That same afternoon, Stanley Holcomb turned into Rittenhouse Square, a park in downtown Philadelphia, checking his watch as he walked past the elegant townhouses with their white marble steps and brass doorknockers. Holcomb, a tall and leanly built man in his thirties, with a mustache and rimless glasses, wore a conservative business suit and dark topcoat and carried a briefcase which he shifted to his left hand to push through the revolving door into the lobby of the Barclay Hotel.

Holcomb took an elevator to the fifth floor and let himself into a three-room suite with windows facing the trees and park pathways of Rittenhouse Square. Hanging his topcoat in a closet off the drawing room, Holcomb removed several bulky files from his briefcase and tapped on the oaken doors of his employer's study, waiting to open them until Andrew Dalworth's muffled voice told him to come in.

Dalworth, seated at a desk near windows, was wearing flannel slacks and a white shirt with an open collar. Without looking up, he said, "Well, what did they tell you over at Keystone, Stanley?"

"The new position is—and this is from Norton—they don't feel they can include their reps in Tokyo on the present terms."

"Well, they're not paid for their feelings, Stanley. They're paid for yes or no answers."

"What it comes down to, sir, Norton wants more time . . ."

"I don't want any more ifs and ands. Give Norton an extension we can live with, say—at the close of business, Tokyo time, Friday."

At fifty-nine, Andrew Dalworth was an impressive figure, over six feet in height, with the firm and still-powerful body of an athlete. Flecks of red glinted in his graying hair and his face was so tanned from sailing and bill-fishing that his eyes seemed almost unnaturally blue under the thick wings of his dark brows. His nose was jutting and authoritative, its bent conformation stemming from a fight he had won in a Golden Gloves tournament against a light-heavyweight brawler almost two generations ago.

Dalworth turned and stared out the windows of his suite, absently watching the city's pigeons and starlings rocking along the sidewalks or skimming through the thinning crowns of dark trees. Something was bothering him, he realized, distorting the normally routine order of his thoughts, but he couldn't for the life of him determine what it was. Frowning at the neat files of paper on his desk, he saw that he had covered a half page of a legal tablet with sketches of small airplanes.

Then he glanced up at Stanley Holcomb, realizing with some embarrassment that his aide had asked him a question.

"I'm sorry, Stanley. What's that again?"

"I have the specifications on that property in Ireland, sir. It's a fine old mansion, thirty rooms or more, called Easter Hill. With it comes about six thousand acres of good hunting in Connemara, and, of course, solid barns, stables, kennel runs, and so forth. A promontory with splendid views is also part of the estate. I have aerial photographs here and a breakdown of the price with local taxes computed in. Perhaps you'd like to glance through them now, sir." Holcomb checked his wristwatch. "We've got almost half an hour before the meeting with DuPont."

Andrew Dalworth stood and paced restlessly in front of the windows, staring out at the park with its dramatic backdrop of tall buildings and glittering skeins of traffic. After a moment or so, he turned and said to Holcomb, "Tell me something, Stanley. What was the name of that couple who came to see us in Detroit last month?"

Holcomb drummed his fingers on the back of a chair and then shrugged and said, "I'll have to check, sir . . ."

"Wait a minute. Wasn't it *Mallory*?"

"That's it, sir. Mr. and Mrs. Daniel Mallory. The wife's name was Monica, I believe."

She had waited for her husband in his outer office at the Detroit plant, Dalworth remembered, flipping through a magazine for the scheduled ten-minute interview which had stretched out to almost an hour. Dalworth had been introduced to Monica Mallory at the end of this session. He had liked that couple, admired their handsome buoyant manner, the husband's intelligent, scientific imagination and his wife's warm and understanding support.

Young Mallory's plans, which involved a new concept of solar physics, had not been ready for laboratory research. Brilliant as they were, the plans still required experimentation and finalizing at the drafting board, Dalworth had decided, but he agreed to meet with the young scientist in six months for a progress report on his work. . . .

He had proposed a grant or subsidy but to his surprise (and silent gratification), Daniel Mallory had refused it. The young couple was quite willing to continue on their own for the next half year of research. And Dalworth, although he suspected the Mallorys might be on financially thin ice (they had a young child, after all), had reluctantly allowed them their way in the matter. In fact, their independence and idealism had struck a surprisingly pleasant note with Dalworth, reminding him as it did of his own early enthusiasm, the fierce pride in performance which he had shared with his young bride, Anna. They, like the Mallorys, it was apparent, had only an academic compassion for handouts, advance payments, and the self-indulgence of credit cards, preferring in actuality to put their full energies into their work and then let the world judge its worth. And yet, and yet, Dalworth thought, drumming his fingers nervously, he wished he'd been allowed to make some payments to the Mallorys, if only for the child. . . .

That was what was bothering him so deeply, marring his concentration, Dalworth realized, his memories of those vibrant people starting home so confidently on that fatal Flight 61 to this very town of Philadelphia and their little daughter. He recalled Monica Mallory saying something about the child—that she liked seashells, was it?—and that she was with a sitter and they would see her in the morning. . . .

"About the DuPont meeting, sir, I suggest that we—"

"I'd like you to postpone that meeting, Stanley. Tell them that something came up and we'll get back to them. Assure them we're still interested."

Holcomb nodded without expression and made a notation in his small leather engagement book. "I'll take care of that, Mr. Dalworth."

Dalworth resumed pacing, rubbing a forefinger over the jutting bone in his nose, remembering with a faint smile the name of the fighter who had done it to him—Mace Torrio—and the sudden humiliation, worse than the pain, of landing flat on his green satin trunks, of staring at Anna, rigid in her ringside seat, eyes wide and startled, hardly knowing whether to laugh or burst into tears. He needed Anna now, he had always needed her, and the five years since her death had been a desolate stretch of time which he had tried to conquer with the only therapy he trusted, a furiously escalated work program that had pushed his business interests into dozens of new markets halfway around the world.

"Stanley, I'd like you to find out where that Mallory child is right now. If it's at all possible, I'd like to see and talk with her."

"Yes, sir. When would you want me to set up that meeting?"

Dalworth watched a squirrel stowing a walnut in a small burl of a sycamore tree. "Let's make it as soon as possible, Stanley. This afternoon, if you can."

"I'll get right on it, sir."

Chapter Five —————————————————

Judge Emory Williams' clerk, Adam Greene, a portly, middle-aged black man with gray curls circling his bald head, picked up the ringing phone.

"Courtroom J–11. Judge Williams." Court was in recess until the following morning, and the empty benches and faded brown-wood jury box gleamed softly in the thin afternoon light. "Yes, sir. But she's in a meeting now in Judge Williams' chambers. I can take a message and—"

Adam Greene heard a door opening and glanced past the judge's bench to the chambers. Miss Scobey waved a goodbye to the judge and strode in her energetic fashion down the center aisle toward Adam Greene's desk.

He smiled at her and held out the phone. "Call for you, Miss Elizabeth."

"Thank you, Adam." Placing her bulging briefcase on the desk, she took the phone and said, "Yes, this is Miss Scobey."

After listening for a moment, she frowned and said, "Well, I don't see any reason why not. But I'll have to check with the foster home first. They usually have a schedule, you know. Nap time, play in the park, that sort of thing... Where can I reach you?"

Miss Scobey wrote down the telephone number of the Barclay Hotel on a notepad that Adam Green pushed toward her. Nodding her thanks, she said into the phone, "All right, I'll call you back, Mr. Holcomb."

Later that afternoon, closer to dusk than daylight, Mrs. Farr answered the ring of her doorbell. A tall man in a tweed topcoat stood on the porch. The faint light drifting down through the trees touched the reddish glints in his graying hair.

"Mrs. Farr? My name is Dalworth, Andrew Dalworth."

"Yes, yes. Miss Scobey called."

"It's very good of you to let me come by on such short notice."

At the curb in front of her home, Mrs. Farr saw a long black limousine with a uniformed chauffeur standing beside it. In the back of the car she saw the profile of another man, a younger man, with a mustache and rimless glasses.

"Come right in," Mrs. Farr said, opening the door wider and wiping her hands on her apron. "Just make yourself comfortable and I'll go get Jessica."

Dalworth sat down on a straight-backed chair, unbuttoned his topcoat and placed his hat on his knee. The room was warm and confortable with shining wooden floorboards bordering the edges of a rose-patterned carpet. White china pots of Boston ferns stood on the wide windowsills.

A light step sounded on the stairs. Dalworth turned and saw a small child looking around the bannister at him. For a second or so, neither of them spoke. Then the little girl came slowly into the room and said unexpectedly, "Do you have any dogs where you live?"

"No, I'm afraid not."

"Don't you like dogs?"

"Oh, yes. I'm very fond of dogs. I *do* have some, in fact, Collies and Shepherds on a farm in Kentucky. My wife loved dogs but since she—" Dalworth cleared his throat, wondering why he felt so oddly nervous with this grave child. "By the way, my name is Dalworth. Andrew Dalworth," he said.

"Do you have any horses?" Jessica asked him.

"Yes, there are a few hunters still on the horse farm and I'm developing some racing stock in California."

"Your wife is dead, isn't she?"

Dalworth nodded slowly, again struck with the confusing feeling that the conversation had somehow got out of his control. He was baffled with himself, uncomfortable with this strange helplessness, but he had enough humor to smile at the situation—a man at home with heads of state and captains of industry, shy in the presence of a four-year-old child.

Then he asked. "Do you have friends your own age to play with here?"

She came closer to him and said, "There's a boy in

the corner house. His name is Thomas and he has a pet frog."

"Well, that's nice. What does he feed his frog?"

Jessica shook her head. "I better not tell you, Mr. Dalworth. You might not like it."

Dalworth was beginning to feel more at ease. She was composed and direct. "Well, try me."

"All right. We give it dead flies. We find them in Tommy's attic. We helped by leaving orange peels up there..."

She smiled as she said this and Dalworth was struck with her beauty. A perfect replica of her mother, he thought, with shining dark hair cut in bangs across a forehead whose texture was like ivory with a blush of pink in it. Her eyes were startlingly blue and candid, with lashes so dark and long that they seemed like little shadows over her eyes. When she smiled, her mouth was wide and generous and clean as a small kitten's. She was wearing blue jeans and a T-shirt trimmed in red—an outfit that, even at this age, accented her trim waist and fine, square shoulders. On her feet were red sneakers over short, white socks.

"Would you like to see my room, Mr. Dalworth?"

"Yes, of course, Miss Mallory."

Upstairs, she pointed proudly at the low table near her bed and the two place-settings of milk and cake.

"Now isn't this nice," Dalworth said.

"We can have our own tea party," Jessica said. "You sit over there and I'll sit here and I'll pour the tea. It's really milk, you know."

Dalworth lowered himself into a small chair and held out a doll-sized cup to Jessica, who poured milk

43

into it with judicious precision. Again he wondered at this performance, at what he was doing handling miniature cups and saucers and sipping tepid milk while wedged uncomfortably in the confines of a child's rocker.

"Is your tea hot enough?" she asked him.

"Oh, yes. It's fine, just fine."

"Are you going to get some more horses?"

"I expect so," he said.

"We'll like that."

He was as puzzled by her comment as he was by his own presence here, and he thought of Holcomb waiting for him, and the land called Easter Hill in Ireland with its vast meadows and stone barns, and the men on various boards awaiting his decision in a dozen cities, and he wondered if he could ever explain his behavior to them or to his dear wife, Anna, if she were alive...Was it some kind of illogical guilt on his part, or a stubborn need to joust with fate—to set things right in some fashion?

"I thought you'd come sooner," Jessica said. "I kept watching from the window."

"Didn't Mrs. Farr tell you when she was expecting me?"

"Yes. But I knew before that." She sighed wistfully and said, "I thought you might be here last week."

"I don't understand, Jessica. I wasn't in the city then."

"Well, I don't understand, either. What should I call you? Should I call you Mr. Dalworth? Does "Andrew" sound polite?"

He smiled and said, "I think that sounds about as polite as anything I ever heard."

44

It had become dark outside and the trees created shadows that darkened Jessica's clear blue eyes and, as he looked into them, Dalworth realized that he might never explain how he felt right now to his business associates, but he knew with a sudden confidence that he could have explained his feelings to Anna, who had dreaded so much that he would be lonely.

"Jessica, I must be going now."

What the little girl said in reply to this was so astonishing that Dalworth, who had risen to leave, knelt beside her and stared with wonder into her eyes.

"I'm not sure I understand, dear," he said gently. "Would you mind telling me again?"

"Yes, of course, Andrew." She studied him solemnly. "I said you were right, that she'd understand."

He put his hands on her slim shoulders and shook his head slowly. "How did you know I was thinking of someone else just then?"

The little girl raised her hands and let them fall gently to her sides. "I'm not sure, Andrew. It was something about seashells at first. It was as if I could hear my Mommy talking about them..."

"Yes, go on," Dalworth said. "But you weren't talking about your mommy when you said 'she'd understand', were you?"

"No, I think that was somebody else," Jessica said.

It wasn't guilt, logical or illogical, that stretched between them, Dalworth thought. It was a tangible link, a trembling filament he sensed without understanding....

45

"Who was that other person, Jessica? Who did you think would understand me?"

"I think it was—" The child frowned and put a hand on Dalworth's arm. "Maybe it was—" Then she sighed and the curiously intense light in her eyes seemed to fade slowly away. "Will you come to see me again, Andrew?"

And Dalworth knew then that the link between them had somehow been broken.

"I'd like to visit you again, if I may."

"We can have another party then," Jessica said. "And we can talk about the dogs...."

As the limousine made a left turn toward the expressway, Stanley Holcomb said, "I've checked the airport, sir. They've okayed our revised flight plan. Do you want dinner at the hotel or on the plane?"

Dalworth looked out the shiny windows of the limousine, the headlights of rush-hour traffic moving over him in rhythmic intervals, like the sweep of a metronome. Ahead of them, horns were sounding. The night had dropped swiftly over the city, bringing into sharp relief the long streams of glittering cars.

"I may be staying in town for another few days," Dalworth said. "As you know, I've been thinking about finalizing those negotiations on the Irish property, the Easter Hill place. This might be the time for it."

"Right, sir. I'll rearrange your schedule."

Dalworth laughed. "She definitely knew what I was thinking about."

"I beg your pardon, sir?"

"It's nothing, Stanley. It's not important."

But he wasn't telling the truth, Dalworth knew. It *was* important, as important as anything in his past or future. His thoughts were turning on the Mallorys, all three of them. Jessica had known somehow about the seashells—a casual comment, words lost months ago on the winds of time—and the little girl had known...and she had known he was thinking about Anna. He had been thinking that Anna would understand how he felt about the little girl, and as if that thought had been something physical and tangible, she had taken it from his mind, saying, "Yes, she would understand."

And Anna would, he knew. His wife would have responded with the same warmth that he had, intrigued and caught by the look of her cool blue eyes, the intensity of her expression, and the trust and urgency that emanated from her. He could still feel her light touch on his arm. And he realized there was something...a power he didn't understand.

"Stanley, here's what I want you to do when we get back to the hotel. Call Juvenile Hall and get me the earliest possible appointment—" There was a faint but challenging smile on Andrew Dalworth's face. "I want to talk with Miss Elizabeth Scobey."

Chapter Six ─────────────────────

Several weeks after her first meeting with Andrew
Dalworth—in the late winter of the year—Elizabeth
Scobey sat at her desk to type out the final forms
which defined the custodial arrangements Judge
Harlan Williams had approved the week before in
relation to Jessica Mallory and the adopter,
industrialist-financier Andrew Dalworth.

Miss Scobey was sustained by a sense of euphoria
as she removed the completed papers from her
typewriter and affixed to them the proper stamps
and seals. This was always a victorious moment, she
thought, pausing for an instant to admire the view of
Philadelphia's ornate City Hall and the expanses of
Fairmount Park, sparkling now in sunlight. A
victory and a personal reward to find a good home
for what Miss Scobey thought of as "her" children. It
almost made up for the heartache she felt when she

failed to find a place for the others, usually those not favored with winsome beauty or the proper skin color or eye-shape, or the twelve to fifteen-year-olds who had already developed a resentment against the world for the way it had treated and cheated them. Yet they were always "her" children, and it was difficult to find ways to assuage her disappointment at their rejection.

But it helped when things worked out well, when the smiles of the new parents were as radiant as the smile of the child's.

It had been a close thing with Jessica Mallory, Andrew Dalworth being a single widower and nearing sixty, but Judge Williams had decided for him—not only because of the character references which included clergymen, educators and United States senators, or because of his impressive financial background but because, as the judge had confided to Miss Scobey, in his chambers, "It was the little girl who tipped the scales, to be quite honest about it. She couldn't have been more at home or at ease with Mr. Dalworth. She just seemed to belong with him . . ."

Once Judge Williams had made his decision, the other details of the adoption fell smoothly into place. Even a primary residence in Ireland had been satisfactory to Judge Williams after he had examined the photographs of Easter Hill and made inquiries into the quality of education available at schools in nearby towns.

Finishing up the last details of the clerical work, Miss Scobey tucked the thick file into her briefcase. She walked a short block up Market Street and took one of the birdcage elevators in City Hall up to

Judge Williams' Courtroom J–11, where she gave the Jessica Mallory folder, which included Miss Scobey's personal notes, observations, and recommendations, to the judge's aide, Adam Greene.

J–11 was in recess now and with dust motes in the air and with the long, vacant benches empty, it had something of the look of a deserted village church on a Sunday afternoon.

Miss Scobey sat down in the chair beside Adam Green's desk and popped a mint lozenge into her mouth. She smiled with a sense of shared accomplishment at Adam as he placed the Jessica Mallory folder in a drawer of his desk.

"Well, chalk up another one for our side," he said. "Yes, Miss Scobey, you found another safe pasture for one of God's stray lambs." Smiling at her, he said, "That little Miss Mallory, she's certainly a beautiful child."

Then his smile faded and he said thoughtfully, "To tell you the truth, I'm relieved she's off in Ireland now."

"Why do you say a thing like that?"

"It's just a feeling I've got, something deep in my bones..."

Miss Scobey said patiently, "Adam, I happen to know you graduated *cum laude* from Villanova. So spare me the rabbit's foot and voodoo drums routine. What is it?"

He grinned and said, "White mama tell it like it is." Leaning back in his chair, he rubbed a hand over his jaw, a frown shadowing his eyes. After a moment he shook his head and said, "It's nothing overt or actionable, Miss Scobey. Just a few bad vibes, say. Going back a few months, I had a telephone call here

50

the day after Jessica Mallory's parents were killed in that plane crash. From a man who claimed the Mallorys owed him money—thirty-five hundred dollars—and he demanded to know how and where to file a claim for it. I got suspicious because he was trying to sound like a colored man, but overdoing it, bad grammar and a bit too mush-mouth to be convincing."

Miss Scobey felt an unpleasant chill as she remembered the "colored" houseman who had answered the phone once when she had called the Eric Griffiths at their place in Chester County.

"Go on, Adam," she said quietly.

"Well, the next thing the man asked me about was flight insurance." Adam Greene frowned and drummed his fingers on the desk. "And right there, Miss Scobey, is where I may have messed up. You see, the first thing Judge Williams asked me to do was to check the Mallory family's assets and insurance. I shouldn't have said anything but I was irritated with that darkie act—so I came out and told him that the Mallorys hadn't signed up for flight insurance."

So that's how the Griffiths had known, Miss Scobey thought.

"If that's all there was to it, I wouldn't have worried," Adam Greene said. "But that same man called me again, Miss Scobey, although the next time he wasn't hiding behind a darkie's drawl."

"When was this second call?" Miss Scobey said, a sudden sharpness in her tone.

"I'll bet you could guess," Adam Greene said with a small, unamused smile. "It was the day after the newspapers ran that first story about Andrew

Dalworth's petition to adopt Jessica Mallory."

"Yes, I could have guessed," Miss Scobey said.

"He told me he was Jessica's uncle, and he wanted to know where she was and where Mr. Dalworth was. When I told him I couldn't give out that information, he started hollering about his rights, about blood being stronger than money—" Greene shook his head. "He really went ape when I told him to write a letter to Judge Williams, that it was the court's authority—that's when he hung up. But the next day his wife called, all sweetness, and said that it was a matter of grave family importance that she get in touch with the child."

Miss Scobey remembered then the look of Maud Griffith's eyes, cold and unrevealing as globes of glass, as cooly removed from the pain and drama of Jessica Mallory as those of a sleek and selfish cat.

"Why didn't you tell me this before?" she asked Adam.

"I didn't want to worry you, Miss Scobey. And besides, I didn't think you could do anything about the calls anyway."

"But it's always good to know these things anyway."

Adam Greene said somberly, "I'm gonna give you another rumble on the tom-toms, Miss Scobey. Something in their voices made me very glad to shade the truth, tell them that Miss Mallory's whereabouts were no longer the business of this office."

"Alright, Adam," Miss Scobey said. Her voice was more concerned as she added, "If the Griffiths ever call again, tell them the same thing. That as far as this court is concerned, the Jessica Mallory case is closed."

"That would be a pleasure," Adam Greene said and locked the drawer containing the Mallory folder. Then he tucked the key carefully into his vest pocket.

- CITY OF PHILADEPHIA -

MUNICIPAL CODE NO. 257346
FOR INTERNAL DEPARTMENTAL USE ONLY
ADOPTEE: JESSICA MALLORY
ANNUAL RESUME REPORT: ELIZABETH SCOBEY

INFORMATION AND EVALUATION SOURCES:
Andrew Dalworth: responsive, semi-annual communications.
Stanley Holcomb: local reference, financial and educational
                                 backgrounds.

U.S. Embassy, Dublin: per attached forms.

U.S. Emmigration Department: as above.
Eric and Maud Griffith: adoptees's next of natural kin: no
                                         communication.
Jessica Mallory: postcards, holiday greetings, letters and
                            poems attached.

CASE WORKER'S REPORT: Exemplary conditions and developments through past four years. Records indicate Miss Mallory two years ahead comparable U.S. school programs. Adoptee obviously benefiting from secure physical and emotional environment, re Irish residence and adoptor, Andrew Dalworth. Attends Catholic school for convenience, religious preference left open.

Child makes friends in own age group easily, excellent adjustment to authority figures, school and parish personnel, household staff. Miss Mallory beneficially exposed to animal

53

husbandry; rides well, has been schooled in equestrianship, is allowed responsibility for own pets.

Present overview and prognosis: Excellent.

Perhaps this final comment is redundant, since attached medical records indicate the child's overall physical well-being. But I would add that photographs of Jessica Mallory, who is now eight years old, suggest to the undersigned that she is a beautiful child and should continue to develop in that fashion and that she has—in a special way—a quality that sets her apart from all "my other children," adopted through this bureau.

Signed: Elizabeth Scobey

Chapter Seven ——————————

Easter Hill was a slate-gray mansion on high ground that dominated a coastline of rough, wild beauty, steep cliffs and rolling meadows spiked with shale and fieldstone. The gray waters of the north Atlantic fused in these southern seas with the Gulf Stream, producing, in season, warm winds and a climate that nurtured the incongruous palm trees swaying above the Connemara shores from Ballycastle down to Galway Bay.

At eight years of age, Jessica Mallory had become securely adjusted to the rhythms of a convent school and to the surface tranquility of Irish country life. She thought of Andrew Dalworth, whom she called Andrew, not as a second father but simply as an "older" father. She still remembered her own father and mother, like images from a dream, as a tall, patient man with books and pencils, and a smiling lady who hugged her and played games with her on the floor in a room filled with bright posters.

Sometimes, when her school schedule permitted, she went on trips with Andrew, to Paris and London and on occasion back to the United States. When she couldn't go with him, her life at Easter Hill revolved around the people who looked after them there; Flynn, the butler; Mrs. Kiernan, the cook; Rose and Lily, the housemaids. Taking care of the grounds and stables were Kevin O'Dell, a young groom, and the gardener, Capability Brown, who had explained to Jessica that he had been named after an English landscape artist—the famed Capability Brown who had designed the gardens and lakes at Blenheim, country seat of the Marlboroughs and Churchills.

And, of course, she had friends at school, and in the nearby village of Ballytone there were Father Malachy and his housekeeper, and Charity Bostwick who gave her riding lessons.

On this late spring afternoon, Jessica rode her brown hunter, Windkin, up the promontory known as Skyhead, a broad point of rocky shoreline directly above the northern pastures of Easter Hill. Holding Windkin's strength easily but surely in one hand, she leaned her slender body into the salty winds coming in off the sea, her knees guiding the horse up to the highest peaks from where she could see the stretches of beach where Holly liked to chase and frighten the seagulls.

Jessica reined in the big hunter and turned in the saddle to study the rocky shoreline and narrow beaches far below her. There was no sign of her brown and white fox terrier scampering and barking after the strutting gulls and the crying terns, and

Jessica suddenly felt a sting of tears in her eyes as she realized that she would never see Holly again. . . .

In her years of growing up in Ireland, Jessica had had only occasional promptings from the strange mental phenomena which she thought of as her "colors." There had been no recurrence of the diamond-bright whiteness that had glowed so terrifyingly in her mind the night her parents had crashed to their deaths. There had been other colors from time to time, warm and comfortable, moments of excitement in the schoolyard when she had "guessed" the winners of foot races and the time when she had "guessed" what grades several of her classmates would get on certain written exams. (She'd been right, too, and what a scene that had caused!)

Some of the things that Jessica seemed to know in advance, she had learned to keep to herself, like the time she had known that Andrew was having Windkin sent over from Kentucky as a Christmas present for her.

Staring along the distant, frothing beaches, Jessica said a silent goodbye to Holly in her mind, remembering with an ache the joyous barking and fierce loyalties that were gone forever. Then she swung Windkin around and spurred him into a full gallop down the broad slopes leading to Easter Hill.

Kevin O'Dell heard the sound of the horse's hooves on the hard spring earth and stepped from the tack room, still holding the bridle he'd been oiling. He was fourteen, tall for his age, with burnished red hair, dark gray eyes and a complexion that remained fair despite the hours he'd spent working with horses in all kinds of weather.

Watching Windkin and Jessica coming down the hill, their figures blurred by ground mists, he wished she would take the slope more carefully, but Miss Charity had trained the girl well and Windkin was a dependable, sure-footed mount.

Kevin O'Dell's chores were finished for the day, the stables smelling of fresh hay and water, the tack oiled and ready for tomorrow. He had waited for Jessica to return in case she wanted him to hot-walk Windkin, although she usually preferred to do this chore herself. In truth, he didn't mind spending extra time at Easter Hill, because his home in the village of Ballytone wasn't a cheerful place these days. His father was dead and his two older brothers had gone off to work in the German-owned factories in the south, leaving him and his mother to share a silent supper at night, and then to watch American-made police shows on television. In the half-darkness of those evenings, Kevin could see his mother moving rosary beads through her work-rough hands and he knew her mind wasn't on the television show at all, but on the gray headstone up at the church and on her sons in strange rooming houses waiting for the early morning factory whistles.

When Jessica cantered up to the stables, he saw the tears on her cheeks and his first thought was that she had taken a fall.

"Are you all right, Jess?" he said, as she swung down to the ground.

"Would you walk Windkin for me, Kevin?"

"Sure, but tell me what happened."

"It's Holly. She's gone."

"You can bet she'll be back for supper, Jess. She's

probably up in the woods or over in the meadow chasing rabbits."

"No, she's gone," she said again but in a voice so quiet that he barely heard the words above the winds coming down Skyhead.

Andrew Dalworth was at his study desk, speaking to Stanley Holcomb in New York. The study was a small teak-panelled room connected by double doors to Easter Hill's library and furnished sparely and functionally with a writing desk, Telex equipment, phones and filing cabinets. In one corner of the room was a triangular glass wall-case which contained a collection of antique and historic hand-weapons with the ammunition arranged in small drawers. The case was locked and only the butler Flynn and Dalworth himself had keys to it.

Dalworth said into the phone, "Here's a change of instructions, Stanley, for Tom Bradley at the farm. We'll want Yankee Drummer sooner than we'd anticipated. By the third of the month at the latest. The trainers here want her to get used to the track and climate at the Curragh."

Dalworth heard the front door open and close and he knew that Jessica was home. After completing his business with Holcomb, he walked into the library, whose walls of books were burnished bright by the late afternoon sunlight. It was his favorite room in the rambling old house with a great stone fireplace, tall leaded-glass windows, a scattering of mellow Aubusson carpets on the parquet floors, and deep wine-red leather chairs around a pair of reading tables.

It was not only his favorite room but his favorite

time of day, he thought, as he poured himself a sherry and waited for Jessica to join him. He moved to one of the windows and looked out at the view of meadows and ponds stretching toward Skyhead. It had been a damned fine four years for him and he was profoundly grateful for them, even the times with Dr. Julian and their mutual concern over Jessica's gifts.

Dalworth had been alerted decisively to the phenomenon of her precognitive skills when Mother Superior Agnes had asked him to join her for a private meeting at the local convent school. Mother Agnes, an old woman with a face pale and hard as a white-washed wall, had accused six-year-old Jessica of going through a teacher's desk without permission to look at grades on certain examination papers. The Mother Superior's evidence had been circumstantial but impressive. Jessica had, in fact, been in the classroom alone. No one but Sister Malvern, who had marked the papers, could have seen the test grades. One conclusive fact remained— Jessica had known the grades and given them to four of her older classmates.

Mother Superior had sent for Jessica then. The child had joined the two adults in the spare office, where pictures of saints stared from the wall like stern jurors and the candle before the Madonna flickered across the frosted windows.

Dalworth had been very proud of her as she stood stiffly but respectfully facing Mother Superior, her face not much higher than the old nun's desk, her blue school smock matching the color of her bright eyes.

"Yes, I told them their grades, Mother Agnes," she said. "I saw the numbers in my mind and I didn't think it was wrong. I would never go into Sister Malvern's desk without permission."

"You're asking us to take a great deal on faith, my child. You say you didn't look into the desk. You say the correct numbers just appeared in your mind? Is that it?"

"Yes, Mother Agnes."

"Tell me then—has this happened to you before?"

"Sometimes, Mother Agnes, when I'm excited." A cloud had seemed to pass across her small, pale face. "Or when I'm frightened . . ."

The old nun had looked dubiously from the little girl to Dalworth. "Perhaps we can test the truth of what you're saying. In the drawer of my desk, is a test paper I graded myself only minutes before Mr. Dalworth came into my office. It belongs to a student in the upper grades. Could you tell me the grade on *that* test, Jessica?"

Dalworth recalled vividly that instant of time, the blank eyes of the Virgin glinting in the flame from the votive light, the sound of voices murmuring in unison from a nearby classroom, the old nun's sceptically pursed lips and the tension visibly straining Jessica's expression.

"Could you tell me that, child?"

The mood of the room dissolved into something unreal as Jessica said quietly, "The grade is an 87, Mother Agnes, and the test paper in your desk belongs to Chalice O'Reilly."

The silence that had followed had been broken at last by the Mother Superior's startled gasp as she blessed herself with a large brass crucifix which hung around her throat and exclaimed, "Praise be to God, the child spoke the truth."

It was at this period of her life that Jessica began to experience a profound curiosity about her powers. Her speculations and intuitions amounted to a certitude that seemed to come to her from somewhere beyond the realm of her physical senses. She knew in some fashion that she occasionally was better informed about what was going to happen in and around Easter Hill than Mrs. Kiernan, the cook, and Lily and Rose, and even, on occasion, than Kevin in the stables. This made Jessica feel triumphant because Kevin knew so much about horses and foaling, and tides and weather, that he was always quick to forecast sailing conditions to Andrew or to predict the exact day a foal would be dropped.

In many small and personal ways, Jessica liked to test her powers to herself. Most of these experiments were innocent and blameless. Often in the early morning she would go down to the hatching house, count the eggs in the brooder and make a mental guess about the color of chicks that might emerge, scoring herself in predicting accurately the nests that had chicks in black, beige or shades of creamy yellow.

Seated in her tower refuge, she sometimes watched the sky during thunderstorms, anticipating what distant crag or tree might attract the next jagged thunderbolt.

Dalworth was aware of her powers, although at that time he still preferred to think of them as "gifts," the natural intuitions of a perceptive, sensitive growing child. But he began to realize that Jessica's gifts were not wholly unremarkable and innocent, as on the occasion of his trip to Dublin. It was a curious business. The train had been due in Ballytone at nine. Jessica told him it would be an hour early, but he hadn't listened to her. When he got to the station, he found that she had been right. Schedules had been changed because of track repairs, and the train was already on its way to Dublin. Dalworth's point of contention with Jessica was admittedly weak.

"You should have *insisted* I call the station," he told her.

She had looked evasive then, and he had let the matter drop, knowing it was as much his fault as hers that he had missed his train. After all, Jessica *had* got what she wanted—his continued presence at Easter Hill for the weekend.

Chapter Eight ────────────────

It was after this experience that Andrew Dalworth decided to get professional advice to define and evaluate Jessica's psychic capacities. Prior to this, and seemingly independent of her prophetic gifts, Jessica had begun to write poetry, simple poems printed in round, babyish letters which she brought proudly to Dalworth for his consideration and approval. Many of these expressed the wonder and surprise of any small child beginning to examine the world of her feelings, although some were informed with an oblique gravity.

One read:

> Don't watch those midnight stars
>   too closely.
> Sometimes one falls.
> Sometimes it's an airplane.

And later in the same month:

> Last night I asked my dolly why
>   she was crying.
>
> Poor dolly couldn't answer me.
>   Her mouth was full of tears.

Using contacts at the universities of Duke and Stanford, Dalworth had been put in touch with Julian Homewood, a young Dubliner who conducted advanced seminars in psychic research and experimentation at Trinity College. Dr. Homewood—or Dr. Julian, as Jessica and Dalworth soon came to call him—had taken a degree in medicine at the age of twenty-two at Cambridge in England, doing graduate work later at Trinity in parapsychology and extrasensory perception.

Dr. Julian was the son and grandson of medical doctors who had been interested in what Julian had once described to Dalworth as "the facilities and powers of the mind that you can't measure with stethoscopes, calipers, or least of all, with what passes for common sense."

A bachelor, Dr. Julian Homewood lived in the Ballsbridge section of Dublin in a Georgian townhouse with a fan of windows over the door. In the last two years he had interviewed and tested Jessica Mallory on a dozen or more occasions. It had been his intention from the start (a point of view which Dalworth shared wholeheartedly) to assist her to accept her psychic abilities with serenity and confidence. Never to let them become a burden—the baggage of a laboratory guinea pig or a drawing room freak....

Dalworth, Jessica and Dr. Julian had become

good friends, a close knit unit, over the years, and they had enjoyed each other's company, not only during professional sessions, but at the theatre and often at race meets and on long weekends at Easter Hill.

But it was after one of her very first meetings with Dr. Julian that Jessica had written a poem which had startled Dalworth with its bitter-sweet mystery and maturity.

> Time is a river
>   arching like a blue rainbow
>   through the landscape of my mind.
>
> I watch the flow of the great stream,
>   I hear the tumble of its white waters.
>
> I see the small crafts of life,
>   bobbing and listing and sailing on.
>
> But ask me not the captains or the cargoes.
>
> Not now ... Not now. ...

Andrew Dalworth glanced at the grandfather clock that stood in a niche between the bookshelves and decided that Jessica wasn't planning to join him, unusual because as a rule she seemed to enjoy spending this time of day with him.

Putting aside his sherry glass, Dalworth walked through the great hall that gave on the shadowed dining room and through other rooms in to a salon used only when guests gathered for a hunt tea or when Charity Bostwick or Father Malachy stopped by for Sunday supper.

The light from the chandeliers and the fading sun was soft now, gilding the old furniture he had bought in France and England and Belfast, sideboards and highboys and antique fruitwood chests. Jessica had accompanied him on several of his trips to the continent and had shown a precocious and healthy interest in his choice of tapestries and jades. She had been equally fascinated by the silver vaults in London and the narrow streets twisting crookedly from the Seine near the Quai D'Orsay, where they had discovered unique collections of candelabra and clouded mirrors with hand-crafted frames.

Dalworth crossed the dark dining room with its panelled walls and medieval concert loft and went into one of the kitchens where Mrs. Kiernan was stirring soup at the stove and Flynn was decanting the dinner wines.

Flynn turned to him with a smile and said, "May I get you something, Mr. Dalworth?"

"No, thanks. I was looking for Jessica. I heard her come in the front door a few minutes ago...."

But no, Jessica hadn't gone to the kitchens.

In the second-floor corridors which ran the width of the huge home, Dalworth met Rose and Lily coming out of a suite which, because of its view, was called the Orchard Rooms. Rose and Lily looked enough alike to be sisters; fair, sturdy village girls with chapped red cheeks and hair tied with dark ribbon at the napes of their necks. The maids had changed into their dinner uniforms—black silk skirts and white blouses with flat, round collars.

They had not seen Jessica either, so Mr. Dalworth walked along the corridor to her room. It was empty, the bed neatly made, her books and playthings in orderly rows on the table before the fireplace.

Then a worried thought occurred to him. There was a cushioned seat under the bay window on the third floor, the highest view from Easter Hill across the meadows and past Skyhead to the sea, which Jessica called her private tower. And what was worrying Dalworth as he started up the stairs was that Jessica retreated to the tower only when she was in a lonely, withdrawn mood, when she felt a need to wrote poetry, when her normally exuberant spirits were weighed down by a gravity which Dalworth could not completely understand and was helpless to relieve.

The wide, deep embrasure of the bay window formed the shadowed refuge of Jessica's "tower." Its leaded windows gave her a world view, an exclusive solitude that complemented and reflected the insights and probings of her own powerful mental visions. It was here that she could see everything, as she could sometimes "see everything" in her mind. Here she watched the lightning, knowing where it would strike. Here she could see the trains enter the valley and wind their way into Ballytone...see unborn foals in her mind-span, foals that would one day charge up Skyhead...see eagles' nests that would fill the skies with wings in the coming spring. This was her place of strength, as familiar as a chapel to a priest, as beads to a nun. She felt comfortable here with the muted tapestries, the beige cushions, the deep carpetings. They were as familiar as old friends. Jessica's tower was a place where she felt both the pain and the strength of her gifts most keenly.

Now Jessica was seated there, staring out to the distant sea. Dalworth joined her, put a hand on her shoulder. When she turned, he saw the stain of tears on her cheeks.

"What's the matter, Jess?"

"It's Holly, Andrew."

"What's the little rascal been up to now?"

"Nothing, Andrew." He heard the catch in her breath. "She's dead."

"Let's hope you're wrong this time. You know, that's a possibility."

"I've been praying I'm wrong, but it's something more than Holly..."

Dalworth patted her shoulder gently and said, "What do you mean, Jessica?"

"I don't know," she said, and shook her head helplessly.

"Holly will cheer you up," Dalworth said. "I'll take Flynn and young O'Dell."

"I'll wait here for you," Jessica said.

Parking his Land Rover on the southern slope of Skyhead, Dalworth followed a rough foot-trail down to the beach, his torch cutting an arc of brilliant light through the gathering darkness and the opaque, misting spray churned up by the surging waves.

Flynn had gone on foot to the meadows behind the stables, and Kevin O'Dell had ridden Dalworth's hunter up to the rim of the woods.

Dalworth followed the shoreline for several hundred yards, picking his way carefully through beds of slippery kelp and feeling the battering force of the winds against his sheep-lined jacket.

Possibly the little terrier had found her way to Angel's Cove, he was thinking, a favorite spot where they had picnicked on quiet summer afternoons.

Perhaps she'd buried chicken bones or some cheese there and was foraging for it when the tides cut her off.

Wrong, he thought, after covering another fifty yards and stopping, the waves foaming around his boots. He knew he wouldn't make the long hike to Angel's Cove after all, because in the glare of his flashlight, at the water's edge, he saw Holly's furry brown and white body wedged in a natural vise of stone, battered by the waves, blood gleaming bright on her skull and muzzle.

The dog's body was wet and cold, pathetically small in Dalworth's hands. As he cradled it in his arms and started back toward Easter Hill, he concluded that the fierce little terrier had probably braved the waves after gulls and been struck by a piece of driftwood spinning about in the powerful currents.

And that's what Jessica had known, he realized—that the dog was dead. But in his suddenly worried heart, he knew that the child had seen something else.

Chapter Nine ————————————————

DR. JULIAN HOMEWOOD
PSYCHOMEDICAL GROUP, TRINITY COLLEGE
CASE FILE 111
SUBJECT: JESSICA MALLORY

      To summarize the past year: I have succeeded in gaining Jessica's confidence. To summarize the two years prior to the past year: It was not an easy task, not without its up-and-down crises. A tentative conclusion: While a subjective relationship has been achieved, I'm not quite sure that's for the best. That, however, may be a dysfunctional conclusion.

      A friendship does exist between us—among all three of us, for that matter—Dalworth, Miss Jessica and myself. While I have supervised tests, some written and others under lab conditions, we have also enjoyed a number of non-working "social" interludes, such as soccer matches, trips with Andrew Dalworth to horse shows, art auctions and so forth. Naturally and inevitably I have been able to draw further conclusions about Jessica Mallory from these ostensibly social occasions.

For example, a picnic at Skyhead beach. Luncheon packed by Mrs. K. Jessica in a triumphant (almost malicious mood) about the rabbit incident. (In brief: Mrs. Kiernan planned a dish of braised hare for dinner the previous weekend. The usuals expected: Charity Bostwick, the local priest, etc., plus two of Dalworth's business friends from Paris. At breakfast the day of the dinner, Jessica warned Mrs. K. that the rabbits would not be delivered by Mr. Cobb, the local purveyor of game. Apparently Mrs. K. dismissed this without much tact. We learned later that Mr. Cobb had suffered an accident with his wagon several hours earlier, but Easter Hill didn't get the news till later in the afternoon and this threw the kitchen staff into a near panic. Instead of braised hare, there was a great scrambling about for substitute items. I sensed that Jessica enjoyed the confusion and Mrs. K.'s discomfit hugely.)

In attempting to analyze this nuance of character, I taped the following exchange with Jessica at the picnic on Skyhead beach:

"Tell me the truth now, Jessica. Why were you pleased that Mrs. K. was so upset?"

"Oh, she just likes to bang pots and pans around to scare Rose and Lily...."

"Don't give me that, Miss Mallory. The poor woman had planned that special dinner for weeks. She'd even made the wine sauce."

"Then she shouldn't have treated me like a child. She should have taken me seriously."

"But you must understand, Jessica, that what seems so clear to you isn't always that way to others."

"I'd better take Andrew a sandwich...."

"You better sit right where you are and listen to me. Never mind Andrew *or* your big, theatrical stares out to the sea. Talk about banging pots and pans around...."

"But Dr. Julian, I'm so tired of feeling *responsible*."

"Jessica, I've explained to you that knowing about something in advance doesn't make you *responsible* for it."

"Dr. Julian, I don't *always* know what's going to

happen. *Don't you understand that?*"

"It's clear enough. You don't have to shout about it."

"Well, it's not easy not to. I try to stay calm. Things *are* easier that way. When I'm sad or frightened or angry, everything gets sharper, pushes at me. *I don't always like those colors....*"

"I'm trying to understand, Jessica. And I'm trying to suggest that you be more patient with yourself *and* other people."

"It's difficult, Dr. Julian, because—well, if they'd *listen* to me, there wouldn't be such troubles."

QUESTION: Might the subject's rebellious mood in this interview be ascribed to the fact that we were on the beach near where the dog Holly had drowned?

In reference to the above query, several thoughts occur to me, all of them disquieting. At times a darkness settles over Jessica. I don't quite understand it. It is dissimilar— more pronounced, more foreboding—to attitudes I have encountered in other psychic-clairvoyants studied.

I related it at first to the tragic death of Holly and the overt demonstration of Jessica's powers to Andrew Dalworth this occasioned. Perhaps this display of her psychic capacity has become fixed for her in an unsettling way with her feelings as an adopted child.

If this is true, if the death of Holly is a simple, triggering incident, it is hardly a serious matter. But I must try to ascertain if something else, something presently unknowable, may be causing these deep moments of anger and resentment, emotions which could be dangerous not only to Jessica but to others.

I think I must review her case histories with particular attention to testing and scoring on the one hand and related ephemora on the other. I must ask Dalworth to bring Jessica down to Dublin as soon as possible.

Chapter Ten ─────────────────────────

Two days later, Dr. Homewood parked his two-seater sports car in the area reserved for staff near the quad at Trinity College. It was a brisk, spring morning. Sunlight brightened the immense cobblestone quadrangle surrounded by gray buildings and crowded now with students in duffle coats and boots hurrying toward classes, bookbags looped over their shoulders.

Mingling easily with these undergraduates in his jeans and loose tweed jacket, Dr. Julian went to his office on the fourth floor of the science building. He dropped his briefcase on a chair stacked with books and pulled up the window shades which gave him a view of college halls and the bulk of a steepled church, its dark stone walls scored with scaffoldings.

Then he opened Jessica's files. He started in chronological order with their first meeting on the tenth of April, several years ago. Her blood pressure had been normal, her height forty-two inches, her weight fifty-one pounds. She had started a poem for him that first day, handing it to him without embarrassment after Andrew Dalworth had left them alone in the doctor's office.

"I can't finish it till I know you better," she had said, seated in the chair opposite him, her shoes swinging free above the floor.

There was a copy of the poem in her files.

> "My dreams are like green balloons
> on a long white string.
>
> Take my hand...

Dr. Julian sorted through the results of examinations he had given Jessica over the years, noting again her records and reactions to the Berenreuther Personality Inventory, Rorschach and Thematic Aperception Tests, the Stanford-Binet and the Pinter-Patterson Performance Scales.

During this period, Jessica had participated in most of the laboratory and field tests available to modern psychic researchers. Identification of numbers written on concealed blackboards, blindfolded guessing of playing cards, identification of persons and objects in sealed rooms, with therapeutic breaks to eliminate the decline effect (or plain boredom) associated with repetitious lab experiments.

Other tests included a reading of Jessica's attempts to physically affect a supersensitive magnetic compass needle, which registered to one-millionth of the earth's field. Jessica's performance had been inconclusive; the change in the output recording was insignificant, the frequency of the oscillation increasing only 1.2 percent for perhaps fifteen seconds.

Dr. Julian studied the results of a test which had particularly interested him at the time, a Global Targeting Examination on a run of ten. Jessica had scored six H's (Hits), three N's (Neutrals) and one M (Miss), identifying salient characteristics of areas known only to her through their grid coordinates, latitude and longitude, in degrees, minutes and seconds. Her degree of success had been gratifying. She had, in fact, looked at numbers written on a notepad in an office in Trinity College, Dublin, and had related them—six times out of ten—to the geographical areas they represented, places in the world she had never been—the Ripon Falls, Africa, Lopez Bay, the Philippines, an island in the Celebes Sea near Borneo, stretches of ocean off the Cornish coast. Her one Miss and three Neutrals (too ambiguous to fit into an equation) scarcely detracted from her performance, particularly since it had been conducted under strict laboratory control of defense against unconscious iedetic assistance (after all, Jessica *might* have at some time seen and memorized maps of those areas). Also, Dr. Julian understood that the object under scrutiny (Jessica) could be affected by the analysis of the witness (himself)—in some cases by his mere physical presence.

> "My dreams are like green balloons
> on thin white strings.
>
> Take my hand . . .
>
> If we walk together,
> the path is wide enough.

At first, Dalworth, the executive accustomed to computerized, corporate decisions at the highest

level, had demanded answers, decisions, *results*—
God, how he had demanded them, Dr. Julian
thought.

"I want to know *why*, Dr. Homewood, *why*
Jessica sees these things we don't, *sees* things beyond
our senses and perceptions. My experience tells me
there are always explanations if you dig deep enough
and hard enough."

They had been sitting in a pub on the Liffey at the
time and Julian remembered his exasperation with
the older man. "Then dig deep and hard into this,
Mr. Dalworth," he had said, giving him a poem that
Jessica had presented to him that same day, four
stanzas of free verse which she called *Pussywillows*.

> I am puzzled by pussywillows.
> They bloom in the chill winds
>   of March, when frost
> Still touches the north bark of trees.
>
> They could be small fur hats.
> They could be mittens without thumbs.
>
> But I think they are bedsocks
>   for the little people who
> wander in the night-time meadows
>   outside my window.
>
> While I am safe in my bed,
> Safe in my bed.

Dalworth read the poem twice, massaging the
bridge of his broken nose with a thumb and
forefinger.

"Well, you're the expert, Homewood. What do
you think it means?"

"I don't know," Dr. Julian said and sipped his ale.
"I mean that in the most literal sense we can
conceive. I simply do not know. There is a breadth

and depth to Jessica's perceptions and precognitions—call them what you will—that brush against the parameters we've established so far. Her intimacy with the strange side of nature, the warnings she sees from colors, the oblique alarms running through her poetry—much of that is beyond my experience with run-of-the-mill psychics and clairvoyants, Andrew. And beyond that of my colleagues for that matter."

Dalworth had looked at him thoughtfully. "All right, I can accept that. Jessica is different. She's unpredictable. Is there a danger in that for her? Or—for others?"

"I've already given you my answer to that, Andrew. I simply don't know..."

When Andrew Dalworth dropped Jessica off at the north entrance to the Trinity quad at ten o'clock, she and Dr. Julian then drove in an open sports car down the coast to Dun Laoghaire, a seaside resort town a dozen miles south of Dublin. A pier jutted from the shore almost a mile out into the Irish Sea. Some of the sails on the boats were bright red, others striped blue and yellow, and still others white against the gray waters, gulls sweeping and crying everywhere. The great white wooden hotels were not yet open for the season, their shuttered windows looking down blindfolded from perches on the gray cliffs.

It was a favorite spot of theirs. Instead of in his office or a laboratory, Dr. Julian had discovered that Jessica—with her love of the sea and the outdoors—was much more relaxed out here in the open, feeding the birds and hiking along the breakwater, the spray hanging above them in the occasional sunlight like dozens of tiny rainbows.

"Are you going to be warm enough, Jessica?"

She looked down at her slim flannel slacks and then at the backs of her leather-and-knit gloves. She fastened the top button of her mulberry-red jacket and said, "Yes, of course I am."

"Fine. You want to race me to the end of the pier?"

"No, let's walk, Dr. Julian."

He looked down at her and saw a certain mournful delicacy in the set of her expression, something wistful in her eyes as she looked at the circling birds, their orange beaks garish against their white plumage.

"Come on, Jess. I'll give you a head start."

"I don't need a head start. Your pipe's out, Julian."

"It's very difficult to keep it lighted in an open car. Which is beside the point, isn't it? So let's walk, and you can tell me what's bothering you."

They sat talking on a stone ledge at the far end of the breakwater, discussing what had happened to the dog Holly and the other things Jessica had seen in her luminous visions. They didn't realize how cold they were until a tea-vendor came their way, an old man bent against the winds, pushing his wares in a three-wheeled aluminum cart.

Julian bought cylinders of hot tea and a pair of pigs-in-the-blankets—steaming sausages wrapped in brown pie-crust and laid on a paper napkin.

Jessica sipped her tea and threw the last bite of her sausage to a gull circling only six feet above them.

"Did you say a prayer for Holly?"

"Please, Julian, I'm tired of it."

"Then we might as well drive back."

"Oh, all right. I'm not sure, I don't think so." Shaking her dark hair back with a feminine swing, she smoothed it down to her shoulders with her gloved hands and tilted her head to stare out across the gray waters.

She would be a beautiful woman, he thought, watching her in profile. It was there in the child—the fluid movements of her slim body, the high candor in her eyes and expression, the whiteness of her forehead beneath the dark spray of hair tumbled now by the salty winds.

"We buried Holly in the orchard where you can see the grave from my room," she said. "Mr. Brown made a cross from the branches of an oak that fell last week. Everyone was there—Lily and Rose, Mrs. Kiernan and Mr. Flynn. And Charity Bostwick brought Father Malachy up. He said some prayers in Latin."

Jessica looked directly at Dr. Julian. After a moment, she nodded and said, "Yes, I said a prayer, Julian."

"For Holly?" he asked her quietly.

"No, Julian, it wasn't *for* anyone." She turned away from him and stared again at the rolling seas. "It was *against* something. I've told you—" She shrugged helplessly and smoothed her hair down again, the ends curling softly around her gloved fingers. "I didn't feel responsible for Holly. It always helps, Julian, to remember what you told me about the view from the hill..."

"I'm glad you remember, Jessica. It's only a metaphor, but sometimes that's the only way we can get a glimpse of things that we can't weigh or measure but still perceive in ways we're at a loss to define or understand."

When she was young—Jessica sighed at her thought; she'd been seven—Dr. Julian had likened her perception of coming events to that of a person standing on a high hill with a view of a river sweeping about its base.

"Imagine that you can see a boat coming down the stream. Think of that as the past," he had said. "As it comes abreast of you, that, in our figure of speech, is the present. Now imagine you can see farther downstream to a waterfall, its spray leaping high in the air but still not visible to the people on the boat. From your view, you know what might happen. The boat may turn a bend in the forked river and be drawn into the currents of the waterfall. But the people on the boat can change course, drop anchor or find a safe cove. They have choices. You aren't responsible for what they do or the possible consequence of what you see."

Dr. Julian wadded up their napkins and poked them into the aluminum tea cylinders.

"We're good friends, aren't we, Jessica?"

"Of course, we're good friends," Jessica said. "I think we always will be."

"Then answer me this: Is there any reason you won't tell me what you're afraid of?"

She shook her head slowly. "I've tried to understand it. I didn't feel responsible for Holly— just sad and lonely. But the other thing is different. Cold brightness in the future, and it frightens me. Someone who had a small blue car and a pet—a black cat, I think. It was when I was very young, and mostly before Andrew." She shook her head with a sudden stubbornness. "I don't want to talk about it anymore, Julian. Please. Let's go back now."

"All right, Jessica," Julian said, and put an arm around the girl, holding her against the winds that hurried them along the breakwater toward the blank eyes of the hotels above the resort town.

Chapter Eleven ——————————————————

Eric Griffith's eye and interest were caught by a
magnificent thoroughbred whose name he fancied:
Yankee Drummer. It was a scene handsome enough
to dispel his gloomy thoughts—the turf in Ireland,
splendid crowds in tweeds and bright silk scarves,
ladies carrying walking sticks, gentlemen with
binoculars, placards showing the current odds above
the betting stalls, and horses parading toward the
race course at the Curragh.

Eric sat in a doctor's waiting room—a depressing
annex with wicker furniture, artificial green plants
and botannical prints on the walls—reading *Town
and Country* magazine. It was winter-dark outside,
the streets noisy with traffic. A black woman with
two small children sagging against her knees looked
stolidly at the details of a large red kidney, which
faced her at eye level from a medical layout on the
opposite wall.

Eric and Maud had been driving to the country from Philadelphia when the pain had struck, starting at the base of her skull and fanning out into her shoulders. He had tried to persuade her to stick it out until they got home where a brisk rub and a whiskey might put things right, but oh, no, she wouldn't have *that*, she thought she was dying as usual (naturally, since she'd had that damned foolish dream again last night), and so here they were in a strange doctor's office, Maud closeted with some old black medicine man, while he sat with kids staring at him like zombies, his nerves twitching for a drink.

Thank God for small favors. In a dusty heap of *Ebony* magazines and old comic books, with a couple of *Popular Mechanics* and *Modern Screens* tucked among them, Eric had found a recent copy of *Town and Country* with pictures of good-looking people and horses to distract him from his simmering resentments.

In grim defiance of a "no smoking" sign on the wall, he lit a cigarette and made a point of dropping the match on the floor. Feeling that he had evened some unspecified score, Eric inhaled the acrid smoke and casually turned the page.

Almost immediately he gasped, the smoke choking him as he fought for breath. A name leaped out at him from the caption under a picture: Jessica Mallory. The girl stood with a group of men holding the halter of the same horse he had admired on the preceding page, Yankee Drummer, international industrialist Andrew Dalworth's entry in a spring race at the Curragh.

Eric Griffith felt the irregular stroke of his heart as he stared at his niece's face, his eye switching from the men around her down to the copy to identify them: the grinning young fop with a beard was a Dr. Julian Somebody, and there was Andrew Dalworth himself—tall, reeking of privilege, the wind in his rusted white hair, a big hand on Jessica's shoulder— and then a beefy country boob in a tweed cape and derby hat, a lawyer named Ryan. All of them were up for the weekend from Easter Hill...

Eric experienced a spasm of anger so intense and acute that it was like physical pain. He clamped his teeth against an impulse to spit at their pictures. Instead, perversely, he forced himself to stare at the photographs, absorbing like gall the look of complacent privilege, the strength and power of the men grouped around *his* niece, his dear sister's only child, his very own flesh and blood...

She was tall and slim, the top of her head nearly level with Dalworth's shoulder, casually at home with the trappings of the race meet, with stewards in boots and tall hats, jockeys saluting with their bats, owners with the colors of their stables pinned to handbags and scarves. Yes, little Jessica was right at home there, he thought, using in his mind a word he despised and resented: she "belonged" to that exclusive world. His own blood niece. A pretty child, blooming into young girlhood. How old was she? When had the social worker come to see him and Maud? At least six years ago. And what the hell was *her* name? All Eric remembered was that she was stocky, disagreeable, and making damned little effort to conceal her disapproval of them. A Miss Scoffey, Scorbey, something like that. Silly woman, holier than thou, getting her jollies with moral superiority, an arrogant *"I've Found Jesus!"* sticker on the back bumper of her cheap blue car. Well, now that you've found Him, he thought, tuck it in a side pocket, and he blew a plume of smoke into the face of the little black boy who had come closer to him smiling tentatively. If that visit had been six years ago, that would make Jessica—what? The little boy backed away, his head again on his mother's knee.

Eric looked at the caption of the pictures and saw a phrase that answered his question: "Eleven-year-old Jessica—" And never a word from her in all that time . . .

And it was while these roiling thoughts of disloyalty and unwarranted loss simmered in his consciousness, that he heard the doctor's mushy voice saying, "Ma'am, I can't find a thing wrong that some aspirin and hot tea won't set right . . ."

"You don't understand. The pain isn't constant, it comes and—"

"But to be on the safe side . . ." The voice was bland and dismissing. "I've written this prescription for a muscle relaxer."

The doctor's receptionist, a black lady with a spray of artificial flowers pinned to the shoulder of her white uniform, smiled and said to Eric Griffith, "Eighteen dollars, sir."

And when he drew out his checkbook, she smiled even more pleasantly and pointed to a sign that said, "No checks."

The ride to Chester County over the Philadelphia Pike through Media was a dismal one. It was a time of year Eric hated. Even though the countryside was lost in darkness, the headlights on curves revealed winter-black trees and limbs shining wet with the first humid, thawing winds of March.

"Eric, I'm sorry," Maud said. Over the hiss of the tires Maud's voice was muted and mildly desperate. "Maybe it *is* nerves, as you say, but the pains are real. I'm frightened, Eric."

"Everybody's frightened of something, Maud." He patted her knee. "It's just a question of getting used to it."

"It's not easy," she said. "That's what you never understand."

"Of course, it's not easy. But if you don't stand up to it, it's just that much harder."

"Oh, bull!" she said, in a harder voice. "When have you ever stood up to anything?"

"Goddamn it, let's not get into that. We'll both feel better when we're home."

"I almost smothered this morning. I thought my fingers were bleeding trying to open that door . . ."

He had heard this particular dream of hers a thousand times. When Maud was eleven years of age, she had been sent to visit relatives in Sea Island, Georgia—an older cousin married to a retired navy commander. They were a childless couple and quite well off, with an ornate beachside home, a cook, a maid, and a gardener who changed into a white jacket at night to serve drinks. One afternoon when her relatives were out playing bridge, Maude had slipped into a walk-in closet to try on her cousin's furs and ballgowns. The maid, seeing the closet door open, had closed and locked it, trapping Maud inside. She had been terrified of the darkness and the frightening feel of fabric against her cheeks, the brush and scratch of chiffon and sequins, the dusty smell of old furs, and the cold rasp of rhinestone

87

shoebuckles across her knuckles. She had given in to panic, screamed for help. Maud had always been convinced that the maid had locked her in deliberately. The maid was a sallow-faced, jealous little darky resenting that she had to serve and pick up after Maud, who was only a few years younger than she was. No one heard her cries (or Coralee ignored them), and it wasn't until seven o'clock that night when the commander brought what he called "a dressing drink" up to the bedroom that Maud was released, at which time she was in a state of shock, eyes rolled up in her head, her pulse pounding at an alarming rate. A doctor was called and he put her into a deep sleep with sedatives.

"I wish to God we could get away somewhere, Eric," she said, looking out at the black, dripping trees. "Someplace where there's sun and we could rest."

"Damned little chance unless my luck improves. I had the long shot yesterday at Hialeah. I doped that race backwards and forward and I knew Adios was ready. I was on the phone to Sam, fifty on the nose, when I realized I had no stake, that I had to bet the favorite."

He slammed the steering wheel with the palm of his hand. "If I weren't always so goddamned strapped for cash, Maud!"

"Somewhere only for a week, to get the smell of that perfume out of my head. When I think of that lying little bitch Coralee . . ."

"Forget it. Until I hit a streak, we'll stay right here. Unless you want to tap your ex, Tony Saxe, for ten fun-filled days in Miami."

"He'd like me crawling to him for a favor." Maud

snuggled deeply into her wool coat, hugging herself with her arms, feeling suddenly small and pitiable and lonely. It wasn't only the memory of the closet she was terrified of. And her resentment wasn't directed solely at the thought of Coralee's smirking lies ("If'n I'd hear Miss Maudie, ah'd let her out surely, ma'am."). It wasn't that. It was the simple awareness of death that had been driven into her consciousness like a heavy, cold spike, not as something vague and dark at a comfortable distance, but as a thing that lived beside and within her. It was the casual inevitability of death that had been forced on her in those hours in the dark closet, the air soft with perfume and terror.

The only specific against it was money, Maudie thought—sunshine, clean winds, being taken care of. She had a fantasy of someplace high in Switzerland, a chalet on a lake, a place where there were saunas, health clubs, masseuses. Fur lap-robes and real old fashioned marvelous doctors, not the golf-playing creeps and their crowded waiting rooms here in the United States, but doctors who made house calls, chalet calls, she thought, arriving at any hour in business suits and purring brown Mercedes-Benzes, prepared to listen to you, to give you tests, to hold your hand, to stay as long as you wanted them to and to tell you at last, over a glass of champagne, that you were blooming fine, just fine.

She was jarred from the reverie by the slap of Eric's fist on the steering wheel. She looked at him and saw that his jaw was set in a hard line, muscles bunching at the corners. The wind from a cracked rear window swirled furiously around her and the noise of the tires had grown louder. The speedometer needle was touching seventy.

"Hey, luv! Watch it." She looked at him closely. "What's got you so stirred up? Certainly not that eighteen dollars ...."

"Here, look at this." He took the issue of *Town and Country* from his pocket and shoved it onto her lap. "Just take a look at the pages I've turned down."

Perplexed, Maud hunched forward on the seat and opened the magazine to the thumbed-over pages, placing it below the faint light from the dashboard clock.

"Well, well," she said, her eyes running across the pictures of the spectators at the Curragh and at Jessica Mallory surrounded by important-looking ladies and gentlemen. "Why, it's your niece, Eric." She smiled at the pictures but there was an expression of rueful envy in her expression. "She's come up in the world, I'd say."

"Yes, indeed. The Curragh, that's one of the finest race courses in Ireland."

"Now, who's the chap with the nice brown beard?" She glanced down at the caption. "Dr. Julian Homewood. I could take him on toast, Eric. He's sexy looking."

"That's my Maud. *I* was all eyes for the horse. Good-looking animal. Sixteen hands at the least."

Maud read from a caption. "The Andrew Dalworth party, up from the Dalworth country home, Easter Hill, in Connemara, with the Dalworth stables entry, Yankee Drummer."

Maud settled back in the seat and let her hands rest on the open magazine in her lap. She looked at Eric's tense profile, eyebrows drawn together in a frown, the wind touching his fine, thinning hair.

"Listen, old pal," she said, a stir of amused excitement in her voice.

He knew that tone. "What is it, Maudie?"

"I just had a thought."

"The usual?"

She poked his arm and said, "A few variations occurred to me. I'll light a fire in the bedroom and you bring up some drinks...You'll think better when you've had a chance to relax."

They drove on in silence until they turned onto the gravel surface of Black Velvet Lane. With the rasp of the tires on the tiny stones, Eric heard another sound, dry and whispering. When he glanced at Maud, he saw that she was carefully tearing the picture of Jessica Mallory and the Easter Hill crowd out of the magazine.

Chapter Twelve ————————————————

In the next years, Jessica lived and grew at Easter Hill in tune with the wheel of the seasons—long, green summers with white caps rolling like lace across the rocks of Connemara's shores, and gulls wheeling against blue-gray skies; and winters that gripped the land in icy hands, with seas dark and heavy and Windkin's hooves like hammers on the frozen meadows. The wave of spring and autumn marked these extremes of weather, bridging them with greening colors and carpets of turning leaves.

Glossy ivy covered the cross Capability Brown had made for the spirited terrier Holly. Another dog had taken her place, a sable collie named Fluter who raced with Windkin and Jessica through the hills above Easter Hill and over the measured runs at Charity Bostwick's small farm.

When it rained in the bitter weather, lightning

storms brilliant above the cliffs, Jessica played chess inside with Andrew, Scrabble alone for practice in her private tower, or games of hide-and-seek with Fluter and the Irish maids—giddy times when they'd take turns hiding in attics or down in the secret priest-hole, which had been cleverly constructed a century ago in a camouflaged alcove off the main dining room. Brocade and panels concealed its entrance. Andrew had explained to her the history of these hiding places for the hunted Catholic clergy, in times when the priests and their vestments and Eucharists had to be spirited quickly to safety when the soldiers of the British Crown were seen in the neighborhood or on the highways. These concealed places were designed so skillfully there were hardly any master builders or architects with tappings and measuring rods who could detect their existence behind seemingly innocent walls of brick and plaster.

Easter Hill's old priest-hole was snug and dark, the air dry with age. Rush matting covered the floor and beneath this a trap door led to cellars. Air filtered in through six small circles which penetrated the walls into corded vines that covered this wing of Easter Hill.

This was a time of growth for Jessica. She was tall and slim and wiry, her eyes a deeper blue, her dark hair hanging to her shoulders. She would be thirteen on her next birthday, and Andrew Dalworth had resigned himself to the fact that she would be going away in the next year or so to a school in England or perhaps Switzerland.

This spring, as a birthday treat since he would be in New York, Andrew Dalworth had agreed to let

Charity Bostwick take Jessica on a vacation tour up the coast and into the upper counties of Ireland. At first he had not been sanguine about the idea, which had been Charity's suggestion, but she had eased his misgivings in her frank, direct way one evening over brandy in the library.

At forty-three, Charity Bostwick was still a handsome woman with prematurely white hair, a deeply tanned complexion and startlingly lively gray eyes.

"We don't understand her gifts, perhaps, Andrew, but we know such things are almost normal in this part of the world. So does Jessica. She doesn't live in London or in a block of flats in New York. She's part of the old countryside of Ireland where the people pay as much attention to stones and earth, to the legends and headstones in the cemeteries as they do to the blathering idiots making time-and-motion studies in factories in the rest of this modern, sterile world. It's still a land of myths and dreams, Andrew, and I think you'd be wrong to try to shield Jessica from it."

"That's certainly not my intention."

"Then let her come with me. Her own father came from up north. There might be some of his people there..."

"I rather doubt that, Charity. We've made extensive checks. The only family of Jessica's we've ever pinned down are an aunt and uncle somewhere in Pennsylvania, and they made it quite clear they wanted nothing to do with the child.

Julian Homewood checked his watch. Eight-thirty of a brilliant spring morning, the first promising softness of summer on the air. He stood at the windows of the Orchard Suite, sipping tea that Rose had brought him earlier. He saw Jessica riding up the rocky promontory, giving Windkin his head, the big hunter and the slim rider blurring as they went through a stand of breeze-bent trees on the way to the summit of the hill.

Jessica had been silent and reserved at dinner the night before, declining politely to make a fourth at bridge, excusing herself and withdrawing to her own room. Yet only yesterday morning she had been in one of her buoyant, tomboy moods, riding with him in the morning, enjoying the excitement of racing him from the top of Skyhead down to the stables. And when Julian had gone up to the Orchard Suite to change for lunch at Miss Bostwick's, there had been a poem from Jessica waiting for him in her dramatic, back-slanted handwriting on Easter Hill's creamy stationery, the folded paper propped up on his dressing table.

Sipping the last of his tea, he looked at the poem again, puzzled by the sharp contrast between its transparent exuberance and Jessica's present subdued mood.

> I think I caught a trout today,
>> a speckled trout, scales of flint-fire,
>> a silver tail.
>
> It flicked in and out,
>> first a shadow in the fern-shade,
>> then a glitter in the sunlight,
>> bright on bright.
>
> It led me up the brook, a sequined tease,
>> pink with sunlight,
>> daring me to catch it with my lure.
>
> I think I did.

And did we dine on it for lunch?
I shall never know. A clever fish...

Perhaps we dined on broiled sunshine.

After breakfast, Julian pulled on a tweed hacking-jacket and rode up the meadow to Skyhead. He tethered the chestnut mare young O'Dell had tacked up for him to a stunted tree near a patch of grass where Windkin was grazing free, held in place as he'd been trained by the weight of his hanging reins.

The day was brilliant. The sun climbed up bright, white skies. Breezes off the sea smelled warmly of kelp. And new spring gorse grew over the Connemara cliffs.

Walking along the bluff, Julian saw Jessica sitting below him on a ledge of rock that gave her a lee from the wind, her yellow scarf and black hair stirred by occasional, erratic breezes. He walked down the narrow trail, finding a perch of rock to sit on. Dr. Homewood took out his pipe and looked appraisingly at her. She was squinting slightly, her long, dark eyelashes lowered to screen out the blinding track of the sun on the water.

"All right, Jess. What's the matter?"

"What makes you think anything's wrong?"

"Well, because I'm extremely clever about things like that. I see a cheerful young girl, happy as a sandboy, writing poems that sound like a flock of larks at play..." He filled and tamped his pipe with a mixture of rough-grain tobacco. "...and the next minute she's frowning like a thundercloud."

"Julian, I am not frowning."

"Technically, you may have a point. But you've

96

hardly spoken a word since last night at dinner."

With a little shrug, shé said, "What's wrong with that? Does everybody have to chatter away all the time like Miss Charity's cousins? I should think they gave you enough talk yesterday to last a week, Dr. Julian, especially the red-headed one."

"Aha!" Julian said.

"Oh, please don't use that silly tone!"

"I can't believe this, Jessica. I think you're jealous."

"I am *not* jealous," she said, a mutinous flash of anger in her eyes. "But you promised to go riding with me after lunch at Miss Charity's. Instead, you took her cousins to the Hannibal Arms where I'm too young to go. So I had the great fun of playing checkers for three hours with Father Malachy."

Dr. Julian puffed on his pipe, hands cupped around the spurting match-flame. When the pipe was going well, he said casually, "Supposing you tell me what's really bothering you, Jessica."

"I know you're going away for a long time, Julian." She looked away and fingered a loose thread on the cuff of her twill trousers. "That's why I wanted to spend as much time with you as I could this weekend."

"I'm sorry. Did Andrew tell you?"

"No, I just knew, Julian."

"I planned to tell you myself today. I'm going to Stanford University in Palo Alto, California, for a year of special seminars and studies. How did that information come to you this time?"

"That you were going? I'm not sure, Julian. I woke up Friday morning knowing it was true." She turned and looked at him directly. "Why are you going away?"

"It's too important an opportunity to turn down, Jessica. It's a chance to work with the top people in the field, a chance to learn more about the work I've been doing—the areas that you and I have been looking into together for quite a few years."

"But we still don't understand all of my feelings."

"Perhaps there aren't any hard and fast answers."

His pipe was drawing well and the strong smoke, streaking blue in the air, eddied about the natural enclosure of the rock. He looked at her and said, "But we do know at least that psychic functioning is much more common than we'd been led to believe. We've learned it's a difficult aptitude to use, or even understand, because it's been allowed to atrophy for centuries. All through history, clairvoyance, precognitive manifestations, were people's perceptual tools, but these tools have been suppressed too often since then, often out of sheer ignorance and superstition. These psychic implements—psychokinesis, remote viewings, out-of-body experiences—have been known to us for ages, of course, but the field of parapsychology is still in its infancy."

Caught up in the subject, Dr. Julian almost forgot where he was. The cliffs of Skyhead and the seas beyond them were suddenly less real than his own thoughts. It was a factor in his personality that made him such an excellent teacher—this mesmerized, and hence mesmerizing, response to the heady reaches of philosophy and science.

"If we imagine our Creator, Jessica—whether we call him (or her) God or Jehovah, the Supreme Force or the Universe itself—if we imagine that ultimate source of power as the ground of all being, the support of all matter and life, it follows that our conscious and unconscious minds, our finite capacities, are inevitably linked to that infinite base."

Jessica had always liked the way he talked to her. It was as if they were both the same age. He never bothered to explain difficult words to her, simply assuming she would understand what he meant to say.

"When a person plumbs the depths of unconscious mind, which you can do so effortlessly, Jessica—the word 'depth' being only a spatial allusion, since I could as easily have said 'height' or 'breadth'—those limits are the approach to the ultimate ground of being. And at that point we can *see* and *know* with infinitely more perception than we can with our senses."

His beard wasn't really brown, she decided, watching his animated face and eyes. It was more like dully burnished copper and nearly red where the sunlight touched it.

Jessica picked a small white flower from a crack in the rocks and said, "But, Julian, Charity Bostwick isn't all that impressed with people who can see things. She told me that half the people in Ireland have some kind of second sight."

"That's just a touch of pardonable chauvinism in the old girl," Julian said.

Jessica studied the small white flower that rested in the palm of her hand, the wind stirring its fragile petals. She sighed and said, "Julian, can I ask you about something else?"

"Of course, Jess. What is it?"

"I've been *almost* seeing something I don't quite

understand. I was wondering—should I try harder to see it? Should I *force* myself?"

"Is it something you're afraid of?"

"I'm not sure. It's not that clear..."

"Then—no. If you force yourself, you'll distort whatever images are coming to you. Because what is *seeing*? Our eyes are only cameras. The brain interprets the picture. And that interpretation is a reflexive, instinctive process, the sum of what we are, what we've been told, the incidence of amino acids in our brains, our response to the external stimuli beating on our nerve endings, waking or sleeping."

He lit another match but went on talking as it burned out in his fingertips. "And in your case, Jessica, there is also a strong input of psychic perceptions. So to force that process would just throw it off balance."

On the occasions that Jessica had attended Dr. Homewood's lectures at Trinity, she had envied the other students—lanky girls and bearded young men concentrating with almost comical severity on Julian's measured word.

When he bent to light his pipe, she watched his hands, clean and brown in the sun, a flex of muscles as he cupped the flame.

She said, "Julian, lately I see a whiteness that alarms me, and touches of other colors."

"Well, then—let's talk about it," he said, and appraising her somber expression and darkening eyes, Julian wondered, as he had so often in the past, at the awesome nature of the burdens they had both assumed. In the years that she had first come to him in Dublin, they had examined the phenomenon and significance of the range of colors that manifested themselves to her inner vision, studying their images as other students and teachers might examine the meanings of words and the symbols of mathematics.

Even her poetry reflected in many instances her awareness of sheen and radiance. The poem she had left in his room this morning was an example of this. He remembered phrases. "—scales of flint-fire, a silver tail," and "a glitter in the sunlight, bright on bright—"

The world of colors, accessible to mystics and psychics, must be one of the reasons, Julian had often thought, why gold and jewels had always been so precious to humanity, symbolizing as they did the world of visions, the infinite beauty of celestial fire. Light over darkness had always been humanity's preference, its need...

One winter when they had been window-shopping together through the streets of Dublin during the Christmas season, they had been impressed by the lights decorating the shops and strung between the lamp posts, and it had occurred to Julian then that these lights, duplicated by the billions throughout the world, were only a simple metaphor for the visions represented in the Star above Bethlehem.

Yet, for all these moments of revelation and excitement and of awareness that they were making progress through difficult, uncharted seas of the unconscious, there was always the element of danger, because Jessica's links to the collective unconscious were so formidably persistent—she was linked not only to vague memories of distant ancestors but to their secret fears and compulsions, which Dr. Julian knew could be a perilous and sensitive connection.

"I've seen this distinctly three times, Julian," Jessica interrupted his thoughts.

"At any particular time of day?"

She nodded and said quietly, "Yes, it was always when I awakened in the morning, just as if it were waiting for me."

"What is the first thing you see?"

"There's a tunnel of whiteness, but this time it's flecked with red. And sometimes I see a memory there."

"Do you know what it is?"

"I think so. It's like when I knew something terrible was going to happen to Holly." She drew a deep breath and watched the wind blow the petals from the flower in her hand, catching them softly and spinning them out above the rocks. "When my mother and father died, there was a lady who looked out for me for a while. Her name was Miss Scobey..."

Julian studied her pale face and shadowed eyes intently. "Why do you think you're remembering this lady now?"

"I'm not sure. There's a sadness about her, Julian, but I don't know why."

"And is that all?"

"I see nothing else. Only the sadness."

A chilling premonition gripped her then and she could feel the wind cold on her sudden tears.

Later that morning, Andrew Dalworth stood at the bay window of his library and watched Jessica ride down from Skyhead. He felt a surge of affection at the sight of that slender figure, hair and scarf flying, guiding the big hunter expertly over the rolling meadows.

In their years together in Ireland, she had turned his empty life around. In his daydreams he often talked to his late wife, Anna, about Jessica, telling her of the child's love and companionship, a tonic that had strengthened and refurbished every fiber of his being. He would have dearly loved to have shown Anna the poem Jessica had written for him last Christmas, neatly printed and tucked with other gifts at the base of the tree in the great hall.

The poem was titled "For Andrew."

> If he were a tree, he would be a great oak,
>   tall and strong-timbered,
>   red in the chills of autumn,
>   whispering green in the coolness of spring.
>
> He would be ships' hulls,
>   trusted strength in deep waters.
> He would be a painted rocking horse
>   with a mane of shavings, waiting for a rider.
>
> He would make a fine wall,
>   a house without wind-cracks and
>   a dormer window looking on a smooth lawn.
> He would be the sharp, shafted
>   arrow in my arched bow.
> He would be the glowing log
>   for the hearth-side of my heart.
>
> And he would scatter, year after year
>   into eternity, the acorn fruit of his branches
> For all the quick, brown squirrels
>   who seek the comforting shade
> Of Andrew Dalworth.

Under the same tree that Christmas morning had been an honorary life membership granted him by the stewards at the Jockey Club in Maryland, a pair of antique dueling pistols from Stanley Holcomb, and dozens of other objects in leather and bronze and silver, all stamped with the unmistakable patina of costly workmanship. But Andrew Dalworth would have traded any or all of those gifts for Jessica's poem, which he always kept with him in his wallet.

As he watched her canter across the courtyard where Kevin O'Dell was waiting for her, he realized how much he disliked having to be away for her birthday, but he also realized that his reaction was to some extent that of an indulgent, possessive father who wanted Jessica close to him constantly, because she brought a flash of laughter into his life, a gleam of quicksilver through the echoing halls of Easter Hill.

Turning from the window, he picked up the phone and put in a call to his New York office to confirm all appointments and travel arrangements for the ten days at the end of this month that he would be in the United States.

In his room that night, moonlight shadowing the old tapestried walls, Dr. Julian wrote a summary report of his conversations that weekend with Jessica. His mood was somber, stirred by forebodings, as he dated a page in his notebook and identified it again as CASE FILE 111.

It is far more than concern and fear for that figure from her distant childhood, Miss Scobey. On one level, these memories should be reassuring ones. But Jessica's preceptions here are on a level I cannot reach. The danger, if indeed it does exist, and her intuitions about it seem to employ Miss Scobey as a triggering agent (cf. notes on Holly). I've given Jessica my address in Stanford, where she's promised to write me, and my phone number in case of emergency. What concerns me most gravely is this: Jessica's psychic capacities expand enormously under stress. She is frightened now, which leads me to one tentative conclusion. The dangers she perceives extend beyond the Miss Scobey "agent" to areas that are immediate and personal, which—of course—embrace her present ambiance, Easter Hill and Ballytone, and everyone here.

Dr. Julian put his notes into his briefcase, locked it, and placed it on the bed beside his other luggage. Then he went to the window and pulled back the tapestries to look out over the cliffs and onto the sea. A fine rain had begun to fall. It was a wet and windless night, more gray than dark, the moon screened in by clouds. Dr. Julian felt a stroke of uneasiness; a sudden chill went through him. For a quick moment, he had not been sure if the fearful thoughts belonged to Jessica or to him.

Chapter Thirteen ─────────────────

On a fine clear morning a week later, Charity
Bostwick and Jessica left Easter Hill for Donegal,
the northernmost county of Ireland, traveling in
Miss Charity's open roadster with their suitcases on
the luggage rack and bundled up against the coastal
winds in tweeds and scarves and leather-palmed
driving gloves.

Fluter followed them to the end of the long
beech-lined lane, the breeze stirring his heavy gray
ruff, but stopped obediently and raised his head for a
last look at the bright green car winding into the
hills. Then the big collie barked at the gulls riding in
on thermals from the sea, and trotted back to the
house and the figures that stood on the terrace of
Easter Hill—Lily and Rose, Mrs. Kiernan, old
Flynn, Capability Brown, and Kevin O'Dell, who
still had a hand raised in the air.

They traveled up the coast to Galway and Connach and Mayo, stopping at inns along the way, and dining in lounges with handsome plates displayed on wall racks and swords crossed above big fireplaces. They reached Sligo when fogs covered the old town and the darkness was sprinkled with city lights.

In a cemetery there, Jessica brushed a film of gray moss from the letters carved on William Butler Yeats' headstone. And when she read the words, she felt a stir of nostalgic affection for the poet and for all the other souls stretching away from her in the reaches of the old graveyard.

> Cast a cold eye
> On life, on death.
> Horseman, pass by!

They visited famous views and landmarks and ancient monastaries, great grey dolmens and crumbling shrines. And in the little town of Glendrum, they learned through an innkeeper of an elderly couple named Mallory—no kin of Jessica, but the old man, Liam Mallory, was well known for his strangeness, his stories and the deep poetry of his speech.

They spent an evening with the couple in their cottage high in the wooded hills above Glendrum, a dwelling of one huge room with an earth-packed floor and a tall stone fireplace where Corinne Mallory, wrinkled and shy in her black shawl and bonnet, sat knitting while her husband talked and an immense silky wolfhound lay at her feet.

During their long swing up and down the western coast, Jessica managed to write postcards at every stop to the staff at Easter Hill and to Andrew and

Dr. Julian in the United States. And between gathering rock specimens, having roadside picnics, and taking the wild-bird count for Miss Charity's records, Jessica also absorbed a fair share of Irish history, partly from her own observation of the land and its landmarks and in part from Miss Charity's rambling, disconnected anecdotes, which ranged from the time of the British Tans to the present troubles with intervening accounts of the activities of her own family and of Capability Brown and the other residents of Ballytone.

Yet among all the crowded, vivid memories of the trip, the one that stood out most clearly and distinctly from all the others in her mind was the one of old Liam Mallory and the strange and marvelous things he had told her, the way he had looked at her when he'd said goodbye—a huge figure of a man with a staff in one hand and tendrils of sea mist curling around his white beard and streaming hair.

"You were sent back to this soil to replenish your gifts," the old man told her. "We need all the wild geese, the second sights, now as never before, not just for this poor, tortured country but for the whole world.

"Once we lived with our gods and were close to them. But man with his bricks and buildings and motor cars and science is always building Towers of Babel that are doomed to drown out the true language of the human spirit."

"And if the gods aren't close to us anymore," she asked, "are they lonely for us?"

"Ah, you're a wise child," Mallory said. "They're lonely for us, dearie, like fathers and mothers for lost, crying bairns. But it's the nature of things. We must go and seek them. You see that, don't you? And for those like you and me, with the gift, that search and its need gives us the power of the elements, the strength of archangels."

"How do we know that that strength is wise?" Jessica asked him.

"You'll know, child. You'll know when the time comes . . ." and he thrust his staff against the roaring winds and held it there as a shield for the two of them.

This was the way Jessica would remember him in all the years to come, a patriarchal figure struck from the myth and rock of Ireland, as dauntless in the face of time as the elements themselves.

The morning after she returned from Donegal, Jessica breakfasted with Andrew Dalworth, who had flown into Shannon the night before. Then, with Fluter wheeling about her in excited circles, she ran down to the stables to tell Kevin O'Dell that she was back at Easter Hill.

O'Dell was working in the blacksmith shop, his collar open and his sleeves rolled up, and Jessica was proud of the look of strength in his arms, muscles coiling as he shaped a horseshoe with powerful hammer blows. He listened with interest as she told him of Sligo and Connach and Yeats' grave, the old churches and the inns and pubs they had stopped at, and raised her voice to make herself heard over the clanging hammer and the explosive hissing sound when O'Dell plunged the white-hot horseshoe into a bucket of water.

At first, he smiled at her enthusiasm, seeming to relish her account of the journey. But as she recounted what Miss Charity had told her of Capability Brown and the troubles and of the time they had spent with the old couple above Glendrum, his mood changed, and he shook his head in obvious exasperation.

When she finished her account of that hillside visit, trying to recreate for him the fantasy and wonder of old Liam's visions, Kevin put his hammer down on the anvil and looked directly at her, a controlled impatience in his expression.

"What is it, Kevin?" she said, "What's the matter?"

"Jessica, this talk about charms and spells and elves dancing on shamrocks or whatever you're saying, it's a lot of nonsense," he said.

"You wouldn't talk that way if you'd heard Liam Mallory."

"He wouldn't waste his time or breath on me, Jessica. Those old-timers save their talk of leprechauns and widows' curses for children and gullible American tourists."

"Just because you're growing a mustache, you think you know everything, Kevin."

Kevin looked embarrassed, but he continued. "I'm sorry, Jessie, but it's true. Those old people may be harmless enough but in a way, they're the curse of Ireland. They're living in a past that never was or truly existed. They don't contribute anything to us except superstition and ignorance. They're simply not part of the real world."

"If they're not, then what *is* the real world?"

"I can show you where that is, Jessica. Just take the Number Ten bus south from Shannon to where the German-owned factories are today. It took foreign brains and foreign capital to teach this old country about reality. Our choice was always to half-starve, digging for potatoes or finding a boat to take us to America or New Zealand. So there's your real world, Jessica: my brothers in factories making tools and goods, not old men in the mountains believing that every sparrow coming in a window was chased by the Devil."

He didn't understand, Jessica realized. It wasn't the literal sense of what the old man had told her that was important. That the seventh son or a Mac or a Mc had the powers to cure sickness in farm beasts. "A Mac can spit in his own hand and wipe the pain from a mare's flanks," old Liam had told her. And he had spoken that night, his voice rumbling like the waves below them, of priests hidden away in the homes of the Catholic faithful, of the Black and Tans spying on men in pubs or out searching the houses, of a chance word or drunken whisper often leading to the betrayal and death of loyal countrymen.

And more about the strengths of curses and visions and specifics against evil... It was valuable not because it was *true*; it was valuable simply because it *was*.

Like their own Father Malachy's talk of gentry bushes inhabited by the wee folk and strange, unexplainable happenings in the woods in winter moonlight. Once he had told Jessica of seeing a woman in a black dress in the shadows at the back of his church. Struck by something terrible in the woman's expression, the old priest had asked her if she'd wanted to confess her sins. In a low, trembling voice, she had said, "It's too late for you to hear my confessions, Father. I am damned."

The woman had placed her bare hand on a

wooden crucifix above the baptismal fountain and then—Father Malachy had blessed himself at this point—she had fled the church, and Father Malachy had told Jessica, whispering now, "You can still see the imprint of her hand, the mark of her fingers burned into the sacred wood."

Jessica had turned her eyes to where Father Malachy's finger had directed them, to the cross above the baptismal fount where there was, in truth, a warp or shadow on the grain of the wood. She knew it could have been made by freezing winter temperatures or shafts of strong sunlight through the stained glass windows, and that it could well be that Father Malachy had fallen asleep in a pew and dreamed the whole thing. Yet the truth of it one way or the other didn't seem to matter very much, she decided; what mattered was the faith of the old priest. Just as the important thing about Liam Mallory was not the exact truth of his words but the magic of belief that charged his life and his energies with significance.

As Kevin turned to pick up another strip of metal with a pair of tongs, Jessica said, "You're welcome to your real world, Kevin. I like old Liam's world and I like feeling a part of it."

"That's an easy choice for Miss Jessica Mallory of Easter Hill to make."

"Now what is that supposed to mean, Mr. Kevin O'Dell?"

"It means that you don't have to worry about Number Ten buses, factories or anything else in the real world. You'll be off to boarding school next year where you'll have a toff's education, a nice little Jaguar or Mercedes when you're old enough, lots of time for theatre and musicals. You'll find you'll miss Fluter and Windkin more than you do the human beings here at Easter Hill."

Tears of hurt and anger started in her dark eyes. "That's a terrible thing to say, Kevin."

"Now listen, Jessica, I didn't mean—"

"If you didn't mean it, why did you say it?"

"But, Jess, let me—"

The young lad stopped there, startled and almost frightened by the cold intensity of her expression, the dangerous anger in her eyes. Taking a deep breath, he said, "I'm sorry, lass. I mean it. I'm sorry."

A strange, little chill went through Jessica. She had experienced something unfamiliar to her, a stir of resources, a surge of power that made her apprehensive. "It's all right, Kevin," she said, troubled by the hurt in his face and frightened by her own anger. "It's all right."

Then Jessica turned and ran with Fluter from the blacksmith shop and up the lawns to Easter Hill.

She had never had a quarrel with Kevin before, not even a misunderstanding, and the memory of it disturbed her the rest of the day. At dinner she was quiet, and Andrew wondered aloud if she might be coming down with something.

"No, I think I'm a little tired from the trip," she said.

"Yes, you look a bit pale. Why not tuck in early, Jessica?"

"I think I will, Andrew."

He folded his napkin and held her chair as she rose from the table. "Mr. Brown's been damming up two streams in the south pasture. He thinks they'll make fine duck ponds." He glanced at his watch.

"Since it's such a fine evening, I'll take the bay hunter out for some exercise and see how the project's coming along."

In the great hall, he put his hands on her shoulders and smiled into her eyes. "I missed you very much on this trip, Jessica."

"I missed you, too, Andrew. There's still so much to tell you."

"All right, run on up now and I'll come in to say goodnight to you." He kissed her on the cheek and she would always remember the feel of his big, caring hands on her shoulders, the roughness of his tweed jacket and the familiar smell of his worn, leather cigar-case.

Jessica stood at the windows of her bedroom looking down at the gathering dusk toward the stables. A yellow rectangle of light glowed and she could see Kevin's shadow occasionally as he moved about tidying up.

It seemed to Jessica then that she had somehow become older than her years. A breeze from the terrace outside her room stirred her long hair which was still damp from the bath. She recalled a game they had played on soft dusky nights like this, with Andrew reading in the library and Mr. Brown putting the last touches to the rosebeds.

From her window she would signal to the stables with a flashlight and Kevin would answer with a light of his own, then he would collect "messages" from Windkin and bring them to Jessica, climbing the big oak tree and swinging from its top limbs to the mansard roof and on down thick clusters of ivy to Jessica's terrace.

They talked in whispers until it was dark, Jessica

with her elbows on the windowsill, Kevin kneeling on the terrace. Their happy acceptance of a make-believe world had added a sweet and exciting innocence to their friendship.

But she remembered one experience that hadn't been so casual and tranquil. They were exploring caves on the beach below the house, searching for shells and mosses and sea mollusks. Kevin was about to plunge his arm into a dark pool formed in a crevasse by the waves when Jessica was seized suddenly by a vividly ominous premonition.

"Don't, Kevin!" she shouted. "Don't!" Running to him, she grabbed his shoulder and threw him aside with such a burst of strength that he went sprawling onto the wet floor of the cave.

"Damn it, what's the matter with you, girl?"

"Look, Kevin, look!" Using a piece of driftwood, she probed into the small dark pool of water and finally brought up the pale, gelatinous form of a poisonous ray-fish, swollen as big as a soccerball.

"Lord Almighty, how did you know it was in there, Jessica?"

"I *knew* it was there. Haven't I told you to listen to me?"

"Yes, Jess, but I never know when you're serious. I mean, *real* serious."

"Well, you'd better start learning..."

"That I will," Kevin said. He smiled and rubbed his aching shoulder. "You got a grip on you like a blacksmith, Jessica. You could have broken my arm."

"I'm sorry, Kevin. I was frightened for you."

Acting on an impulse now, Jessica found her flashlight and played it across the weathered boards of the stables. Within minutes she heard the sound of footsteps above her and then the creak and rustle of the stout, ropey ivy as Kevin dropped lightly onto the terrace.

"I'm sorry I spoke as I did, Jessica. Everything seems to be changing so fast."

He was feeling the same bittersweet loss which she had experienced, Jessica realized as she watched him pick up a handful of leaves from the terrace and let the wind blow them from the palm of his hand and spin them off into the darkness. A frown darkened his face.

"It used to be that all this was home, Jessica. Ballytone, Easter Hill, the Head and shores, all the country around here. A place where the O'Dells belonged."

"But you still do, Kevin."

"It's different now. My brothers are gone south to work and that's more final than when my dad died. I can visit his grave and put flowers at the cross, but Tim and Mike will never come back here, you can be sure of that. Soccer games we played at the top of the street, that's all over now. There's nothing but my mother with her beads at night, the telly and waiting for news from them, the two of us with hardly a word between us when we sit down for our supper."

"And is that why you were angry with me, Kevin?"

"We're friends and I'll tell you the truth. I was angry when you said that Miss Charity had talked about Mr. Brown and the troubles. She has the right to speak her mind, of course, but there are some things better kept silent. It's what's torn us apart as a country, Jessica, the hatred between countrymen over religion and politics."

116

He looked at the moon just slipping up past the crest of Skyhead and said, "It's time I'm going. Mr. Dalworth will be back directly."

He stood and looked steadily at her. "I won't be coming here again this way, Jessica. It's no longer a game and we're no longer children. Do you understand what I'm telling you, Jess?"

"I think so. It's what you said about things changing."

He smiled and said, "And something more than that, too."

"But, Kevin, I don't want things to change. I know that's foolish, but it's the way I feel."

"And I know how I feel. Things *have* changed, so goodnight, Jessica."

When he had gone, Jessica closed her windows and sat down on the edge of the bed, her hands locked tightly in her lap and the faint moonlight glinting on tears in her eyes.

She looked at the clothes laid out for tomorrow morning and realized that there was something mocking and irrelevant about them now, the boots upright in their blocking stays, the gray jodphurs, the blue jacket and yellow silk scarf. She knew she wouldn't be wearing riding clothes in the morning and she realized with a twist of terror that Kevin had lied to her tonight, unwittingly, but lied nevertheless. She knew he would come to her room again on another occasion...

Jessica saw then a play of shifting colors in her consciousness and the shapes behind them were so suggestive of menace that she shook her head quickly and helplessly. Closing her eyes, she covered them with her hands, but the childish gesture

117

couldn't erase the blazing white radiance in her mind, diamond-sharp reflections as clear and pitiless as a cold winter sun.

She saw with hideous clarity, as clearly as she had seen the bloated form of the poisonous ray-fish with Kevin, saw there in her scented room exactly what would happen to Andrew.

She leaped to her feet and faced the door of her bedroom, hearing voices raised in the great hall below and knowing what they meant. Then another sound, the frantic footsteps coming up the stairs, and Jessica knew with a sad and terrible certainty just what message was being brought to her.

Old Flynn's voice sounded in the hallway, breaking with anguish. "Come, Miss Jessica, come at once! Mr. Dalworth's had a terrible fall. They've sent for the priest and the doctor..."

Chapter Fourteen —————————————————

The point-to-point race over four miles of rough country was underway, and when the powerful field of hunters came into view from the low meadows, an excited cheer rose from the crowd, but Eric Griffith thought bitterly, "I should have bet Plover's Egg...dammit, dammit, *dammit*!"

The big roan mare, notably a strong finisher, had a length on the favorite, High Pockets, as they swept past the tawny row of maples that marked the start of the last quarter-mile to the finish line. Instead of Plover's Egg, Eric had committed a reckless share of his dwindling funds on Harlequin, because he had overheard Colonel Innis making a sizeable bet on that entry, and now the pig was running dead last, its tail swishing about like an electric fan.

The crowds watching the point-to-point had gathered on the sprawling Cadwalader estate in eastern Maryland for a day of spring racing. In tweeds and cashmeres and burnished boots, they lined the homestretch, cheering on the tightening contest between High Pockets and Plover's Egg. Others watched from cars on the high ground above the race course, tailgates loaded with wicker baskets and sparkling cocktail shakers.

"Plover's Egg," Eric thought again. Then he repeated the name aloud and a group of grooms standing near him laughed and one of them, without glancing at Eric, said, "He could be right, of course, which would make it an even once ..."

The groom, a stocky man in his forties, was employed at the Cadwalader stables. His name, Eric knew, was Hank Dunker.

"That's pretty good, Hank," another groom said and laughed again. "Plover's Egg ... just to make it an even once."

When Griffith realized they were referring to him, he felt a sudden warm and prickling heat in his cheeks. Sly, boorish louts, he thought, a sustaining anger growing inside him.

So far, it had been a disastrous day. He had lost the last four races and there was no hope for this one now, with Harlequin forty lengths behind the leaders. This was his last chance ....

"Hank!" he said suddenly.

The groom turned and regarded him with masked eyes. "You call me, Mr. Griffith?"

"That's right. I gather you don't agree with my estimate of Plover's Egg."

"Well, you're entitled to whatever you think." His friends grinned and looked away. "But I don't see this here Plover's Egg holdin' off High Pockets."

"How would you like to back your judgment for, say, fifty dollars, Hank?"

"I expect you know the books are all closed on a race that's runnin'..."

"Yes, I'm aware of that and I know from the fumes drifting my way that you and your friends have been drinking rot-gut. But isn't that all beside the point? I have fifty dollars that says Plover's Egg wins it."

Hank glanced down the home stretch at the horses, only two hundred yards from the finish line now. His eyes narrowed alertly, and he rubbed his stubbled beard with the back of his hand. "Thing is, Mr. Griffith, I know where them horses will be after the race, they'll be back in their stables. And I know where *I'll* be after the race. Thing I'm not sure about is where *you'll* be..."

"I see they're teaching impudence on welfare now," Eric Griffith said angrily, and pulled a fifty-dollar bill from his wallet. "Here's my money. I suggest you put up or shut up now, Hank."

Obviously resenting Griffith's tone, the groom said in a surly voice, "All right, you got yourself a bet." Climbing onto a fence that kept spectators off the course, Dunker cupped his hands around his mouth and shouted toward the charging horses.

"Move it, High Pockets! Stir those damned stumps of yours!"

The groom's friends fanned out behind him, pounding each other on the shoulders and yelling encouragement at the favorite.

And to Eric's dismay, he saw that the tide of the

race was turning inexorably to High Pockets, who was now running like a smooth and effortless engine, while the roan mare was fighting the reins, her ears twitching—a sure sign she'd lost interest in the race.

He couldn't even win here in a country meet, he thought in rage, with the purses provided by local charities and the proceeds from the refreshment booths marked for a pumping engine for a volunteer fire company. No, not here, and never mind the dream that had become a tiresome exercise in futility over the years—the thoughts of vindication in singing, winning weather at Hialeah or Del Mar or the fabled courses at the Curragh or the fence and brush at Aintree where they ran the Grand National.

Christ, Eric thought bitterly, feeling the familiar but always dreadful loser's knot of anxiety tightening in his stomach. Dunker and his friends were still looking in the opposite direction, shouting boisterously now as High Pockets lengthened his lead over the field. Griffith took that opportunity to put his money away and slip off into the crowd.

After crossing the meadow on the opposite side of the finish line, he hurried off between rows of cars parked on the hill. He soon became aware that Hank Dunker and his cronies were pursuing him relentlessly through the crowd, leaping up and down to keep track of him, spreading out through the paddocks and behind the refreshment booth where the ladies from the local fire-company auxiliary were serving hot dogs and coffee.

Eric found sanctuary for several hopeful minutes in the narrow confines of a yellow metal portable privy. Then someone hammered on the door and a voice thick with laughter said, "Come on, pal, or there's gonna be a damned Johnstown flood out here..."

Griffith took cover after that near the judges' tent where Colonel (Lord Douglas) Innes, Mrs. Cadwalader's houseguest for the weekend, stood talking to his hostess. He joined them, smiling, and pulled off his tweed hat in a deferential gesture to the old lady.

Secure for the moment, he relaxed and listened to Colonel Innes, a stocky, graying Highlander who was complimenting Mrs. Cadwalader on the organization of the day's events. Then the colonel stared at Eric, his bushy eyebrows coming together in a straight line above his clear, cold eyes.

"Where did you get that tie, Griffith?"

"We dressed at the crack of dawn and there was barely any light—" To his chagrin, Griffith heard a stammer of nervous conciliation in his voice. He was caught; there was no way of conning this shrewd old colonel. Still, Eric made a weak effort saying, "I shared a room with a chap and we must have switched ties."

"Probably didn't belong to him, either. It's the Scots Grays, of course."

"Well, I wouldn't know, sir," Griffith said, glancing nervously at the red and orange stripes which had looked so festive and stirring in the Olde London Shoppe in Philadelphia.

"I can assure you *I* know it." The colonel laughed without humor. "It's my own regiment and we fly two hundred years' of battle flags."

"I wonder what Hank wants," said Mrs. Cadwalader, a stout graying woman in mauve tweeds and low walking boots. "I believe he's beckoning to you, Mr.

Griffith. Did you have a bet with him? He's making that rather timeless gesture with his thumb and forefinger."

"As a matter of fact, I believe I did. It was such a small amount, it slipped my mind."

"Then you'd better pay him what you owe him," Mrs. Cadwalader said, and Griffith was stung by the fact that she hadn't for an instant assumed that it might have been the other way around, that he'd won a bet from her boorish little groom, that the impudent bastard owed *him* money. But on second thought, he wouldn't take it so personally. What churl, of Dunker's caliber, he mused, goes in hot pursuit of a creditor? Griffith fished the fifty from his pocket and made his way, only slightly begrudgingly, to the gesturing groom.

Plover's Egg, Eric Griffith thought with searing exasperation. He twisted on the hard narrow bed and reached for his glass of whiskey and water. He had stopped off at a motel on the outskirts of Lancaster, a row of dingy cabins that stood across the street from a storefront mission, whose facade was garish with flashing neon signs.

Griffith sipped his drink and put the glass back on the table beside the bed. His thoughts were rancorous and self-accusing. His ego had been shredded after all, by the abrasive encounters with Mrs. Cadwalader's groom and that arrogant Scots bastard, Colonel Innis.

Plover's Egg, he thought, disgusted with himself. What had made him bet on that glue-factory reject? In his heart he knew the answer to that, realized it was the toney, plummy sound of the name that had attracted him, words redolent of country estates and ladened sideboards and cheerful servants, the kind of life he had envied so long and pointlessly that it sometimes made him weak with anger to even think about it.

Over the years, as a kind of masochistic hobby, Eric Griffith had collected menus of hunt breakfasts and debutante teas, mortifying himself by studying the varieties of food and beverage laid out for the rich and privileged—tables of cold meats, York ham and roast beef; other tables for hot dishes, lamb chops, filets, sausages, and kidneys. And spread between them on snowy linen, silver dishes of kippers and grilled salmon, marmalade and muffins, creamy mounds of Scotch woodcock, fluffy omelettes and plovers' eggs... There it was, as plain as day, the reason he had made that humiliating bet with Hank Dunker. Eric, driven by the man's sneering familiarity, had played the squire of the manor then—"They teach impudence on welfare now...." He heard his own words again and was glad he said them.

Eric poured himself another touch of whiskey, and stood to turn down the volume of the television set. An announcer with a long, gray face was discussing the plight of the dollar in the Scandinavian countries.

He'd taught that coarse loudmouth a little trick or two after all, he thought, sipping the watered whiskey. Eric saw himself in a mirror hanging above an unpainted chest of drawers, the bare overhead light glinting on his blond hair and the bright stripes of his tie. He raised the glass to his image in an ironical toast.

"Here's to you, Mr. Griffith. And screw everybody else, including those fancy Scots Grays."

In a better humor, he stretched out on the bed, shifting his position to avoid the glare of the neon sign across the street. The "Jesus Saves" legend was flashing rhythmically and creating broken shafts of orange illumination around his room.

He smiled, thinking of the Cadwalader groom and relishing the inevitable scene, the sputtering denials, the flushed looks of shame, the stammered protestations of innocence.

Chuckling, he sipped his drink, only half-aware of the news bulletins from the television announcer. After the races that afternoon, Eric Griffith had unobtrusively joined the crowds flocking across the estate to the tea Mrs. Cadwalader had given in honor of Colonel Innis. Avoiding the hostess and the colonel, Eric had gulped down several large whiskies which was why he had stopped here in Lancaster for the night, too tired and boozy to drive the extra hour or so down to Chester County.

And it was while he stood quietly in the corner of the Cadwalader's crowded library that the idea had come to him, complete and perfect in one exciting flash. He noticed a bronze incense burner which he identified as authentic Ming, his envious eye having become sharp and knowledgeable over the years. An ornate censor, sun-spotted with gold, and no bigger than a baby's fist, sat next to a vase of daffodils on a table near an open window, a pie-crust table of shining cherrywood whose raised edges and detail of hardware told him its provenance, a mint Chippendale.

That's when it had struck him, while he was

nursing his drink and his grievances against a society whose conventions seemed designed solely to frustrate and humiliate him. You could damn the booze to your heart's content, he thought, putting an arm across his eyes to shield them from the flash of the sign across the street. Sing the praises of clean living, all true enough, but when you needed a touch of guts and nerve to get you through a tight spot, nothing did the job better than a few jolts of whiskey.

Bolstered and assured by drink, his hand had moved with unerring speed to the Ming censor and he was gone with it in the same movement, easing through the crowd to the pantry and kitchens where he exchanged a few genial words with the staff before letting himself out into the gathering darkness behind the manor house.

In the grooms' changing quarters near the horse barn, Eric had found Hank Dunker's footlocker and wedged the Ming burner into a pair of sweat socks, stuffing these back under an assortment of trousers and knit underwear. (A friendly but anonymous telephone call to Mrs. Cadwalader in the morning would close the trap with finality. "A word from a friend who must be nameless . . . A pity. Your groom Hank, after all, probably has imprecise notions of right and wrong. But I did happen to see him reach through that open window in your library and snatch that little treasure. . . .")

Eric stood and toasted himself once again in the mirror.

The television announcer said, ". . . drew Dalworth, one of the world's wealthiest and most famous industrialists, injured earlier today, remains in a coma, his condition listed as grave at his country

127

estate, Easter Hill in Ireland."

Eric Griffith smiled at the imaginary phone he was pretending to speak into. "Please, Mrs. Cadwalader, you mustn't thank me. If our sort didn't stick together, I can't imagine what the world would come to."

He went into the bathroom and splashed cold water on his face. Reaching for a towel, he frowned suddenly, trying to grasp and remember what the announcer had just said. His thoughts swirled with whiskey, and he couldn't pin it down. Somebody hurt, injured. An accident?

Turning on the water tap, he splashed more cold water on his face, feeling the coldness pierce his eyes and bring reality once again into focus. *Dalworth*, that was it, and *Easter Hill*, he knew those names. At the TV set, he knelt, drops of water streaming down his face, and listened with frustration to a beaming sportscaster talk about basketball and somebody setting picks.

Eric flipped from station to station, but there was nothing on but local news and police shows, cars racing into alleys, machine guns flashing like fireflies in the darkness. Gripped by a sense of excitement, Eric dressed hurriedly and left the room.

At the first intersection, he bought a newspaper from a battered vending machine. The story was on page one, below the fold, an old picture of Andrew Dalworth descending from an aircraft in Athens. The headline read: "Industrialist in Coma After Accident." A subhead read: "Thrown from horse on Irish estate." The dateline was UPI Dublin.

Standing there on the sidewalk, a wind stirring refuse in the gutters and the flashing lights of the

"Jesus Saves" sign falling across the paper, Eric Griffith read the story twice, experiencing a thrill of personal involvement at the sight of familiar names and places. Easter Hill and Jessica Mallory and Andrew Dalworth, the Honeybelle stock farms in Kentucky, the Dalworth Holding Company... He knew them all, he realized with sustaining excitement, a sense of growing power.

Since the time he'd come across Jessica's picture in *Town and Country* in the doctor's office, Eric and Maud Griffith had kept a file on his niece, newspaper clippings and articles, items from the sports and financial pages relating to the Dalworth Stables and business enterprises, a piece in *Vogue* on the jade animal collection, a lay-out on Easter Hill in *Architectural Digest*, and other articles.

His thoughts were polarized, tightly circling two facts: in a coma... condition grave...

In his motel room again, he read the story a third time, aware of the sound of his heart thudding against his ribs. He felt wrapped up in this business, in some way an essential, vital part of it. He almost felt sorry for Dalworth, leaving so much...

And what of Jessica?

Eric Griffith sat sipping whiskey judiciously now, just a touch to keep his thoughts spinning smoothly, while a gray light of dawn mingled with the flash of the neon sign on his hard, thoughtful features.

Jessica... She would need help now, counsel, advice. Not the nudgings and maneuverings of managers and lawyers and accountants—cold, impersonal bastards out to fleece the child and feather their own nests. Now she needed, *desperately*

129

needed, the warm and loving strength of her own family.

He stood and began pacing, twisting his big hands together and casting sidelong, almost furtive glances at the mirror, analyzing his appearance as he might a horse in an exercise ring, giving himself points for a high forehead, a straight nose, and eyes that appreared, when he smiled, to suggest an amiable honesty.

There were, on the other hand, the thinning blond hair, the fine network of cracked veins across his cheeks and, deep inside him—fortunately where it didn't show—the self-pity and angers that could only be dissolved in whiskey or by Maudie's annealing administrations.

He stared at himself in the mirror, knowing that he was close to something very important, quite literally the chance of a lifetime. Yet, in his envious observations of privilege, Eric had learned a great deal about the very rich. And he knew from bitter experience that they despised, above all, not the nouveau, because all money had become nouveau today. Oil money bred indiscriminately, after all, with sterling and Marks and Eurodollars and produced bastard offspring that deposited Iranian sheikhs in the delis of Beverly Hills and Greek shipping merchants on Park Avenue so scared of kidnapping that they instructed the doormen to address them by assumed names. No, nouveau was acceptable, Eric thought, with a flash of anger. Nobody gave a damn where you came from once you had it, but what the rich really hated were the *pretenders*, because they could truly and finally

130

screw up the game for everybody.

And so, from the outset, he must establish credibility, deal from a secure financial base. Not join the whining beggars with cups who would be drawn toward Easter Hill like bees toward honey. He wouldn't go through that groveling performance because the essential thing about Eric Griffith was not what the mirror reflected of him, and not even what the world might think of him, but the very genes and cells that linked him to Jessica, the blood from the same family that flowed through their veins.

He scooped up the phone and dialed the house on Black Velvet Lane. When Maud answered, saying, "Hello? Hello?" in a sleepy, irritable voice, Eric said quietly and insistently, "Maud, I want you to listen carefully to what I'm going to tell you. Don't ask questions. Just listen to what—"

"Is that you, Eric?"

"Of course, it is. Did you think it was Sinatra with a singing telegram?"

"You said you'd be home tonight. Where are you, Eric? I've had this funny ache in—"

He sighed and said, "I'm sorry, Maud. Now forget that and *listen to me*. I want you to call Tony Saxe first thing in the morning. Set up an appointment for both of us tomorrow at his club, anytime that's convenient for him."

"Eric, what have you been up to?" Her voice was sharper.

"I'll explain when I see you at Tony's."

"Well, okay. I guess I wouldn't mind seeing the old place again."

Maud had sung at Tony Saxe's club in Camden, New Jersey when she was married to Tony, crooning of lost loves and smokey afternoons in a pleasant but reedy little voice, whose vibrations went largely unnoticed by the patrons—hostile people with a look of challenge about them, talking usually of sex and fixed fights and ward politics.

"You've got just one other thing to do, luv," Eric said into the phone. "Bring along that file, the manila folder in my desk. It's in the top drawer, the one with all that stuff on Jessica Mallory..."

Stretching out on the unmade bed, Eric laced his hands behind his head and smiled thoughtfully at the ceiling. He felt charged with confidence now, unintimidated by the thought of mingling his interests with the world of Tony Saxe, an arena of cunning tricks and deceits, a world of street-smart hustlers.

Eric felt keenly alive and hungry. He wanted breakfast, a big one, eggs and a ham steak, the yolks pricked and running into the hashed browns, a stack of buttered toast to mop it up with, and cups of hot black coffee. He wanted a woman, achingly and surprisingly, and a stinging shower, fresh clothes, wanted to be in one of those dark New York bars, the faint, smoke-streaked light breaking on rows of bottles and glasses, and a girl, perhaps a young actress, glancing at him from the corner of her eyes, wondering at his secret, confident smile.

The neon sign from the storefront church across the street flashed against his face, the garish tones softened by the spreading morning light. He wondered why he found it so exasperating. Perhaps it was just his normal reaction to fanatics with their convictions of eternal chumminess with the Lord, hopeless losers with their ridiculous, credulous Faith and Tithings, their tiny plastic saints hanging from windshields, blatantly arrogant bumper stickers proclaiming their faith in the Second Coming, their rapture in spiritual sex or unisex or some damned thing, their joy in having found It or lost It or shot It into a side pocket, every car begging to be rear-ended.

Suddenly, an involuntary shudder went through Eric's body. Sitting up, he stared in a growing understanding and consternation at the tremor in his hands. He reached for the bottle and drank the last half-inch of whiskey straight from the neck, feeling the raw heat of the drink in his throat but realizing it wouldn't touch a deep, anxious coldness that had settled in the pit of his stomach.

He knew now why those flashing church lights had irritated him at first and why they frightened him now, bringing with them as they did the nearly-forgotten memory of a disapproving lady with cold eyes and a bumper sticker on her blue Volkswagen.

Chapter Fifteen

Several days later, Miss Elizabeth Scobey sat at her desk facing the view of Philadelphia's center city. It was a brilliant spring morning, and on such a day, superb with clean, cold winds off the rivers, she could see beyond Ben Franklin's statue to the green expanses of Fairmount Park and from there all the way to the stone steps of the art museum.

Her phone rang suddenly.

"There's a man to see you, Miss Scobey." It was Emily at the front reception desk. "He doesn't have an appointment but he says it's personal and urgent.

"What's his name, dear?"

"Griffith, Mr. Eric Griffith."

The name rang a vague bell. Miss Scobey glanced at the clutter of files and forms on her desk and said with mild exasperation, "I honestly don't have a moment to spare. What does he want to see me about?"

After a minute, Emily was back on the phone saying, "It's about an adoption you processed through this office about eight years ago. A little girl named Jessica Mallory. Mr. Griffith is her uncle. He wants to talk to you about something that happened back then. He insists it's terribly important."

Staring out at the gray-stone, gingerbread mass of City Hall, a vague, uneasy memory of a wintry countryside and Eric Griffith stirred in her. "Well, all right, send him in..."

"—I believe the human spirit is malleable, Miss Scobey. I believe it can be reshaped in the image of our Lord God, Jesus Christ. I believe in the phenomenon of redemption and rebirth—"

"Mr. Griffith, I don't disagree but I have a deskful of—"

"—and that is why, I entreat you to hear me, Miss Scobey, that is why I've presumed on your valuable time. Because you, dear lady, in the mysterious ways of the Lord, may have been His instrument for the therapy of humility that led me to the higher plateaus of grace. Since you helped me once, even unknowingly, to be born again, I pray—"

"Mr. Griffith, I have every sympathy with what you're trying to say, but would you please tell me what it is you want?"

"May the Lord bless you, Miss Scobey. Eight years ago, you came to my home to see me and my wife, Maud, to discuss our niece, Jessica Mallory..."

As Eric Griffith recreated that scene in the past, talking in a rambling, circuitous fashion, with evangelical sweeps and frequent invocations of the Deity, Miss Scobey remembered in considerably sharper detail her trip to the Griffith place in Chester County so many years earlier. And the memories were far from pleasant—Griffith with his nervous posturings, and his wife, eyes wide and round as the keys of a cash register glinting in her doll-like face, slamming the car door hard.

"Our unChristian selfishness has been a heavy burden, Miss Scobey, but like the cross itself, I have carried it as a sweet penance for my many sins."

Suddenly, Miss Scobey realized why Eric Griffith was here. Of course. Andrew Dalworth, on the TV news and in the papers this week, still in a coma, near death from his injuries in a riding accident . . .

"Just what is it you want with this office, Mr. Griffith?"

"My beloved wife, Maud, is close to death, an incurable disease. I want you to help us, to join with me in bringing her into the presence of a forgiving God *in this world*—before she must account to Him for her sins in the next."

Miss Scobey looked at him without expression. "Just how would you expect me to do that, Mr. Griffith?"

"You took extensive notes when you talked to Maud and me, Miss Scobey. I want to show those actual notes, that evidence of our callousness, to my wife, Maud. To make her understand how desperately she must seek the Lord's forgiveness for having closed her arms and—yes—her heart, against our own flesh and blood."

Miss Scobey's phone rang. After listening a moment, she replaced the receiver and said, "Would you excuse me, Mr. Griffith? That was my boss. I'll be back in a few minutes."

136

Eric Griffith relaxed and looked with a musing smile at the views of the city stretching out toward cloudless horizons.

Suffused with a glow of superiority and a confident anticipation of victory, Eric savored the view along with the recollections of his meeting with Tony Saxe the day after the point-to-point at the Cadwalader estate.

Oh, yes, Tony had seen the money in it, that was clear enough, poring over the news items about Dalworth, the pictures of Easter Hill that Maud had brought to his club, holding them up for closer inspection, muttering statistics aloud in an excited voice, his face sharp and cunning as a vole's, the smokey light in his office catching the glint of his diamond-chip cufflinks and the rings on his fingers. And the greedy glint in his eye had become as bright as those rings when Eric had pointed out that Andrew Dalworth was a widower with no children of his own, no living relatives and no one in the world with stronger emotional and legal claims to his affection and wealth than his adopted child, Eric's own dear niece, Jessica Mallory.

Tony Saxe's club, The Rhinestone Quaker, was located near the river on the outskirts of Camden, New Jersey, just across the Walt Whitman Bridge from Philadelphia—in a neighborhood gray with decay and noisy with funky jazz bars, with massage parlors and adult bookshops balanced in a precarious equipoise with the few respectable jewelers and furriers and pawnshops struggling for honest livings in a pocket of urban decline.

Saxe had paced behind his desk, the piano from the lounge sounding faintly around them, only the

137

quick puffs on his slim brown cigar betraying his excitement. He hadn't aged since Eric had last seen him, but it would have been difficult to tell in any case, because Saxe's deeply tanned face was not only without lines or wrinkles but almost totally without expression. His eyes were dark, so dark the whites seemed strangely vivid in the frame of his hard features and cropped black hair. And he still favored the characteristic decorative and sartorial embellishments—jewelry, rings and tie-pins (this one a gold eagle with a small ruby in its claw)—and neat, dark suits, mohairs, Italian silks and gabardines.

Eric remembered that an incautious female companion of Tony's had once told him that he looked like a Lebanese rug merchant who had struck oil. Tony Saxe had shown his appreciation for her humor by smiling and putting out his cigar on the back of her hand.

"But, Eric, you haven't been in touch with this kid, not even a postcard, for eight years," he had said. "With that kind of money, there'll be vultures flocking down from everywhere. Who do you think you'll fool?"

"I expect that. I'm prepared for it."

"And so far, I've only got your word on what the stuff's worth, the jades and antiques and all."

"Check it out. Check with your friendly neighborhood shylocks—just show them those pictures of Easter Hill."

"Then how do we pull the handle on the slot machine? How do we cash in our chips?"

"We'll need a crooked cop or two in Belfast and an international fence. You should be able to set that up, Tony."

"So all you're asking is that I finance the deal to ease your way into that kid's life?"

"You'd be a fool if you didn't, Tony. And Maudie insists you're no fool."

Tony Saxe had stared hard at the photographs of Jessica and Dalworth taken at the race course of the Curragh, and then at the entrance to Easter Hill where a gray-haired butler held open the door of a Daimler.

He said then, "What I'm staking my loot on is whether you'll keep your mind on the job, Eric. You gotta play a role, no slip-ups, stay nice and sober for as long as it takes. What it comes down to, pal, is whether you want it bad enough."

And it was at that moment that Maud burst into the room, like some howling Cassandra—Eric recalled with amusement—accompanied by Benny Stiff, Saxe's professional muscle. She had just remembered Miss Scobey, the way they'd treated her, the things they'd said eight years ago, with Miss Scobey's busy little fountain pen taking down every word of it.

Studying the skyline of Philadelphia, Eric savored the memory of their faces, Tony Saxe's and Maudie's and Benny Stiff's, when he had said blandly and casually, "You needn't worry yourselves about that. I'll take care of Miss Scobey. I've already set up an appointment with the good lady."

And yet, as he sat beside the social worker's desk, fingering the cross in his lapel and watching the pigeons flying their strafing runs above City Hall, and yet—his thoughts drifting without direction—there was something unappealing, in fact, downright distasteful, about these sordid details. To be forced to include such brazen thugs as Tony Saxe and Benny Stiff, to con a pious gullible fool, to soil himself with talk of theft and crooked art dealers and alibis. What the devil did he need *alibis* for? How could he, in fact, "steal" what practically belonged to him as the child's only blood relative?

Still, Eric thought, there was a catch to that, a brutal, frustrating flaw to his claim. While he had certain "rights" to Easter Hill, it came down to that—they could only be exercised at the whim of distant fates, far, far down the long roads of chance, when Jessica—perhaps an old, old woman by then—might die and leave her estate to the next of kin. But, and God, what a bleak thought this was, where would he and Maud be then? Long past any hope of enjoying the monies, the luxuries of Easter Hill, of savoring that life with its privileges.

And even if Jessica wanted to throw them a bone out of charity's sake, she wouldn't be in a legal position to do so until she was twenty-one, years and years from now. And Tony was right. With lawyers and administrators watching her estate, shrewdly eyeing those millions, there was no way they'd appoint him her executor or legal guardian, no way that could ever happen. But as a favored uncle, a needed and trusted companion, a beloved mentor, he might be a guest at Easter Hill . . . At least until he had won her confidence and set up the scheme he had let Tony Saxe in on, the deal that would give them all a load of loot from Easter Hill.

But still it was enraging, thought Eric, to have to settle for a pittance of what he felt was rightfully his . . . His middle name was hardly a coincidence; Boniface, the Irish saint, the confidant of kings and popes; Boniface, the legendary patron of inns and hostels, a name that symbolized a spirit of grandness in style, lavishness in hospitality, connoisseur of all gracious material pleasures.

That was his birthright, what was owed him by the covenant of primogeniture, not the role of petty thief snatching up a crust of bread with the silverware and fleeing from his own estates with the dogs after him...

He smiled at these reflections but when he heard Miss Scobey's brisk footsteps, Eric Griffith quickly composed his features into an expression of suitable gravity.

"I'm sorry, Mr. Griffith," she said, sitting down behind her desk. "What you're asking is simply not possible. All of those files and notes are confidential, under the seal of the Court which presided over the child's adoption."

Eric Griffith sighed and said, "Well, I imagine I was hoping for some kind of miracle, Miss Scobey. I was clutching at straws. If I must lose Maud, well—" He smiled directly at Miss Scobey, feeling with an actor's gratification the cool glint of tears in his eyes. "You must understand how desperately and terribly I need the hope, for myself and for my dear wife, that she will be in heaven when I join her with our Lord Jesus Christ..."

Miss Scobey was suspicious, but troubled by his obvious pain and misery. It was difficult for her to relate this unhappy and shattered human being with the whiskey-drinking braggart she had encountered at their first meeting eight long years ago. Now the bogus tweeds and foxhead tie pin had been replaced by a plain black suit with shiny elbows, a dark narrow tie, a pale blue shirt. The thinning blond hair was neatly combed. Even his eyes seemed different to her, luminous and moist behind wire-framed glasses. In his lapel was a tiny silver cross with a filigree of metal forming a Crown of Thorns around it.

Elizabeth Scobey had deliberately chosen a profession which gave her a constant and ample opportunity to help people—childless couples, abandoned infants, lonely children, all the helpless and needy of the world, that's what this warm, stout-hearted woman felt she had been put on earth to do something about.

"Mr. Griffith," she said impulsively, "could you bring your wife to this office? Maybe, just maybe I can have an exception made in this case and have the files transferred here."

Eric stared down at his hands. "I've waited too long. Even a month ago, she might have—. But she's bedridden now, weaker every day."

"Mr. Griffith, you have my sympathy. I do hope you understand, however, that I can't do anything about the regulations."

"Of course. This was just—" He sighed wearily. "...a last chance, a plea to St. Dismas." Standing, Eric smiled into her troubled eyes and then, with a gesture that surprised and moved her, he patted her hand. "You mustn't worry about us, Miss Scobey. But there is something you could do for both of us which would be a great kindness."

"Certainly, Mr. Griffith, if I can."

"Would you pray for us? Please..."

Miss Scobey felt a sting of tears in her eyes. "Of course, I will, Mr. Griffith. Of course, I will."

"Thank you, Miss Scobey. God bless you."

But before he had taken two steps away from her desk, the social worker was on her feet, a quick, restraining hand on his arm. Despite her earlier skepticism, her religious impulses overcame her. "I'll arrange to have your wife look at those files. We are all on this earth to do the work of the Lord. I feel our dear Lord would want me to—" Her quick mind was already managing the details. Adam Greene was still Judge William's bailiff at Court J-11. There would be no need for a formal requisition.

"Are you at the old address in Chester County, Mr. Griffith?"

"Yes, Miss Scobey, we're still in the same place, R.D. #1, Black Velvet Lane."

"Then you may expect me about ten Saturday morning..."

Eric Griffith had been expecting approval from Tony Saxe, had quite frankly, in fact, been anticipating a pat on the back for a job well done, but when he completed his account of the meeting with Miss Scobey, Saxe looked despairingly at the ceiling of his office and said, "Goddamn amateur night! You sitting there telling me—"

"What the hell do you mean 'amateur night'?"

Tony Saxe stood and paced behind his desk, a hand massaging his tanned jaw, light refracting in brittle slivers from his ringed fingers. "It's just what I figured—you don't want it bad enough, Griffith."

A knock sounded and the door opened.

Benny Stiff—stocky, in his forties, with broad, hammered features and skin that looked like it had been baked too long in the sun—held a piece of paper in his thick, muscular hands.

"I just took a call from Chicago, Tony."

"Yeah, yeah, what is it?" Saxe said irritably.

"They gave us a name. Simon Ethelroyd. Britisher working out of—" Benny glanced at the paper in his hand. "—a place on the east coast of Ireland, Ardglass, the man calls it, about thirty or forty miles south of Belfast. Handles imports, exports, with a boat at St. John's Point."

"That's about as useful as last week's newspaper," Tony Saxe said.

Eric said angrily, "If you'd stop this infantile posturing, Saxe, and just tell us—"

Saxe cut him off with a gesture—an abrupt, chopping motion with a glittering hand. "You still haven't thought the damned thing through," he said. "You pulled a little showboating con game on this dumb broad, and you think that hacks it. Just tell me this, Eric, just tell me one damned thing," Saxe said. "What're you planning to do when she shows up at your house? Sprinkle salt on her tail and grab them records when she turns around?"

"I'm glad you haven't lost the light touch, Tony. I'll tell you *exactly* what I'm going to do," Eric said, speaking in measured accents. "I intend to take those files and notes from Miss Scobey and destroy them. End of scenario. What in hell did you *expect* me to do?"

"Christ!" Saxe slammed the palm of his hand down on the top of his desk. "So what do you think she does then?"

"It sure ain't the end of the script," Benny Stiff said.

"You think she'll just drive back to Philadelphia

and forget the whole business? Take a nap, watch television, and never mention to anybody that some crazy madman named Eric Griffith gave her a big snow-job about a dying wife and then snatched a bunch of official records from her? You think she won't mention that to her neighbor, her boss, her boyfriend maybe? Hell, no. She'll drive to the nearest police station and blow a whistle you could hear all the way from City Hall out to the Main Line."

"Well, ultimately it would be only her word against mine, which is a risk we'll just have to take."

"You still don't understand. We can't afford *any* risks in this deal. No flaps, nobody blowing whistles." Tony Saxe was speaking slowly and quietly, but with bitter intensity. "Maud filled me in on how it was when that old broad came out to interview you and her. Told it back with all the trimmings. So just you try to make a play toward the kid, Eric! Try for adoption or power of attorney, or just to get her confidence—with shrewd lawyers and accountants watching your every move—"

Saxe made a helpless gesture with his hands, then let them drop to his sides. "That's when this Scobey character is pure poison, because she can finger you for a phoney and a liar. Christ, do I really have to spell all this out?"

"I'm afraid you will," Eric said. "Frankly, I know no way to guarantee her silence."

Tony Saxe exchanged a tight smile with Benny Stiff and said, "You don't have much of an imagination, Eric."

"Now what's that supposed to mean?" Eric said, but his throat was suddenly dry because he saw now what was expected of him.

"It's like I figured," Tony Saxe said. "You just don't want it bad enough. You like the idea of you and Maud living it up like royalty, putting the con on a helpless kid. But for the hard work that's got to be done, you got a pair of blinders on. Because you won't face the problem staring you in the face."

"Wait a minute. Are you suggesting that I—?"

"I'm not suggesting one damned thing. Benny? You hear me suggest anything?"

A smile flared across Stiff's hard face. "Not a damn thing, boss."

"I'm not *telling* you anything, and I'm not *suggesting* anything. Maybe you understand the problem now, maybe you don't."

Tony Saxe leaned forward over his desk, supporting his weight on his hands, staring evenly into Eric's eyes. "But I just got one more thing to say. My gravy train just stopped, Eric, and it don't move until you solve your little problem. Otherwise, I can't risk it."

"I think we understand each other," Eric said at last, relieved at the solid timber of his voice. "Of course, a bit of plain speaking would have cleared matters up at the outset. Still, the sunburst of the English language never shone too bright on the Levant, did it, Tony?"

The grinning black face, the rolling white eyes, the tittering malice of Coralee's laughter shot in a frightening fashion through the clouds of perfume, the smothering weight of furs and gowns, the unendurable pressure of the walls closing in on her,

146

constricting her lungs and throat, compacting her body into a squeezed and hobbled mass on the floor of the musty closet... ·

Maud struggled to free herself, her lips flattened over her teeth, a strangling sound breaking past her corded throat muscles.

And Coralee was laughing at her, the sound rolling like thunder through her dream.

Striking out with her arms and legs, Maud kicked the sheets and blankets into a tangle at the foot of her bed. She lay still then, gradually waking as the dread, familiar dream faded away into the depths of her mind.

There were tears on her cheeks, and she could feel her heart racing and striking against her ribs. She turned on the bedside lamp and picked up the pills she laid out each night beside a glass of water. Two blue and two yellow and four sips of water... after which she lay breathing deeply and waiting for the residual fear of the dream to disappear and her poor laboring heart to slow down.

"Eric," she said. "Eric, please. Hold my hand."

There was no response, no sound from his bed. When she raised herself on an elbow, she saw he wasn't there, saw his robe and pajamas neatly folded over the bedstead.

She lay back, darker thoughts streaking her mind, remembering last night. Eric had been preoccupied at dinner, hardly touching his food, and then had shut himself off in the small bedroom he used as a study, drinking and playing old jazz records until at last Maud had guessed the reasons behind his strange behavior. Even now, the memory of the

147

scene with him held blurred edges of terror, an awareness of implications their strained words had only hinted at.

"Would you please turn that damned music down?"

"I'll do precisely what I like, Maud. I'll do what I must."

"And I know what that *must* is, don't I, Eric . . . ? What you and Tony Saxe are planning."

"If you know so much, why are you asking me about it?"

"For God's sake, do you have to?"

He had said something then she didn't understand. "There'll be no singing or winning if I don't."

"Then I want you to promise me something, Eric. You know I'm not too strong, you know how I worry. So, unless you promise me never to mention this subject again—"

"You'll what, my dear?"

"Don't make me say it, Eric."

He had laughed drunkenly. "Ira Washburn would replace you with your understudy. You'd make a ridiculous Lady MacBeth with that attitude. Goodnight, Maudie. I haven't heard a word of this . . ."

From the garage behind the house, she heard the station wagon starting up. Feeling bereft and vulnerable, Maud stood and went to the window, pulling back the curtains on an early spring morning still gray and chill, the mists rising like fogs from the patch of lawn behind the Griffiths' home.

The black station wagon was pulling out of the driveway, Eric at the wheel, but this would have been only a guess if she hadn't known his profile so intimately, because there was little visible of him now, what with the collar of his jacket pulled up high around his turtleneck sweater, the big, dark sunglasses and the peak of a tweed cap shadowing his forehead.

The Saturday morning turned clear and bright with the rising sun, dissolving a ground mist as fine as lace and revealing the first of the spring flowers—snowdrops and yellow star-grass, Miss Scobey noticed, identifying these along with pinkings of early clover.

On her drive to Chester County that morning, Miss Scobey's Volkswagen threaded the narrow roads, twisting through rolling meadows and open country, where horses were out to pasture and winter-rotted haystacks and manure piles were steaming in the first heat of this sunny day.

Despite the glory of the weather, for which she had duly and enthusiastically thanked the Lord, Miss Scobey's thoughts were again censorious as she reflected on that strange gentleman, Eric Griffith, and his troubled wife, Maud, at death's door and still unrepentant in the shadow of her Maker.

The files and notes relevant to the Griffiths were on the seat beside her, tucked into her old leather briefcase. She had reread them last night and once again been filled with exasperation at the Griffiths' heartless indifference to their orphaned niece, Jessica Mallory.

Turning onto a narrow black-topped secondary road, Miss Scobey resolved to temper her judgment with Christian mercy, putting out of mind the abrasive evidence in the files and remembering instead the miraculous transformation, the growth in grace that had occurred in the case of Eric Griffith. And perhaps there was hope as well for his wife, and if Miss Scobey would be the instrument of the Lord in Maud's salvation, then she would, she must, perform the role with forbearance and kindness. As a token of this Christian goodwill, Miss Scobey had stopped at a health food store in Philadelphia to buy a suitable present for the ailing Mrs. Griffith—a round, squat jar of rose-hip jelly now tied with a fancy green ribbon and resting on the seat beside her briefcase.

Frowning, Miss Scobey braked her car, slowing it down to a stop at a road barrier, a long wooden sawhorse with lanterns suspended at either end of it. A crudely drawn sign reading 'detour' and an arrow were tacked to the crossbar, diverting traffic (for no good reason that Miss Scobey could understand) into a narrow dirt road flanked by stands of timber and deep, cavernous excavations which had been dug out many years ago for their rich veins of feldspar and mica.

The silence out here in the back country was restful and almost complete, the stillness trembling now and then with the cry of birds and the sound of spring winds high in the trees.

Turning onto the dirt road, she saw that the steep, downward sides of the old mica pits still sparkled in the sun where sharp bits of the spikey mineral pierced the brown earth. She drove on slowly, her car dappled with the light filtering through the big trees that arched over the road.

Glancing up, she saw in her rearview mirror that a black station wagon had turned into the lane behind her and was closing the distance between them rapidly. Miss Scobey slowed down and angled off as far as she could toward the right side of the road, straightening the wheel when she heard the thornbushes brushing the side of her car.

Cranking down the window beside her then, she waved to the station wagon to pass—overtake was the word the British used, she recalled from the first and only time she had been abroad, a charter flight which had included a walking tour of the Cotswolds and a weekend of sightseeing in London. She checked the rearview mirror again and saw to her surprise and irritation that the big black car gave no intention of going around her but had slowed to match her speed and was now only six or eight feet behind her bumper.

She despised this sort of motoring discourtesy, so unnecessary, so stupid, but there was nothing for her to do but move back into the middle of the lane, because directly ahead of her there was the lip of a deep mica pit, its steep, bramble-choked sides cutting sharply down into a gorge, whose floor was covered with shards of rock and winter-black shrubbery.

What happened next was as unexpected and ghastly as a fatal lightning bolt. Swerving to the left, the station wagon's motor roared with a rush of crescending power and then it was abreast of Miss Scobey's small Volkswagen, the driver looming high above her on this rutted country road. There was something familiar about him, the set of his shoulders, a reddish-blond glimpse of sideburns, but Miss Scobey couldn't be sure if she knew him or not because his features were almost completely obscured by the collar of his tweed jacket, sunglasses, and the pulled-down peak of his cap.

The big black vehicle angled sharply toward her and she cried out desperately, "Watch it, watch it, you idiot!" but even as her straining voice echoed on the cool and fragrant spring air, there was the hideous sound of grinding metal. The station wagon crunched heavily into the side of her car and sent it spinning out of control down the steep side of the mica pit, turning and crashing end over end until it landed on its roof on the bottom of the man-made ravine, wheels spinning futilely in the air.

Miss Scobey lay in a tangled heap in the wreckage of her car, upside-down and hopelessly disoriented, her head and cheek pressed harshly against the windshield and dashboard, one of her arms twisted at an unnatural angle through the spokes of the steering wheel.

In her shock and confusion, she felt no pain at all, no particular concern or anxiety, remembering only the crash of the two cars, the grating metallic wrenchings and ruptures that still seemed to be exploding in her eardrums.

Later, in her drifting, dreamlike condition—she couldn't guess how long it had been since the accident—there was the sound of footsteps, and she saw—and how bewildering this was—a man's arm coming through the open window and a hand closing on her briefcase, snaking it free from the car.

There was some pain now, a sharpening clarity, and Miss Scobey was grateful when the man's arms and hands came through the window once again. Touching her shoulders, the hands moved along her arms to her throat, strong hands, warm, strong hands, tightening now, slowly but inexorably, and

Miss Scobey realized with a touch of wonder that these hands had not come to help her. Her second-to-last thought was how grossly unfair this whole business was. Her last thought was, what a shame to waste that lovely jar of rosehip jelly, smashed and broken against the windshield.

Miss Scobey did not live long enough to see the smoke begin to curl from the rear of her car or to hear the crackle of flames.

Chapter Sixteen ——————————

A clean, hard wind was blowing down Skyhead and through the trees at Ballytone the morning of Andrew Dalworth's funeral. There had been a formal memorial service the previous evening at Easter Hill. The names of mourners from Ireland and the United States and other countries were now listed in the registry book which Flynn had set out on a rosewood table in the great hall.

The final ceremony at the cemetery with its weathered headstones beside Father Malachy's church was reserved for members of the household staff and close personal friends.

In a bottle-green coat with a black velvet collar, Jessica stood close to Charity Bostwick. Fluter lay at the girl's feet, his head resting on white forepaws, his liquid eyes fixed on the casket with its coverlet of lilies and white carnations. The wind stirred Jessica's long black hair and brought a pinkness to her cheeks. She stood with her head held high, determined not to cry, because she believed that holding back the tears she wanted to shed was a way of saying (childishly and helplessly) that Andrew wasn't really gone from her yet, not yet...

Holding a long silver aspergillum, Father Malachy sprinkled holy water on the casket and began to recite the funeral prayers.

"Into Thy hands, Oh, Lord, we commend the spirit of Thy humble servant—"

The old priest wore the vestments of a Requiem High Mass—black chasuble figured with silver threads, and a stole in a matching pattern. On his white head rested a dark, four-cornered biretta with a silver tassle.

"As a stranger, he entered our land; as a friend, he entered our hearts..."

Standing in the crisp winds, fragrant with flowers, Jessica did not feel lonely. How could she with her friends gathered at his grave... Miss Charity, Capability Brown, Kevin O'Dell, and Rose and Lily, who wore simple white dresses in the Irish tradition, which held that such pristine apparel symbolized the joyous welcome of the dear departed's soul into the Kingdom of Heaven. No, Jessica didn't feel alone at this hour, but she had never felt so shattered and forlorn in all her life—not even after the death of her parents—because she couldn't conceive that anyone, anywhere could ever replace Andrew Dalworth.

"There was never a time I asked this good man—" Father Malachy stopped and shook his head vigorously. "No, I'm telling a lie, for I never had to *ask* this good man for help of any kind. He always offered it before I could ask."

Mrs. Kiernan wept openly into a lace handkerchief. In the open fields surrounding the burial site were groups of people from Ballytone; Tige Wicks, publican of the Hannibal Arms; classmates of Jessica's and their parents—the men with heads bared, and the women with rosary beads, lips moving in prayer.

Angus Ryan, Dalworth's solicitor from Dublin, stood directly behind Jessica and Charity Bostwick, the breezes stirring his white hair. They had talked of the inevitable future, seated at the fire in the library, while Rose and Lily went quietly about their work, eyes red from weeping, fetching and caring for the doctors and nurses who tended to Andrew Dalworth in the last unconscious days of his life, his lined face liked old ivory against the pillow in his darkened bedroom.

"We aren't giving up hope, little lady. Not for one minute," he had said to Jessica. "God willing, Andrew will be sitting hale and hearty at the head of his own table in a fortnight. But in the meantime, I'm sure he'd like you and me to have a practical chat."

That afternoon, with the first signs of spring heartbreakingly evident in the trees and shrubs outside the library's great leaded windows, Angus Ryan had explained the nature and function of Andrew Dalworth's principal trusts and foundations. The first represented his business interests, and the second, his experimental farms and breeding ranches. Both were administered by a board of directors in New York with monthly resumes sent directly to Easter Hill by Dalworth's personal aide, Stanley Holcomb. The third trust, administered by Angus Ryan from his Dublin offices, provided for the maintenance of Easter Hill and all such personal expenses as might be incurred by Jessica Mallory, including education and allowance until she reached the age of twenty-one, at which time she would, as Andrew Dalworth's sole heir, become the legatee of his entire fortune.

"When he enters into the Kingdom of Almighty God, the blessed immortal soul of our friend, Andrew—" The old priest's voice trembled on the cold air, fragrant with the faint sweetness of floral wreaths.

To distract her during these past sorrowful days, Capability Brown had allowed Jessica to help him with the gardens, and they made a good pair—the wiry old man in tweeds and a bog hat, the slim youngster beside him. Together they had lined the borders of the flagstone paths with primula and marguerite daisies, circling the bird fountain with alyssum seedlings. In the sally garden, Mr. Brown had showed her how to disc the ground and to grind the bone-meal and manure from the stables into the fertile, black earth.

And during those dreadful final days, Dr. Julian had called frequently from California. The connections were excellent, and his voice had sounded so warm and clear and close that it brought tears to her eyes. She hadn't told him that she was frightened, but he had sensed it.

"What is it, Jessica? I know how you feel about Andrew, we all do. But something else is bothering you."

"I'm not sure, Julian. I can't quite see it..."

A BBC helicopter flew a circling pattern above

157

Skyhead, photographing the funeral services for the evening news and the staccato beat of its rotaries mingled with the distant boom of the surf in coves up and down the shores.

Whatever her fears were, she must face them, those ephemeral, elusive shapes with glittering colors spun out in her consciousness. With a sense of strength and purpose, Jessica stood by Andrew Dalworth's grave and thought of the old man she had visited with Miss Charity on that stormy night in Donegal, and how she had felt when Liam Mallory had led her up a path to the brink of the precipice from where they could hear the waves crashing below them and see masses of scudding dark clouds tumbled by gusting winds across the moon.

In an almost frightening fashion, the very essence of her soul had been drawn to something older and infinitely wiser than herself then, and that something was the very earth and wind of Ireland and all the people who had lived there and now lay under headstones in all the sodded graves across the land.

Old Liam Mallory had put an arm around her shoulders and held her close to him, and when he spoke, voice as strong as the waves pounding the cliffs, she was no longer afraid.

"Jessica, I know you have gifts. Trust in them and trust your bright colors. Never doubt and God will make you wise, but against evil sometimes wisdom and trust are not enough. If their forces gather against you, remember me and I will give you strength . . . What we are is what we must be, child, and it is beyond us."

On a narrow road that curved through an open field toward the cemetery, a green Ford sedan came into view, stirring up dust as it turned and stopped in the parking area near the rectory. Villagers turned to glance at the man and woman who stepped from the car and walked toward the group of mourners clustered about the open grave.

"And as man was born of dust, he shall return to it ... to be given everlasting life through the Grace of Almighty God."

It was over.

Jessica knelt for a long moment in silence, her thoughts turning on the last words she had composed in Andrew's memory.

> In the dark skies of life
> I shall find you,
>
> My star-father. I draw spirit
> from your dear and distant light.

She broke off a single white carnation from the coverlet that draped the casket and pressed it carefully in her prayer book. Then she whispered, "I hope you know, and always knew, how much I loved you, Andrew. When we have a son, we shall name him after you. We'll call him Andrew and pray that he will be as good a man as I knew you to be ..."

A shadow fell across her kneeling figure, and Fluter growled softly. Jessica looked up and saw a man she had never seen before, a man with thin blonde hair who smiled down at her and said, "Dear, we came as soon as we possibly could."

He helped Jessica to rise and then introduced her to the woman who stood beside him, a tall lady with a wisp of black veiling shadowing her bright, polished eyes. "This is your Aunt Maud, my dear."

Still smiling, he placed a large, strong hand on her shoulder. "And I, Jessica, I am your Uncle Eric."

Chapter Seventeen ─────────────

The last guests and mourners departed Easter Hill
later that afternoon, with only Eric and Maud
Griffith and Angus Ryan staying on in the library
with Jessica, a quiet group seated at the glowing
fireplace.

The household staff had found a therapy for their
grief during the long day by caring for friends and
visitors who stopped by to pay respects, setting out
sliced cold meats, preserves, and custards on the
sideboard of the dining room and passing drinks and
sherries on silver trays to those in the great hall and
drawing room.

The tones of the library were soft in the fading
spring sunshine, the carved arms of chairs and sofas
and the leather bindings of books catching golden
reflections from the shining bay windows.

Eric found himself comfortably at home here,

relaxed in a huge leather chair with a glass of whiskey in his hand and a view of meadows and trees stretching off to the sea. He liked the look of the books reaching to the dark timbered ceilings and savored the perfection of his Waterford goblet, the smokey taste of the Irish wiskey.

What a blissful, relaxing change from the haste and confusion of the last few days. After the first televised reports of Andrew Dalworth's death, they had scrambled frantically to get their tickets and pack for the trip to Ireland, with Tony Saxe haggling over money and Maud being her usual pain-in-the-derriere, matching silk scarves to tweed suits, and pearls to black silks—a petulant, time-wasting process—all of that plus the last detour on the way to the crowded airport, the cab ride to the dingy shop off Front Street to bargain with the bald old man about the silly trinket till they almost missed the plane.

With the taste of sour copper in his mouth, the nerve-frazzling Customs at Shannon, the disorientation of jet lag, the expensive rented car and driving on the wrong side of the curving country roads—well, it was good to stretch out his legs and sip a whiskey and feel at home.

Maud was making herself agreeable to Jessica and Angus Ryan, something she was proficient at when such efforts coincided with her own interests. Jessica told her about Windkin, her studies at school, and her stamp and coin collections, while Eric allowed Angus Ryan to ramble on in his boring brogue about the industrial expansion in southern Ireland and the present offerings at the Abbey Theatre in Dublin.

Eric's mood was ambivalent. He relished these graceful surroundings, so subtly speaking of privilege and class, yet the knowledge that they belonged, not to him, but to his solemn and haughty little niece was stirring resentments in him.

Mrs. Kiernan, the stout old biddy from the kitchen, had sniffed in disapproval when he had gone to the sideboard for this last whiskey. He knew from experience how long a nose house-staff had for money: they peeked at labels in jackets, they heard the gossip behind your back when you were gone, and if you happened to be out of a job or overdrawn, it was like wearing a leper's bell around the neck. Even the lumbering brute of a collie (Fluter, was it?) had taken a dislike to Eric, growling and baring his teeth when he only so much as poked his head into Dalworth's private study, a teak-pannelled room connected to the library and fitted with files and phones, a desk, and a display of antique hand-guns.

Angus Ryan pulled an old-fashioned gold watch from his vest pocket. "Well, I'd best be thinking about my train." With a smile at Jessica, he said, "Lass, shouldn't you be wanting a little rest?"

"I'm all right, sir. I think I'd prefer to go down to the stables to talk with Windkin for a few minutes. But I'll wait till you're off to the station."

I'd prefer this, I'd prefer that, Eric thought moodily. Such a high-toned little miss with her fine manners and Dalworth's millions, and not toddling off obediently with a swift smack on her behind if there were any complaints about it. That was very likely what she needed, spoiled rotten by an indulgent old sugar daddy, the same as the staff in the kitchen, who could also use a reminder about

162

who were the servants and who were the masters here.

Maud said, "Eric, we've got to be leaving, too, but first I want to show you this view from the bay windows ..." Taking the glass from his hand, she put it on a table and led him to the far end of the library where she pointed out over the fields and spoke to him in a low, angry voice, "Goddamn it, get your mind onto why we're here. Stop swilling whiskey and playing the lord of the manor."

"I've got as much right here as anybody," Eric said sullenly.

"Talk to the old fool, talk to him *now*." Smiling and raising her voice, she said, "The sun on the hills is just breathtaking."

"Simply marvelous," Eric turned and joined Angus Ryan who had stood to examine a fine woodcut in a hand-carved frame.

"Mr. Ryan, could I have a word with you?"

"Why, indeed you may, Mr. Griffith." Angus Ryan looked steadily at Eric, a faint smile brightening his shrewd blue eyes. "And what word is it you want with me, sir?"

Eric heard (or believed he heard) a dry, pointed tone in the solicitor's voice. And he didn't like the way Ryan was regarding him, sharp eyes glittering beneath tangled eyebrows. Of course, this wouldn't be a country yokel of a lawyer, not with Dalworth's fortune to look after.

Eric glanced over his shoulder to make sure that Jessica was out of earshot. She was indeed, seated at the fire with Maud, leafing through an album of photographs.

"It's just this, Mr. Ryan. Since you are the

executor of the Dalworth estate and Jessica's legal docent or advisor, and since Mrs. Griffith and I are the child's only relatives, I thought it might be useful if we had a talk to discuss our mutual responsibilities."

"If you see the need for such a meeting, of course, I am at your service. But I think you should know in advance that my responsibilities are neither flexible nor negotiable. They are spelled out precisely by the terms of Mr. Dalworth's will."

"Naturally, I assumed they would be," Eric said. "However, as Jessica's blood kin, I also have responsibilities."

"Ah, yes." Again the tone was honed and dry. "I'm sure you do, Mr. Griffith. I take it you and Mrs. Griffith aren't on a rigid schedule?"

"That's right, Mr. Ryan. We're at the Hannibal Arms."

"It is indeed fortunate that you have this free time coincident with Mr. Dalworth's demise. May I suggest we meet in my offices in Dublin, say, a week from today?"

Eric smiled. "Perhaps I could give you lunch, Mr. Ryan."

"The office will do nicely, Mr. Griffith. Shall we say eleven o'clock?"

As they turned back toward the fireplace, Maud opened her handbag and removed a heart-shaped golden locket on a fine, slim chain. "I'd like you to have this, dear," she said to Jessica.

"It's very lovely," Jessica said. "But I think I'm too young to wear jewelry..."

"What a sensible attitude," Maud said with a quick smile. "But this is special, my dear, and I think you'll enjoy having it. You see, Jessica, this locket belonged to your mother."

For the first time in that long and painful day, there was a glint of tears in Jessica's eyes. She took the small gold heart from Maud and impulsively threw her arms around her and kissed her on the cheek.

"Couldn't you and Uncle Eric stay here a while with me at Easter Hill?"

"What a very sweet child you are." Maud smiled mistily at Eric and Angus Ryan and touched a handkerchief to the corner of her eye.

Christ, it would soon be slopping over at this rate, Eric thought. Trust Maud for the maudlin . . . At least she hadn't forgot to remove the price tag from the locket, which they'd bought in a Philadelphia pawn shop on their way to the airport.

In the following few days, the Griffiths settled easily into the unhurried existence at Easter Hill, with breakfast trays in the morning, luncheons on the terrace overlooking Capability Brown's gardens, and dinners at night in the large dining room with its inlaid ceiling of harps and shamrocks and—a deference to older customs—the small choir-loft, which, Jessica had explained to them, was used only for holiday programs and pantomimes.

Eric kept a tight rein on his drinking. It required discipline to listen with attention, to stroll as a guest through rooms and gardens, which he was convinced, if there were any justice at all, belonged just as much to him as they did to his preposterously lucky little niece.

The complexity of the plans were a healthy

therapy against his resentments, however, and he spent the first few days at Easter Hill unobtrusively photographing furniture and objects of art in the gardens and in the rooms of the house he had access to—the great hall, the library, the drawing room, and various of the upstairs suites.

For the benefit of the staff, he played the part of the amiable American tourist and uncle, compiling a family album, taking many shots of Jessica walking in the orchards and gardens or posed in front of statues and highboys. And late in the evening, using a night-time lens and flash, he compiled a pictorial record of French chairs and sofas, a Louis XV Bombay commode, an Ormolu-mounted tulip-wood bureau, a Henri II desk chair, a choice collection of Chinese porcelain figurines, Directoire settees, antique Aubusson tapestries and Chinese rugs, many small bronzes, animals studded with precious stones and, in the formal fruit arbor, a pair of garden seats enameled with peacocks and flowers and, at the fountain, a reclining horse in bisque-fired clay and a pair of brass and ivory dolphins.

When the list was as complete as he could make it without arousing the suspicions of the maids or old Flynn, Eric excused himself on a fine, clear morning and drove into the village of Ballytone.

Lunching at the Hannibal Arms, he struck up an acquaintance with two American tourists. One of them had the ridged forehead of a prize fighter, and the other, dark-haired and swarthy, wore several bright rings on his fingers. Both men wore sport shirts and sunglasses and carried cameras. The new acquaintances stood each other rounds of Guinness at the fireplace in front of a low table which was supported by a pair of thick and wrinkled elephant hooves two feet high and trimmed with brass.

After a discussion of prices in Ireland as opposed to New Jersey and the common afflictions created by jet lag, the man with the rings cleared his throat and looked at Eric.

"When do you see Ryan?" Tony Saxe asked him.

"At the end of the week. I have an appointment with him in Dublin." Eric took several rolls of film from his pocket and placed them on the table. "I'd like you to get those developed for our next meeting, Benny. Also, you can make the reservation at the Dorchester in London for Maud and Princess Jessica . . ."

"The *Dorchester*!" Benny Stiff grinned at Tony Saxe. "In the old days, Tony, Maud could make do with a motel and a coffee machine on the Jersey Pike."

Eric said pleasantly, "Benny, it's that kind of birdbrain thinking that's made you a loser all these years."

"Now listen, Eric, don't—"

"I'm not interested in your comments," Eric looked evenly from Benny Stiff to Tony Saxe. "I don't intend to economize on accommodations for Jessica Mallory in London or for my wife, Maud, the child's only living aunt. Have you both got that straight?"

"Well, sure, Eric," Tony Saxe said, shrugging and glancing at Benny who nodded and looked impassively at the backs of his powerful hands.

There had been a subtle change in the relationship of these three men since they had learned what Eric had done on that sunny morning in Chester County, the small, blue car smashed and broken at the bottom of a mica pit, the rose-hip jelly blending with the blood on the windshield.

It had been the kind of absolute gesture they had not truly believed Eric was capable of. But, as was always the case in such surrenders of control or innocence, there was forever-after the ominous and constant implication that such surrenders would only be easier the next time... And it was this awareness that was evident now in Stiff's and Saxe's reluctant acceptance of Eric's authority.

"Well, all Benny meant," Tony Saxe said, "was that we should take it a little easy on the bankroll. But you're right, we can't be chintzy with the kid and Maud."

"Not to worry," Eric said, and for the benefit of the publican, Tige Wicks, he said with a wide smile, "Always good to run into one's countrymen like this. Here, Mr. Saxe, take my number. Perhaps you'd care to come up to the house for cocktails one night."

The following morning Eric asked Jessica to show him some of her favorite views, and while they were walking the horses in the meadows below Skyhead, Eric introduced phase three of his plan.

"Jessica, I wonder if you could do me a small but special favor..."

"What is it, Uncle Eric?"

"It's your aunt. That is to say, it is something you can do for her. She's been more than a bit depressed by the circumstances here. She was just a young girl herself when her own parents died."

"She didn't say anything about that to me..."

Eric nodded gravely, "Of course she wouldn't,

Jessica. That's like Maud. But she needs a change; a week or two in London would be ideal. The trouble is, I can't get away from here. There's a Mr. Saxe, a business associate of mine from America, who's turned up unexpectedly. And I've promised to help him with some breeding stock up north."

"Would she mind awfully going alone, Uncle Eric?"

"I'm afraid she would, dear. She needs a companion. You have probably noticed, Auntie Maud is not too strong."

"And is that the favor, Uncle Eric?" Jessica waited quietly, watching her uncle's face thoughtfully.

"Yes. I think it would be a fine trip for both of you. But there's just one more thing." Eric regarded the young girl with one of his quizzical smiles, the kind that older women so many years ago had savored as "boyish." "Knowing Maud, she would be reluctant to ask you herself, Jessica. She's quite shy and formal in some ways. So I wonder if we could just pretend it was all your idea?"

Eric sighed and raised his eyes to the towering peaks of Skyhead. The faint, salty breezes stirred his fine hair. "How proud my sister would have been of her little girl," Eric said, the words soft and muted by the winds from the sea.

Chapter Eighteen ————————————————

Angus Ryan's offices were on the second floor of a
Georgian building, whose narrow windows faced the
Liffey and the central streets of Dublin.

The reception rooms were done in brown leather
and honest oak, pictures of race meets and the
Dublin dog show brightening the panelled walls.
The offices of the senior partners, Angus Ryan and
the late Dermod Maloney, had been done less
somberly and more functionally—refectory tables in
place of desks, built-in filing cabinets, and silver tea
sets. This had been the original scheme, but since his
death some years before, the quarters of Dermod
Maloney had been converted into book-lined rooms
to house the firm's legal library.

On a week to the day after Andrew Dalworth's
funeral, Eric Griffith, in tweeds and a tattersall vest,
sat in Mr. Ryan's office facing the gray-haired

solicitor across the clean expanse of the shining refectory table.

"—and as I mentioned at our first meeting at Easter Hill, Mr. Ryan, Maud and I both feel we have some degree of responsibility to our niece."

Angus Ryan said gently, "Would you enlighten me, sir, as to the nature of those responsibilities?"

Eric shrugged and, with a practiced and seemingly helpless smile, said, "Well, that's where I was hoping you might help, Mr. Ryan. You see, Maud and I are comfortably off but we're hardly what you'd call rich."

"Ah, is that so, Mr. Griffith?"

"Yes, but we still feel an obligation to Jessica. If there's any way we can help, we'd be pleased to. I know that in the long run Jessica will be provided for, but sometimes in emergencies like this, there's a problem of cash flow and if that's the case, we'd be happy to send our niece a reasonable monthly allowance . . ."

"Now that's quite generous of you," Mr. Ryan said, wondering if he had possibly misjudged these American relatives. "However, that won't be necessary, Mr. Griffith."

Briefly, Mr. Ryan explained the purpose and functions of the Dalworth trusts administered by a board of directors in New York. After which he explained his position as the executor of Andrew Dalworth's provisions in relation to Easter Hill and to Jessica, and his fiscal responsibility for Jessica's allowance, schooling, travel, and so forth.

"I'm pleased to know everything is so tidy," Eric said, smiling steadily at the old lawyer. He was also pleased (and suddenly grateful) that he had made solid plans of his own and was therefore not dependent on a nuisance settlement from this tight-fisted old coot, or on a bone thrown to him with whimsical generosity by his niece.

Yet Eric couldn't help but feel diminished by the role he was required to play, cast as the scoundrel in a bogus necktie, forced to cheat and lie because no other avenue was open to him. He didn't want to spend his life waiting for a hand on his shoulder, a hard, official voice saying, "A question or two, if you don't mind."

Cantering one morning across a meadow above Easter Hill on one of Dalworth's hunters, a pair of Irish lads on a dusty road had greeted him with smiles, and when he had saluted them with his crop they had pulled off their caps in a gesture of deference that had touched him . . . That was the life he wanted, not hiding his face from privileged Scots lairds and the likes of Mrs. Cadwalader.

Angus Ryan made a steeple of his fingers and looked across them at Eric, trying to take a reading on the man. Since he was basically tolerant and charitable, Ryan was thinking his first appraisal might have been hasty.

"Perhaps you could satisfy my curiosity on one point, Mr. Griffith. Handling the business of the estate as I do, forwarding mail and such, how is it I've never come across a postcard or letter from you or your wife in all these long years?"

Eric had rehearsed an answer to this question, and as he met the old man's narrowing eyes, he was glad that he had practiced his responses with Maud and in front of his bedroom mirror—rueful smiles, the sigh of futility at the pain of the past, shrugs of dismissal and helplessness.

"The child had started a fresh new life and didn't need us. But quite frankly, my sister Monica and my wife never hit it off. Whose fault was it?" One of the rueful smiles. "Who can say? My sister didn't like the fact that Maud had been married before. But perhaps she wouldn't have been happy with whomever I married." A shrug of fond helplessness. "I was quite a bit older than Monica, and she may have thought my function in life was to be the eternal big brother, available forever for riding lessons, a partner to practice the latest dance craze with." A sigh at the pain of the past. "Yet, as I'm sure you understand, my loyalty had to be with my wife..."

"Of course," Angus Ryan said.

"But now, at a time when our niece is truly alone, naturally we're standing by."

"I think...I understand your position, Mr. Griffith."

"Now there's something I'd like to ask *you*, if I may, Mr. Ryan. About a picture along the second floor corridor of Easter Hill—an oil painting. A Hereford steer on a winter day with an old barn and some outbuildings at the edge of a field."

There was no such painting, but this was a gamble Eric Griffith had decided he must take. This was the crux of the matter, the reason for this meeting.

"It looks like the countryside where I have my home in the States, Chester County in Pennsylvania. We have a museum there on the Brandywine with dozens of such oils, in the style of the Wyeths and Howard Pyle—a whole school of painters..."

"A Hereford against outbuildings?" Ryan frowned and shook his head, and Eric breathed more easily. "I'm afraid I don't know the picture, Mr. Griffith."

"Well, it's not important. But it reminded me of home."

"I'd been after Andrew Dalworth for a good while to have a curator in to catalogue the collections. He and Jessica were great shoppers, you know."

He smiled at a memory. "It was hard to tell who was the younger when they were out on their expeditions. Still, Andrew felt strongly that a man's home had no business with librarians and accountants and sightseers and the like."

Concealing his relief at this information, Eric glanced at his wristwatch and managed a neatly executed start of surprise.

"I really shouldn't take up any more of your time, Mr. Ryan, but I'm pleased that we had this talk."

They stood and shook hands. Then Eric pretended to remember something. "By the way, Mr. Ryan, at dinner the other night, Jessica suggested that she and her Aunt Maud take a little vacation in London. Naturally, that's a decision we wouldn't make without your approval."

Ryan looked at him keenly. "It was her idea, you say?"

"Yes, she thought it might be a nice change of scene. It will be my treat, of course..."

Angus Ryan rubbed his jaw and then said, "Well, I can't see the harm in a little holiday just now."

"In that case, I'll tell her 'bon voyage' for you."

Mr. Ryan showed him to the doors of the reception area. Eric smiled boyishly at the pair of middle-aged secretaries and took the lift down to the street.

After staring out at the River Liffey for a moment or so, Mr. Ryan turned and picked up his phone and placed a call to Easter Hill.

In the lounge of the Russell Hotel off St. Stephen's Green, Eric ordered a whiskey and made two telephone calls, one to Tony Saxe at the Hannibal Arms, the second to Easter Hill where he found (as he expected) that the phone was busy.

To pass the time, he bought a copy of the *Irish Register* from the concierge and studied the racing columns and turf reports. The attention of the writers and betting commissioners (limey for bookie, Eric knew) was centered on the upcoming Grand National. Heavy favorites at this stage were Daedalus; the French entry, Etoile Rouge; and Kerry Dancer, a great bay from the Muirheads outside Belfast.

Eric's eyes were drawn as usual to the long shots, the predicted also-rans. When they came in, it was so much more gratifying (and profitable) than when the beautifully bred favorites flashed past the finish line.

He tried Easter Hill again. When the connection was established, he said to Maud, "Who was on the line?"

"Just now? Mr. Ryan for Jessica."

"How did it go?"

"Couldn't have been better if we wrote the script." Then, quickly and in a lowered voice, "Call me later, Eric." And in a brighter voice, "Is that you, Jessica?"

From Dublin, Eric drove in a rented Ford to Monaghan, where he spent the night at the

Nuremore Hotel. The following morning, he crossed the border into Northern Ireland and drove to the airport at Belfast, where Tony Saxe was waiting for him at the main cab ranks.

With Saxe tracing their route on an Automobile Club map, they circled the gray stone mass of the city with its armored cars and sandbagged intersections and drove south and east for thirty miles to the town of Ardglass and the port of St. John's Point.

Simon Ethelroyd's warehouse, a long, single story building with boarded up windows, was squeezed between two open produce markets several blocks from High Street, facing a railroad marshalling yard, power cranes, and truck scales.

The proprietor of Ethelroyd Enterprises (thus read the paint-flecked sign on the single front door of the warehouse) greeted them in an office acrid with smoke from a coal-burning stove. The room was small, crowded with packing cases, a rolltop desk and several files.

"Sit down, sit down, we don't stand on ceremony here," Ethelroyd said, waving them to a pair of chairs.

A tall, obese figure in a blue porter's smock, Ethelroyd's eyes were like the tips of daggers deep within the rolls of flesh that bunched up from his ruddy cheeks. His hair was thick and black, and his sideburns came down like jagged scimitars to meet beneath his chin. Ethelroyd sat in an armchair beside the desk and lit a thin, black cigar. When it was drawing well, he looked through the film of smoke and said, "I'll have the photographs now, if you please."

Tony Saxe gave him a thick envelope, and

Ethelroyd dumped the color prints onto his desk, arranging them in tidy patterns with surprisingly deft movements of his puffy hands.

Opening a drawer, he removed a magnifying glass, leaning forward to peer through it at the colorful photographs of furniture and art objects from the salons, halls and gardens of Dalworth's estate. Ethelroyd's breathing was heavy and labored. With each inhalation his stomach swelled forcefully against his loose smock and collapsed when the wind wheezed from his lungs like a hiss of air from a punctured inner tube.

Eric glanced at his watch. "I'd like to get this business settled promptly, Mr. Ethelroyd."

"Of course, of course. But begging your pardon, I'd like to satisy myself that the articles are genuine."

"You'll find everything just as we've represented it," Eric said.

"I'll be the judge of that, if you gentlemen don't mind."

Tony Saxe said, "You come well recommended, Ethelroyd. Buffy Cappella told us you were one of the best."

"Very kind of him, I'm sure."

"Yeah. What was the last job you did for him? It was hash, wasn't it? Morocco, then bills of lading laundered here at St. John's and shipped off to Copenhagen?"

Ethelroyd placed the magnifying glass with a decisive gesture on his desk, straightened, and looked from Tony Saxe to Eric, a malicious hostility glittering in his small eyes. "It seems Buffy has developed a bloody big mouth, doesn't it? I trust you gentlemen haven't succumbed to that affliction..."

"Now listen to me," Eric said. "I've got two things to say, Mr. Ethelroyd. The first is that this is a cash transaction. Not an article leaves Easter Hill until we have the agreed-upon sums of money in hand. That is the number one condition and it's not negotiable. The *second* point I want to make is—"

"Hold on with your points and conditions," Ethelroyd said, standing so abruptly that his chair rocked and teetered on its castings. His cheeks were flushed and his breath whistled in and out of his mouth. "I'm not going to tell *you* fine Yankee gentlemen some of the problems we're up against, certain obstacles which in your innocence I daresay you haven't even considered. Come with me, please."

Opening a door at the rear of his office, he stepped aside and gestured them to proceed, the sweep of his arm eloquent with sardonic servility.

They entered the main area of Ethelroyd's warehouse, a vast structure stocked with tiers of dismantled furniture—chairs, tables, chests; bins of finials, brass hardware, hasps and hinges; shelves of carved arms and legs and fretwork filigrees; rolls of damask and brocades; and a brightly lighted counter, where three brawny men in turtleneck sweaters and leather aprons were working at what looked to Eric like an antique furniture assembly line.

With heavy sarcasm, Ethelroyd said, "Please have the goodness to attend to me, gentlemen. If you think we're a gang of smash-and-grab artists, think again. The nannies and maids and old butlers will have paid loving attention to those objects of art at Easter Hill for many years. They will miss them, as

178

surely as if a baby were snatched from a cradle. So understand me well." Ethelroyd slapped two fingers resoundingly into the palm of his hand. "Each object we take has to be replaced by a reasonable substitute." Gesturing at the shelves and bins of his warehouse, Ethelroyd said, "We'll prepare the facsimiles here and they'll pass muster long enough to give us any lead time we will need."

"So what's the big deal?" Tony Saxe said. "It's what we're paying you for."

"Then let me explain something else to you bloody Yanks. You've come here to a country at war and expect an operation like this to go off like a piece of cake. Well, let me disabuse you of your naive expectations. First of all—" Again, Ethelroyd slapped his plump fingers into his palm. "First, I've got to take my lorries twenty miles west of Dungannon to cross the border. A little exercise which means paying off the following: the Ulster Constabulary, Irish Provos, the bloody Brits, customs agents on both sides, and probably the goddamn Irish Republican Army when we get into Eire—any or all of which will shoot us squarely in the ass if there's the slightest slip, if *anything* goes sour. In addition to which there's an expert forger to pay off for lading bills, a cargo master here on the dock, and a mate and captain on the ship that takes our goods to Liverpool."

He turned and looked at them directly, his chest heaving, a film of perspiration beading his forehead. "So don't try telling me my business, Yanks. *Just don't try it!*"

Eric said smoothly, "I'd suggest you get yourself in hand, Ethelroyd." Pointing at the man's stomach, he said, "All that blubber pressing against your heart isn't doing you any good. I imagine you're already having the odd dizzy spell. And a second tip for your own benefit—*don't ever interrupt me again*!"

The laborers had stopped their work to watch the mounting tension between their employer and the Americans.

"I told you I had two things to say," Eric said. "You heard the first. Now you better pay damned close attention to the second. Buffy Cappella gave us *three* names to check out and yours wasn't on the top of the list. So if you have any more reservations or complaints, we'll consider this meeting over and done with. Clear enough?"

After a moment of silence, Ethelroyd's eyes slid away from Eric's and focused on the backs of his thick hands. "My doctor talked to me about the weight," he said, in a voice shaded with conciliation. "He doesn't take into consideration that I'm heavy-boned and need a lot of nutriments."

"That's the trouble with doctors. They seldom see the whole picture."

"You're right there, Mr. Griffith. I'll tell you what. You gentlemen will come back around tea time, I'll give you estimates on the whole project then, all details worked out, type of currencies preferred and denominations."

"Very well, until tea time then, Ethelroyd."

Outside, in the smokey fogs from the railroad yards and the sea, Tony Saxe looked at Eric with worried, appraising eyes. Taking a silk handkerchief from his pocket, he dabbed at the sweat on his forehead.

"You scared hell out of me," he said.

Eric smiled as they settled themselves in the convertible. "Why were you worried?"

"That was one hell of a bluff you were running about them back-up dealers. Supposing the fat man called you on it...?"

"It wasn't likely," Eric turned on the ignition key and listened to the smooth hum of the motor. "People who let themselves go to seed like that rarely have much strength of character."

Eric glanced at his watch. "Well, you character analyst, we've got some time to kill. I suggest we have a large lunch—to get our nutriments—and some decent wine and count our blessings."

Chapter Nineteen ———————————

Maud was not a good traveller. She liked restaurants and cocktail lounges, snacks from room service and television. London, with its parks and churches and the boldly delicate tracery of the architect Wren had no appeal for her, and the museums with their solemn, dusty silences turned her almost faint with boredom.

She usually napped after lunch, the coverlet of her bed sprinkled with gossip and fashion magazines, and it was at this time that Jessica explored London on her own, using the underground subway, which Andrew had taught her to do, window-shopping in Knightsbridge, visiting the Tate and National galleries, and feeding the pigeons in Trafalgar Square.

One day Jessica became restless during lunch in the dining room of the Dorchester. The sensation was perplexing—not significant enough to make her apprehensive, just the vaguest of premonitions, the most fragile of tremors across her warning systems.

Maud was having an iced Calvados with her coffee and exchanging smiles and pleasantries with the gentleman at the adjoining table, an Arab from Morocco who wore a red fez with his dark gray suit. Jessica asked to be excused and Maud dismissed her with a quick smile.

In their suite facing the park, Jessica sat at the curved-legged escritoire and began a letter to Dr. Julian, hoping this would dissipate her strange, rootless anxiety.

But after she had written his name and started the letter with "We are in London for a week or so, Aunt Maud and I—", she stopped there, mildly irritated and self-conscious at the banality of the sentence.

When she began again on a fresh sheet of paper, Jessica wrote down several unrelated words and then the pen began to move almost by itself, swiftly and reflexively, and she was writing a poem to Julian instead of the simple letter she had planned, putting down her truest and most candid feelings without guilt or reservation. Jessica was plumbing depths of sensitivity she had barely been conscious of, tapping well-springs of emotion at the very core of her being. In a way, she didn't quite understand, Jessica realized that these new feelings were connected with the topsy-turvy change of events in her life—the death of her beloved Andrew, the loneliness for Julian, and the newness of Uncle Eric and Aunt Maud, who were so surprisingly and so constantly at home in what had once been her dearest sanctuary, the lands and mansion of Easter Hill.

With a faint smile, she wrote down the words "sudden" and "sharp" and "silver," savoring their provocative sibilance. And then she looked out the windows at the greenness of the park and thought sadly and somewhat wistfully of the inevitable words that must complete her thoughts: "gemstone" and "childhood."

At noon the following week, cool sunlight lay across the ponds and streams of Easter Hill, gently gilding the feathers of ducks and trumpeter swans. In the stables, Kevin O'Dell pitched hay into Windkin's stall and brought the hunter a leather bucket of water.

From the garden, Capability Brown collected an armload of iris and daffodils and took them to the kitchen where the cook was preparing lunch for Mr. Griffith and an American tourist he had met at the Hannibal Arms.

With a glance at the stove, Mr. Brown said drily, "Would you think, Mrs. Kiernan, that will satisfy the gentlemen till tea time?"

"I grant you, Mr. Griffith fancies a good table."

The trout were ready for the broiler, bright with butter and lemon slices; a heavy brown turtle soup with sherry simmered on a gas ring; and the baron of beef circled with roast potatoes and parsnips was ready in the warming oven. In still another oven, the cakes that Mr. Griffith preferred for high tea were baking—a pineapple upside-down cake and a chocolate to be layered with raspberry preserves.

Rose sat at a wooden service counter using a curved spoon to scoop butter-balls from a delft crock. "It's not like her to be gone a week without even a postcard."

"If the truth were told," Lily said, taking the pineapple cake from the oven, "Miss Jessie didn't fancy going off to London."

"That's nothing for you girls to be gossiping about," Mrs. Kiernan said. "There, Mr. Brown. This will do nicely."

"Himself was asking me again about the silver darning egg and the Chinese snuff box," Rose said.

"If by 'himself' you mean Mr. Griffith, please say so, girl."

"I'm sorry, Mrs. Kiernan, but he stands so grand with his thumbs hooked in his vest pockets, looking at me like I'd pinched them."

"The lass feels as I feel," Mr. Brown said, placing the daffodils in a vase. "There's a cloud over this house since Andrew Dalworth—" Mr. Brown made the sign of the cross on his forehead "—joined his Maker. Uncle or not, I can't stomach that Griffith. He's seen fit to hire an extra hand in the stables, and a rogue at that, if I'm any judge. And what sort of a name has he got? I leave it to you, Mrs. Kiernan—is Benny Stiff any kind of a proper name for a man?"

Old Flynn, in a striped serving jacket, came up from the wine cellar with six bottles in a canvas sling. "He's got an eye for the labels, I'll give him that. Whether there's a palate to match, I'm not so sure."

"Ach, Flynn, you're as much a critic as Mr. Brown here," Mrs. Kiernan said.

"It's the truth, ma'am," Flynn said. "He went like a shot to the bins with the big clarets, the same that Mr. Dalworth, God rest him, sent back from

185

Bordeaux two summers ago. Same with the burgundies—Richebourgs and the like. But at three and four bottles a meal, he and his friend, Mr. Saxe, should be down with gout presently."

"Now, now, what sort of example are you setting for the girls?"

"Pay us no mind," Flynn said, with a smile at the young maids. But something occurred to the old man as he uncorked the wine and he frowned. "Tell me something, ma'am. Have you noticed that Fluter seems off his food lately? No life or bounce to him at all?"

"He's heartsick because Jessie's away," Lily said.

"That's God's truth," Rose said. "I read about it once in a novel with a girl on the cover in a big hat with ribbons."

Mrs. Kiernan stirred the turtle soup with a firm, almost angry flick of her wrist.

"As for Fluter's rations, Mr. Flynn, I wouldn't be knowing. Mr. Griffith is feeding him these few days, say he wants the dog to get to like him better..."

Later that same morning, Eric discovered Lily dusting in the library. Without preamble he said, "Now this won't do at all, Miss. I don't want you girls messing about in these rooms when Mrs. Griffith and I are expecting luncheon guests."

"But, sir—"

"No excuses, I want this work done earlier, before breakfast, if necessary."

"But sir, Mr. Flynn posts the schedules and—"

"Damn Flynn," Eric said with a show of anger, "I'm telling you what you'll do and what you won't do. And in the future, here is something *else* you will not do. You will not work in these rooms *alone*. You and the other girl—whatever her name is—will work as a pair, is that clear?"

Lily said blankly, "I don't understand what you're getting at, sir."

Eric clasped his hands behind his back and looked her up and down. Then he said, "I'll tell you exactly what I'm getting at, Miss. There are valuables in this house and I wouldn't want anyone getting careless. It's for your own protection, girl . . ."

After this incident, Lily reported the whole conversation to Mr. Flynn, saying almost in tears, "I won't be called a thief, Mr. Flynn. I won't."

Tony Saxe arrived in the leased convertible shortly after noon and was shown into the library where Eric sat slumped in a deep chair, a glass of sherry in one hand, staring thoughtfully at the view of the orchards and meadows.

On the table beside him was a leather folder, bulky with typewritten correspondence.

"I think the last piece just fell into place, Eric," Tony Saxe said. A tension and calculation was evident in his expression as he perched on the arm of a sofa. "We must be living right, pal, because this is the pot at the end of the rainbow.

"Last night I got talking to a regular down at Hannibal's, a rummy with a thirst that won't quit. After I hosted him to about a barrel of Guinness, I began pumping him about the kid in the stable and the guy who works in the garden. I was looking for some kind of leverage, because it won't look right if we throw everybody here out on their ass. Somebody's got to stay, you said that yourself.

Otherwise, it's too damn obvious.

"So the rummy tells me that the gardener, Brown, was the wheel man in a noisy IRA caper a few years back, where they knocked over a lorry hauling some terrorists up to the jail at Longkiln . . . With this, we can put pressure on Brown, threaten to turn him and his pals in. That way, it's all smooth as silk. He's got to play along."

Eric continued to stare through the windows, sipping sherry, his free hand drumming restlessly on the leather folder.

"So all we got to do . . ." Tony Saxe looked closely at Eric. "Look, pal. I get the feeling I don't have your attention. I latched onto the last thing we need and you sit there like a damned buddha drinking booze and watching the scenery. Come on, Eric, get with it!" Saxe snapped his fingers irritably. "Ethelroyd called me last night at the Hannibal. His lorries will be here at eleven-thirty tonight, ready to load."

"Cool it, Tony," Eric stood and picked up the leather file from the table. "We're exactly on schedule and the Constable from Ballytone is on his way here right now. But—" Eric hefted the file in his hands, aware of the tension and excitement building in him. "But I've stumbled on something, Tony, that may make this caper with Ethelroyd look like a penny ante poker game."

"I don't like surprises, Eric. I don't like changing the rules in the middle of the game—"

"I'm holding a goldmine in my hands, Tony. Reports and correspondence between Dalworth and one Dr. Julian Homewood. I want you to read it, Tony, every single word of it."

Eric had found the file when he was going through a Chippendale chest in the late Andrew Dalworth's bedroom. He had been cataloguing the possessions and effects of the entire manor house, ostensibly to satisfy his interest in artifacts and period furniture, as well as to make his own gratuitous contribution to the estate of Andrew Dalworth. He used the activity to cover his occasional presence in the servants' quarters.

The correspondence covered a period of eight years, beginning when Jessica was six and continuing until the present. The reports and tests and interviews documented Jessica Mallory's steadily developing psychic abilities.

Eric had read through all of this material last evening, propped up in his bed with a whiskey beside him. Only curious at first, he became deeply interested and ultimately fascinated by the opportunities suggested in the doctor's conclusions.

There had been several poems in the folder, written by Jessica and commented on by both Dalworth and Dr. Homewood. In one instance, Dalworth had written, "Julian, doesn't this strike you as a bit morbid?"

The poem read:

> I see echoes of the future,
> Flowers, white-petalled and evil,
>   with stamens that sting the eyeballs
>   and roiled centers alive with hybrid worms.
>
> Death, too, can smell of blossoms.

The lines had repelled and frightened Eric, a chilling reminder of Maud's preoccupation with dissolution, her fear of an unhealthy attraction to mosses and wetness and the mold forming on damp stones. And yet the smug young doctor in Dublin had dismissed Jessica's poem as the normal, self-drama of a growing girl, a healthy awareness of mortality.

Another of her poems had made Eric uneasy on an even more profound level.

> . . . the small crafts of life,
> bobbing and listing and sailing on.
>
> But ask me not the captains or the cargos.

The words had sent a chill through him. It was how he had felt himself on so many occasions, not knowing any answers and worse, not even the questions . . .

A third poem was accompanied by a sketch of a beach done in blue and green crayon.

> Summer, sand and seashells,
> Nature's hidden trove.
>
> Our secret, mine and Andrew's,
> The beach at Angel's Cove.

As Eric handed the file of letters to Saxe, Flynn the butler appeared in the arched doorway connecting the great hall and library.

"I beg your pardon, Mr. Griffith, but Constable Riley is here to see you, sir."

Eric savored the look of the old servant in his short striped morning vest, white gloves in a pocket (to be worn while serving lunch), but most of all he enjoyed the expression of confusion and concern on Flynn's composed but worn features.

Eric smiled blandly and said, "Be good enough to show the Constable in. And please ask the rest of the staff, including yourself, to assemble in the kitchen."

"May I inquire, sir, the purpose of this?"

"You'll know soon enough, my good man."

After lunch, Maud Griffith had luxuriated in the ministrations of a hotel masseuse, a large and angular Danish lady whose fingers of steel produced in dizzying succession sensations of nearly insupportable punishment and pleasure. Miss Helgar was a sworn foe of cellulite. Detecting a layer of it under Maud's slightly rounded abdomen, she had attacked it with a missionary zeal which reduced her client to a state of breathless, flushed exhilaration.

The masseuse promised Maud that if she would undergo a deep massage each day of her stay in London, the chronic back pain she suffered would be banished—Miss Helgar pronounced the word in three distinct syllables—ban-ish-ed—forever. Maud had not talked to anyone so sympathetic in years, so down-to-earth and sensible about the things that Eric had no patience for—her fears and anxieties and dreams. As a consequence, Maud booked four more appointments with Miss Helgar and then, after her shower and a lovely little nap, Maud dressed and returned to her suite in as fresh and cheerful a mood as she could remember for many months.

To her surprise, when she let herself in, she saw that Jessica had packed her suitcase and was dressed for the street, wearing a bottle-green topcoat with a matching beret.

"What's all this, dear?"

"I'm needed at home. I'm taking the night flight to Shannon."

"What happened? Did Eric call?"

"No. No one phoned." Jessica pulled on short

black gloves. "But I know I'm needed there."

Maud said anxiously, "Are you coming down with something? Let me see..."

But as she raised her hand to the girl's forehead, Jessica twisted away from her and said, "I'm perfectly all right. I've called for our bill and a cab."

"Just hold on, young lady. If you think you're waltzing out of here because you've got some whimsical idea—"

"You can stay here if you like, Maud, but I'm leaving."

"If this is your idea of a game, please stop it. How could you possibly know what's going on at Easter Hill?" Maud squared her shoulders. "Calm yourself, Jessica. I'm *not* going to let you go."

Jessica stared at her aunt, and the older woman took an involuntary step backward, suddenly frightened by the burning expression in the girl's eyes and face. "Don't you *dare* try to stop me," Jessica said in a voice that Maud had not heard before, hard and low and resonant, and the timber of it sent a chill streaking through her nerves.

"Why are you trying to scare me?" Maud said anxiously.

"A darkness is coming. There are shadows on Easter Hill. Is that why it is happening? Is that why Fluter is dying?"

Jessica cried out these words though Maud realized with another spasm of fear that the child was no longer talking to her, but staring beyond to the treetops of the open park. Jessica had seemed to change before her eyes, no longer so delicate and polite but charged with a visible determination and power, currents evident in the movements of her body as she turned to stare again through the windows. And the voice was changed, too.

"You may do as you like, Aunt Maud." Jessica stared at her with hard, glazed eyes. "I'm leaving now."

"No, wait for me. Hold the cab. Eric would want—I've *got* to go with you."

And when Jessica had gone to the lobby, Maud—feeling threatened and vulnerable—picked up the phone and asked the hotel operator to place a call to Easter Hill in Ballytone. She was alarmed to notice how badly her hands were trembling.

At dusk, with the soft tones of evening spreading across the meadows, Eric Griffith walked down to Capability Brown's quarters, one of several small cottages adjacent to the stables. The door stood open and Brown was packing his clothing and personal effects in a worn duffel bag.

The other servants had already left—the girls and Mrs. Kiernan in tears, old Flynn with eyes flashing anger, and Kevin O'Dell giving notice in sympathy with the others—departing with their possessions in the single old taxi from Ballytone.

Eric rapped lightly on the door jamb. When Mr. Brown turned to him, his craggy features set in bitter lines, Eric regarded him with raised eyebrows.

"What's this, Brown? You're not thinking of leaving, I hope."

"Just as soon as I pack my things, Mr. Griffith."

"I think you should reconsider, Brown."

"No way I will, I've had my fill of this place. I won't stay on where good, honest people are called liars and thieves." Turning his back to Eric, Mr.

193

Brown removed several framed photographs from the wall and placed them on a cot beside his duffel bag. "Mrs. Kiernan, the girls, and Jack Flynn—they never touched a farthing that didn't belong to them. So I'll be off with young Kevin."

Eric studied the reflection of fading sunlight on his buffed nails.

"Brown, I'm a reasonable man. If you'll stay on, I'm prepared to overlook your impertinence."

"Don't put yourself to any trouble on my account."

"Impertinence is one thing, stupidity is quite another," Eric said. "In your own interests, Brown, I'd urge you not to indulge the one at the expense of the other."

"Can you speak plainly, as one man to another, or is that beyond you, sir?"

"I'm warning you, Brown, don't test my anger."

"Begging your pardon, I think I'll chance that."

"Let's see if you can, then," Eric said, his voice cold and derisive. "I've got information that you participated in an IRA raid several years ago. I have the date and the names of the men who were with you that night, including your own son, Timothy, now with the Provos in Belfast. Would you like—?"

Brown stared at him with burning eyes. "You'd crush a man for his loyalties to his blood, would you? I say you're no *man*, you're a *devil*, Mr. Griffith."

"That's a matter of opinion, Brown. When I submit those names, if your stubborness forces me, the Ulster Constabulary and the British will call me a friend of the Crown and a gentleman of conscience. Once again, Brown, I strongly urge you to stay on."

Brown sat down heavily on the edge of his narrow

cot and, without meeting Eric's eyes, said, "I'll be staying on."

"Speak up, man. I can't hear you!"

With an effort, Brown said again, "I'll be staying on, *sir*."

"That's a good man," Eric said and walked back through the gardens to the manor house, whistling a light accompaniment to the chatter of starlings nesting in the ivy-hung walls.

As Eric entered the library, Tony Saxe was crossing from the bay window to the fireplace.

"What the hell's wrong with the kid's dog, Eric? He was out on the side lawn throwing up."

Eric shrugged. "He might have caught himself a raunchy groundhog. Was there a call from London?"

"No. You expecting one?"

"Yes, but there's still time." Without explaining this cryptic remark, Eric poured himself a whiskey and looked steadily at Tony Saxe. "Well? Have you thought it over?"

"It's no good, Eric. It's too dicey."

"Then all I can say is, you're a fool."

"Maybe, maybe not. But just for the record, here's what I bought into. I bankrolled the three of us and Benny Stiff, backed your play against the people who worked here, touted you onto Ethelroyd—" Saxe flicked a glance at his wristwatch, "—who'll be knocking at the door of my room at the Hannibal in about three hours. Ethelroyd gives us the cash, you give him the keys to this place. He takes what we've agreed on, makes the substitutions, and splits. That's what I bought, that's what I want."

"You're settling for a cheese omelette when you

195

could sit down to an eight-course banquet..."

Tony Saxe looked skeptically at the leather folder of correspondence on the coffee table. "You want to bet your share of this caper on crystal balls, be my guest. I don't buy any of that crap—tarot cards, astrology, palm readings, they're just rackets to fleece old ladies and hippies."

"Tony, the conclusions in this folder were reached after eight years of investigations, by a doctor who gave my niece every test known to science."

"Hell, that stuff can be faked, Eric. Scientists can go shut-eye just like carny freaks, proving whatever the hell they want."

Eric said, "If you're too lazy or blind to see the gold pieces we could pick up, I'm not going to argue with you. But I've seen the entries for the Grand National. Sterling Choice, Gitano, Bowbells, all going at better than seventy-five to one. Eleven other horses are better than thirty- to forty-to-one. If the winner is in that pack of long shots and my niece—"

Saxe interrupted him with an emphatic head-shake. "I'm telling you again, Eric. No way! My horse is that fat crook Ethelroyd."

He began pacing, rubbing his hands together nervously. His rings and wristwatch glittered with reflections from the burning logs in the fireplace. After a moment, he stopped and stared at Eric. "Look, if this kid is a psychic, if she can really see into the future, then how come she didn't *see* what you and Maudie are up to? You been lying to that kid every hour on the hour, planning to rob her blind. So where was her crystal ball during all that?"

"Dammit, didn't you understand what you've just read? It's not like she runs up a curtain and looks out

196

the window at tomorrow. Her psychic skills depend on her mental condition, her emotional state."

"Well," Tony said with finality, "I'm not risking any money on that kid's moods or daydreams. So she called the shot on her dog and it washed up right on schedule. Maybe that was a coincidence."

"But you're forgetting, she also called the shot on her mother and father."

"So when she blows one, it could be when we got a bundle on a horse in the National . . . and everything I've invested so far is down the drain. I'm wondering, Eric, maybe you didn't read this stuff too good yourself." Picking up the leather file, Saxe flipped through it to a letter from Dr. Homewood. "Here's one from the shrink to Dalworth. It goes: 'What we call your daughter's psychic skills hardly matters, Andrew. It doesn't add to our understanding to classify them as clairvoyance, precognition or second sight, because, in point of fact, we don't have the vocabulary to describe what is actually the man–is–fest—manifestation of an advancing evolutionary process.'"

Tony dropped the folder and nodded at Eric, a glint of triumph in his eyes. "Slice that any way you want and it's a lot of two-bit words adding up to the fact that the doctor *himself* don't know what's going on."

"You're the one going shut-eye, Tony. You don't have the guts to see what's staring you in the face." Snatching up the folder, Eric opened it and said, "Just listen to this. Yes, here it is. 'The most precise comparison I can suggest, Andrew, is *adrenalin*. One function of Jessica's psychic powers is very similar to that bodily secretion. It creates, and reacts to, an

197

awareness of danger, provides for faster reactions, greatly increased strength and stamina.'"

Eric glanced across the folder at Saxe. "Now listen to the rest of it. Homewood goes on to say: 'In a peaceful, tranquil situation, Jessica's precognitive skills are likely to lapse into a dormant state. But in a situation or predicament that caused her deep anxiety, sharp emotional pain, or fear, it's probable that her clairvoyant perceptions would be proportionately more acute and accurate.' You hear that, Tony? Proportionately *more acute and accurate*!"

"Sure, but you're forgetting the biggest thing of all, Eric. What if she finds out we've looted her house? And she'll know when she walks in the door that you kicked all those servants out on their ears. Why should she want to help us?"

"You weren't listening, Tony. Let me read it again. 'But in a situation or predicament—'," Eric spoke in soft but emphatic accents, "'—that caused her deep anxiety, sharp emotional pain, or fear—'"

As Eric looked with a thoughtful smile at the growing understanding in Saxe's expression, the phone in Dalworth's study began ringing. Eric hurried to answer it. A measure of his tension was in the tremor of his hand when he scooped up the receiver and heard the British-accented voice announcing a long distant call from London.

It was Maud from the Heathrow Airport. "I tried to phone you from the hotel but the circuits were busy." Her voice was petulant and exasperated. "And the damned kid wouldn't wait. We're taking the next flight out to Shannon. Can you send Flynn to meet us?"

"No, I suggest you take a limo." Eric tightened his

grip on the phone, hardly daring to ask the next question. Drawing a deep breath, he said, "What made you cut your trip short?"

"You won't believe this, Eric, but your niece insisted on it. She's got a crazy fixation that things are happening to her pets, claims that her dog is..."

From where he stood in the library, Saxe could see Eric at Dalworth's desk, the phone in his hand and the windows of the antique weapons cabinet coated like mirrors with the last rays of sunshine.

After a few more exchanges, which Saxe couldn't hear, Eric replaced the receiver and returned to the library, his eyes bright with excitement and secrets.

"That was Maud. They'll be at Shannon in just a few hours."

"What the *hell* is going on, Eric?"

"Just listen. I want you to get down to the Hannibal and intercept Ethelroyd. Tell him we've got to put everything back at least twenty-four hours."

"I don't budge till you answer some questions. How come they're on their way home? Maud was supposed to keep Jessica in London until she got the okay from us."

Eric made himself a second drink, judiciously adding a touch of soda to a generous splash of whiskey. Watching the amber mixture glinting in the crystal tumbler, he smiled at the play of shifting lights and shadows.

"Tony, you accused me of wanting to take reckless chances, to risk our investment on tea leaves and tarot cards. You should have known I wouldn't move a step in that direction until I could offer you proof—precise, observable proof—that my niece,

Jessica, has precognitive powers." He pointed to the leather folder of letters and records. "Even the doctors don't have all the answers. But now I've proved she can do what I've told you she can."

Eric put his glass down and gripped Tony Saxe by both shoulders and stared steadily into his eyes. "Jessica knows, Tony, *knows* certain things are happening here at Easter Hill, even though she's miles and miles away in London."

"You're talking about *proof*, Eric. I'd like to hear it."

Eric sighed and said, "Well, the fact is, for the last three days I've been poisoning her dog. Frankly, it gave me no pleasure but I needed to make certain."

"You've been *what*?"

"Yes, I've been adding a touch of Mr. Brown's snail meal to Fluter's ground beef. And somehow, in some fashion, Jessica knows the animal is ill."

Tony Saxe shook his head in disbelief and said, "You're something else, Eric. Really something else."

"Yes, you're right," Eric said and sipped the tangy Irish whiskey. "Now you'd better be off to the Hannibal Arms and take care of your end of things."

Chapter Twenty

Jessica and Maud arrived at Easter Hill in an airport limousine shortly after midnight, a damp, spring wind buffeting the car and scattering the last of the winter leaves across the gravel driveway and dark lawns.

Jessica went directly down to the stables. As she pulled open the heavy doors, a man she had never seen before came out of the tack room, a cigarette slanting up from his mouth, the moonlight shining on his flattened nose and on the shock of black hair that stood up like a curry brush.

"Hey, what're you doing here this time of night?"

"I live here," Jessica said. "I want to make sure that my house is all right. May I ask why you're in our stables?"

Benny Stiff grinned and said, "Sure, you can. I work here, kid. You're the little princess. Right?"

"Where is Kevin O'Dell?"

"You mean the young Irisher? He quit. I'm the new groom. Benny Stiff's the name."

Another figure emerged from the shadows and Jessica was relieved when she recognized Capability Brown, but her apprehension quickened when she saw that her old friend's face was set in hard, grim lines.

"Windkin is fine, Miss Jessica," Mr. Brown said. "I've kept an eye on him. But you should know, Miss, there's been some changes at Easter Hill."

"Mr. Brown, please tell me."

"I think that's a task for Mr. Griffith. You'd best go up to the house now and let him explain how it was."

Eric was waiting for Jessica in the great hall. "I'd like you to join me in the library, my dear," he said. "We've had some unpleasant goings-on here while you and Maud were away. Since it's a family matter, I want to explain everything as clearly and frankly as I can."

The lights and colors in Jessica's inner vision were now dazzling and white, shadows forming with a powerful sense of urgency along a corridor of diamond-bright illuminations.

Aunt Maud had seated herself on a sofa in the library, long, slim legs crossed and a drink in her hand. Standing beside her was a man with dark hair and a dark complexion, and an array of rings and cufflinks that glittered as brilliantly as the lights behind Jessica's eyes.

"Jessica, this is Mr. Saxe, an American I met in Ballytone," Eric said. "He's spending a few days with us. Tony, may I present Jessica Mallory."

"A real pleasure, Miss," Tony Saxe said.

"Now, Jessica, I want you to sit down and hear me out."

"I prefer to stand, Uncle Eric."

"Suit yourself." Eric paced slowly in front of the fireplace, rubbing his large, bony hands together, his expression grave and thoughtful. The measured tread of his footsteps and the tinkle of ice in Maud's glass were the only sounds jarring the stillness of the shadowed library.

"It was just a week or so ago when I noticed the antique snuff box was missing." Smoothing back his blond, thinning hair, Eric then closed his hands over the lapels of his tweed jacket. "It was right over there, plain as day, on the teakwood table, a beautiful little thing, as you know, mother-of-pearl insets and carved Chinese characters. At first, I thought one of the girls had taken it away to clean, but a day or so later something else turned up missing—that solid silver darning egg that belonged to some queen or other. That was always in plain sight, too, on the second shelf of the vitrine in the drawing room. Well, I waited another day for that to show up and then I asked the maids. But Lily and Rose and Mrs. Kiernan, they pretended to be as much in the dark as I was.

"I didn't want to act in haste, Jessica. I simply couldn't believe we had a thief in the house. So I waited another day and then I informed the staff that if the objects were returned by the following morning, that would be the end of the matter, that I would consider the incident closed. But the next morning, those objects were still missing."

Eric's histrionic talents were now functioning at their sharpest and most subtle pitch. His expression suggested that of a man wrestling with decisions and judgments that brought him almost physical pain.

"In fairness, I gave them all one last chance. I announced that I was driving into Ballytone for a supply of tobacco and would not return until lunch. In my absence, I expected they would take advantage of this last period of grace."

Eric's hands twisted together with a sound like that of dry, rustling leaves.

"When the objects failed to appear, I had no recourse but to ask Constable Riley to look into the matter. I truly hoped he would find we had been the victims of a sneak thief, a gypsy, or some other vagrant who might have slipped in when the staff was below stairs."

Eric raised his hands and let them fall in a gesture of despair. "Constable Riley searched the house from top to bottom, but there was no sign of forcible entry, no broken locks or window panes."

Eric looked intently at Jessica. "It is now my duty, dear, to tell you where the Constable found those missing objects. The silver darning egg was wrapped in a silk stocking and tucked into one of Lily's Sunday slippers. The snuff box was in the bottom of Mrs. Kiernan's trunk, hidden in a button box. In Flynn's room we found six silver fish knives and a sterling soup ladle bundled up in a towel and stuffed away in his wicker fishing creel. We hadn't even missed those last items, so there's no telling how long they've been robbing you blind."

Jessica said quietly, "This just doesn't make sense, Uncle Eric."

"I beg your pardon. Are you suggesting Constable Riley doesn't know how to perform his duties?"

"But there must have been some reasonable explanation."

"Oh, you can be sure they tried to brazen it out, claimed they had no idea how those things had got into their rooms."

"Then that's the truth of it," Jessica said in a deliberate voice. "If you'll excuse me, I'd like to talk to them now."

"I'm afraid that won't be possible," Eric said. "They've packed and gone."

Jessica looked at him, her expression incredulous. "You mean, they've *left* Easter Hill?"

"I did not make the decision on my own, Jessica. I only acted after consulting with Mr. Ryan's office in Dublin. His people agreed with me that the servants here should be dismissed on the spot."

This last statement of Eric's stretched the truth considerably. He had indeed covered himself by calling the solicitor's office in Dublin, but presented the facts of the thefts to a secretary in so garbled and rambling a fashion that she had at last interrupted him, suggesting he put the whole matter in writing for the benefit of the insurance company.

"After I explained my decision to the guilty servants, Kevin O'Dell and Rose also decided to leave. They talked rather grandly about their loyalty to one another but my guess is they were using that as an excuse to clear out before we caught them at something else . . .

"Just one last thing," Eric said. "Then we can close the book on this unfortunate episode. I took it on myself, Jessica, to inform Constable Riley that we

205

wouldn't press charges against Lily, Mrs. Kiernan, or Flynn. I went farther than that, in fact, and assured them that we would provide them with reasonable character references when they sought other employment. However, I think it's unlikely they'll find positions in this county and so we'll have to mail them their papers when and if they need them."

"If you'll excuse me, Aunt Maud and Uncle Eric, I'll say goodnight."

"Have a good sleep, Jessica," Eric said. "Try to put all this unpleasantness out of your mind. Starting tomorrow, we'll carry on here at Easter Hill just as before..."

Jessica stopped in the arched doorway of the library and looked steadily at the three adults whose figures were silhouetted by the spurting flames from the fireplace.

"Uncle Eric, where is Fluter?"

"I don't have a clue, my dear. I think Brown's been looking after him."

Jessica turned and walked into the great hall, crossing to the corridors that fanned out toward the servants' quarters. She went swiftly through the dark kitchens and storerooms, looking into the shadows behind the salad sinks and pot cupboards, calling Fluter's name softly but insistently. Even the air itself seemed unresponsive to her summons, heavy and motionless in the cavernous rooms.

Jessica walked through the pantry and laundry, opened the door to the rear staircase, and went to the second floor of the sprawling house.

There was no sign of Fluter in her bedroom. Jessica hurried along the corridor, looking into the open doors of the various other suites, calling for the big collie. At the end, she retraced her steps, discouragement settling like a physical weight on her slim shoulders.

The lights of her inner visions flickered constantly now, but she could discern no pattern or meaning in the shadows silhouetted by their illuminations. However, when she reentered her own bedroom, she heard a weak whimpering sound and, snapping on the lights, she saw the great merle collie pulling itself sluggishly from under the bed.

That was why her first quick glance missed him, she thought, dropping to her knees and cradling the big head in her arms. Fluter was gravely sick, she knew at once, his tongue black, his nose hot and dry, the great eyes clouded and feverish, his plumed tail rising and falling feebly.

In the bathroom, Jessica filled a porcelain basin with cold water and brought it to the panting dog, lifting his head so he could lap it with his parched tongue. Someone, she realized with a flare of anger, had tightened the collar to the choking point. She loosened it two notches and almost immediately heard the dog's breathing settle into an easier rhythm.

Jessica turned off the lights in the room and then carefully opened the door to the hall and walked through the darkness to an alcove at the head of the stairs where a French phone rested on a gate-legged table.

Dialing the operator in Ballytone, she gave the lady a number, speaking in a voice that was clear but barely above a whisper.

Then Jessica became aware of two sounds

simultaneously, a windy draftiness in her ear, which told her someone in the house had lifted another receiver, and then the faint tapping sounds of her Aunt Maud's high heels on the parquet floor of the great hall below her.

As Maud peered in her near-sighted fashion up the gloomy staircase, Jessica retreated into the shadows of the alcove, her walking a whisper on the heavy carpet.

"Jessica? Is that you up there?"

At the same instant that her aunt called to her, a click sounded in Jessica's ear and she heard Dr. Julian Homewood's voice.

"Hello. Dr. Homewood here . . ."

Jessica longed to speak to him but she knew now he was too far away to help her. She realized she must solve her own problems tonight, knowing that hesitation at times like this not only compounded one's fears but one's dangers, too. And so, in her heart, she whispered a goodbye to Doctor Julian, replaced the phone and ran swiftly through the hall to her dark bedroom. As she fled, she heard the click-click of doors being latched downstairs.

Maud returned just as Eric put the phone down in Dalworth's study. He glanced at Tony Saxe with an odd smile.

"The little golden princess changed her mind. She decided *not* to talk to Dr. Homewood," he said.

Staring from Saxe to Eric, Maud noted the silent communication between them, an appraisal in their smiles. She said abruptly, "Supposing you gentlemen tell me what the hell's been going on around here?"

Eric lifted the decanter from the bar to add a

splash of whiskey to his glass. "I'll be more than pleased to bring you up-to-date, my dear. Would you hand me that folder, Tony?"

After Eric explained what he had learned about Jessica from the Homewood-Dalworth folder—and after he had outlined their new plans—Maud was silent for a moment. Then she shook her head nervously, distracted by worried thoughts.

"You and Tony may think you know best, but I don't like it. If Jessica's got some kind of kooky gift, she could know more than is good for us. I mean, about more than just horse races."

"Well, that needn't concern us," Eric said.

"But you weren't there at the hotel," Maud said, a thread of fear in her voice. "She was different, Eric. Almost dangerous. More than just a girl—"

Tony Saxe cleared his throat warningly. "Tone it down, luv," he said under his breath. "We've got company."

On his words, they all turned and saw Jessica standing in the arched doorways of the library. She had changed into riding clothes, a paisley scarf pulled loosely about her throat. After an interval of strange silence—a quietness that seemed to stretch and hum through the big room—Maud wet her lips and said, "Jessica dear, I thought you were going to bed."

Eric looked at his niece appraisingly. "Yes, you seemed quite worn out."

Jessica entered the library, her sturdy boots stopping just outside the semi-circle of golden light cast by the burning logs. Her face was in partial darkness, like a faint star against the mass of black hair.

"Fluter is sick," she said. "And someone purposely tightened his collar so that it was nearly choking him."

"I simply cannot believe it," Eric said. "I can't believe the servants would take out their spite on a poor, dumb animal..."

Jessica studied him deliberately and candidly, seeing now what had been obscured by grief and dubious loyalty to family. The death of Andrew, the link through him to her mother—all this had served to camouflage what she was seeing now—a cunning, practiced smile, and words transparently evasive and false.

"I'm going to ride Windkin over to Miss Charity's and bring her back with me. She'll know what to do for Fluter. And when I'm there, I'll phone Mr. Ryan in Dublin and ask him to come over here tomorrow morning."

"What a busy child you are," Maud said, putting aside her glass.

"What in hell do you want that senile shyster for?" Eric smiled as he moved closer to Jessica. "I think you're tired and overwrought, young lady. And I think you can forget this notion of riding across the moors like some Gothic heroine. If you wish to call Mr. Ryan, you can do it right from here."

"I tried to make a call only ten minutes ago and someone in this house was listening in."

"Well, I was phoning Ballytone. Wanted the late racing results. Perhaps our calls got mixed up..."

"I don't believe that, either," Jessica said. "I'm also quite sure you know why I'm calling Mr. Ryan." In spite of her youth and stature, there was something dominant about Jessica then, her eyes tracking across them like the muzzles of small pistols. "I don't believe for a minute that Flynn or Lily or Mrs. Kiernan tried to steal anything."

"You sound like a bloody little district attorney," Eric said, feeling a sluggish but pleasurable anger stirring in him. "I'm your *uncle* and I'd advise you to remember that."

"Then I'd like *you* to remember this," Jessica said. "Easter Hill is *my* home. Those good people you sent away are my dearest friends and they have looked after me most of my life." Jessica paused and drew a deep breath. "When Mr. Ryan arrives tomorrow morning, I want you all to make arrangements to leave here immediately."

"As I suspected all along," Eric said, "you're a spoiled little ingrate."

Maud uncrossed her legs and, with no suggestion of haste, stood and smoothed down the front of her skirt. "You're talking so strangely, dear. I still think you might have a fever..."

She moved toward Jessica, who stepped back at the same instant, retreating from the circle of firelight gilding the floor.

Tony Saxe shrugged. "Kid, I've been thrown out of better places than this, so it don't worry me much."

"You are *my* guest here, Tony," Eric said. "And you'll stay just as long as it suits *me*."

His anger was gathering itself together powerfully, coiling hotly inside him. He wasn't to be humbled this way, not Boniface. In her absence, he had been a generous patron, the master of Easter Hill, approved of, warmly approved of, he thought, remembering the Irish lads who had whipped off their caps in respect and deference when he had cantered past them.

Pointing a long finger at Jessica, he said with intensity and bitterness, "You listen to me, princess. You're not turning your own aunt and uncle out into the cold like some haughty lady of the manor. No bloody way. But I'll tell you what you *are* going to do. You're going to your room without any more of these impertinent theatrics—*and you are going to stay there*. And if you give me any more back talk, I'll give *you* what that indulgent old fool, Dalworth, should have given you a long spell ago—the flat of my hand where it will do the most good."

Jessica was so outraged by what Eric had said that she was momentarily unaware of how helpless she was against three adults. "If you ever raise a hand to me, I promise that you'll regret it, Uncle Eric," Jessica said and turned and walked quickly from the library into the hall.

When she heard the sudden rush of footsteps behind her, the girl started to run, but it was already too late. Uncle Eric's long, sinewy hands caught her wrists and twisted one of her arms cruelly behind her back. And when he increased the pressure, the pain in her shoulder was so fierce that a scream of anguish forced itself past her lips.

Jessica pounded the heel of her riding boot down onto Eric's glossy moccasin and was rewarded by his bellow of anger.

"Little bitch!" Maud said. She stood watching with Tony Saxe in the doorway of the library.

Panting with exertion, Eric said, "You badly need a lesson in manners, young lady, and you are going to *get* it." Tightening his grip on her arm, he forced another cry from Jessica's throat.

From the corner of her eye, the girl saw a blur of movement on the wide stairs, Fluter's merle blue-gray ruff rising like a crest around his powerful jaws.

"Fluter!" Jessica cried.

The huge collie jumped, a snarl breaking past its bared teeth.

Maud screamed and Tony Saxe shouted, "Eric! For Christ's sake—*watch it*!"

Eric wheeled, his face twisting with panic. Fluter's body struck Eric's chest, its weight driving them both in a heap to the floor. Eric screamed, kicking his feet desperately.

"Get him off me! Get him off!" he shouted.

Jessica ran into the vast dark dining room, calling over her shoulder, "Come, Fluter. Come!"

After snarling barks, which chased Maud and Tony back into the library, the collie wheeled and rushed after the girl.

She had by then parted the brocade draperies and pressed fretwork knobs that caused a walnut panel to swing back from the priest hole.

Whispering to the dog, she prodded him down a flight of steps into the cold hiding place, then pressed the lever that forced the panel to swing smoothly back into position.

After a breathless moment, Jessica heard Eric's voice in the dining room beyond the priest hole.

"I'll put a bullet through that damned dog's head..."

She heard footsteps then, the men's heavy on the old floorboards, Aunt Maud's high heels clicking like a woodpecker on a cold day.

When the sounds faded in the direction of the pantries and kitchen, Jessica lifted a corner of matting from the floor and raised the trap door exposing steep steps leading to the cellars.

Jessica went down the stairs and snapped her fingers. When the big dog joined her, she whispered, "Stay, Fluter. I'll come back with Miss Charity..."

On the second floor, Eric and Maud snapped on lights in both wings, checked closets, swept back draperies and dust ruffles, and threw open bathroom doors. Meanwhile, Tony Saxe examined the windows and doors on the first floor. When they regrouped, he said, "No way she could of got outside. The whole place is locked tight."

"Get a flashlight, Maud," Eric said. "Maybe she got to the attic..."

Jessica ran down the dew-slick lawn from the gardens of Easter Hill to the staff cottages and stables.

In the darkness of the horse barn, she felt along the walls until her hand touched a bridle and bit on pegs. Pulling them down, she ran to Windkin's stall, climbed a mounting stool and coaxed the big mare close to her with a cluck of her tongue. There was no time for a saddle; she would ride bare-back to Miss Charity's. But Windkin pulled away from her, neck muscles flexing and hooves pounding in staccato rhythms.

"Now stop it! You've got to help me, Windkin! Please..."

The overhead lights flashed on. Jessica turned and saw the new groom walking toward her, a puzzled smile on his battered features. He had obviously been sleeping. His black hair was pushed up on the back of his head like a cockatoo's crest. His cheeks were creased from a wrinkled pillow.

"Kind of late to go riding, ain't it, kid?"

His smile was easy and insolent and when his eyes moved from her shoulders to her narrow waist, she felt exposed and vulnerable.

She said, "My dog is ill. I'm going for the vet."

"Why don't you make a phone call? Or get your Uncle Eric to take you in the car?" Putting a cigarette between his lips, he slanted it up toward his cheek but didn't light it. "What's going on, little lady?"

"I've told you, my dog is sick."

"You better level with me, kid."

"I'm telling you the truth." Jessica was angry with herself. She felt close to tears, resisting an impulse to cross her arms over the thin twill jacket covering her chest.

"Look. Your uncle and aunt know what you're up to?"

"That's none of your business."

"Wrong, kid. I gotta check you out. There's a phone in my digs. Come on."

"I'm not going anywhere with you," Jessica said furiously.

"Got a hot temper, right?" he said. "I kind of like that." Removing the cigarette from his mouth, he dropped it into his shirt pocket and then, with a powerful sweep of his arm, caught her about the waist and pulled her down from the stool.

He was frighteningly strong. She struggled desperately against him, almost gagging at the smell of liquor on his breath. But his arm was like an iron band around her slender body.

Laughing, he carried the girl from the stables to his cottage where he snapped on a lamp and dumped her onto a sagging leather couch. Seating himself beside her, he pinned her down, his hands locking her arms above her head.

"Hey, cut the act, kid!" he said, and laughed as she struggled.

"You have no right to touch me, you—*bastard*."

He laughed again. "Oh, come on. Old Benny's not such a bad guy when you get to know him..."

There were footsteps then, a shadow from the open door, and a voice loud around them.

"Take your hands off her, you scum," Capability Brown said.

When Benny Stiff spun around, the tines of the pitchfork the old man held were just inches from his eyes.

"Hey, hey!" Benny Stiff raised both arms above his head in a gesture of entreaty. "Cool it, pal. We were just having a little fun."

"On your feet," Brown said.

"Sure, anything you say." Moving slowly, Benny stood and inched back and away from the shining pitchfork.

"Did he hurt you, child?" the old man said.

"I'm all right, Mr. Brown." Jessica said, scrambling from the couch. And it was then, when the old Irishman turned to put a protective hand on the girl's arm, it was then that Benny struck, a savage right that caught the old man in the face and knocked him across the flagged hearth of the fireplace, the pitchfork clattering to the floor from his suddenly limp hands.

"Get up, you old stumble-bum," Benny Stiff said. "On your feet!"

But Jessica knew from the unnatural angle of Mr. Brown's head and neck that he had been badly hurt.

Staring down at the small, huddled figure of the gardener, Benny Stiff's expression changed.

"Hey, get up!" he said, his voice troubled and uneasy.

But the old man didn't stir. Eyes that had appreciated all growing things, that had kept vigil through many nights for his country's enemies, were now fixed and staring on the hearth stones.

"Hey! What's this? Some kind of act?" Benny said. "I didn't hit him that hard."

"You've killed him!" Jessica said, her voice rising. "You've killed Mr. Brown."

"It was an accident, kid, that's the way we got to make it go down..."

With a strangled sob, Jessica wheeled and ran through the cottage door into the darkness. For an instant, Benny Stiff stood paralyzed over Brown's motionless body.

He knew he should do something, take care of this business, save his own hide, call Griffith or Tony Saxe to tell them what had happened, get his hands on the kid before she ruined them all...

Stiff lunged through the door and ran into the night after Jessica. She was only a dozen yards in front of him, fleeing down the sloping lawn, an occasional streak of moonlight flaring on the bright scarf at her throat.

"Wait, kid!" he bellowed, and started after her, his legs churning under him like pistons.

He closed on her rapidly, near enough at one instant to clutch at the sleeve of her jacket, but still she evaded him. Her advantage lay in the fact that she knew every inch of the grounds near Easter Hill. The terrain was hers. When she darted to the left and he jumped to cut her off, he realized only when the stretches of wire mesh stung his face and hands that she had led him into a trap. Jessica had ducked behind a trellis of climbing Guinea beans and Benny had crashed into the wire grids supporting the vines. While he floundered like a rabbit in a snare, Jessica climbed the garden wall and disappeared into the meadows beyond.

Freeing himself, Benny ran to his cottage, snatched up the phone and dialed the manor house.

Chapter Twenty-One —————————————————

A surging wind broke against the Connemara coast that night, pounding the sea side of Skyhead and stirring eddies of sand on the flat beaches running north. The wind rode hard through the streets of Ballytone and over the ridge of hills that rose from the village toward forbidding skies.

It raced along the cragged coasts of Connaught and Mayo, past towns named Castlebar, Innisscrone and Screen, churning up sprays of white water in Donegal Bay before finding its match in the high escarpment that stood above the town of Ballydrum and served as a storm-break for the Mallory cottage where, at this moment, old Liam Mallory had paused with a hand on the tea kettle to say to his wife, Corinne, "I fear something, woman..."

"What are you fearing?"

"I cannot tell. But I have the feel of it."

Placing the kettle on the iron arm hinged to the fireplace, the old man looked through the windows at the mists coming up above the cliffs.

"All week they've been telling me," he said. "The eggs with triple yolks, then the birds—quiet in the trees—stopping their cries, and your mother's wedding plate, for forty years on that shelf wall, falling and shattering itself."

"It's only the winds, Liam."

"Was it just the wind that opened the Bible to the death pages? Showing the names gone before us?"

Staring at the white mists, he shook his head. "No, they're telling me about the girl who was here. Warning us . . ."

The old man tried to remember the name of the lady who had brought Jessica to their cottage but the name remained elusive at the edge of his thoughts. Then Liam recalled that the woman with Jessica Mallory had talked of their village in the south and mentioned the name of the priest there. "Was it not Father Malachy, Father Malachy from the town of Ballytone?" And when his wife nodded, old Liam made his decision . . .

From the top of the meadow, Jessica heard snatches of shouted conversation. Soon afterward came the sound of car engines rising to life, then the orange beams of headlights slashing through the trees.

The green sedan Eric Griffith had rented at Shannon Airport disappeared south of Easter Hill. The black convertible with the new groom and Tony Saxe in the front seat headed toward the road to Ballytone.

Jessica ran across the field, sod springy under her boots. She planned to cross the trout stream at the bottom of the meadow, then climb the next hill toward Skyhead, a course that would take her away from Easter Hill and from the village of Ballytone. She knew it would be foolish and reckless to head for Miss Charity's, even the rectory tonight. With two cars and four sets of eyes, Uncle Eric and Aunt Maud and the two strangers could easily cover all the approaches to the village.

When she reached the summit of Skyhead, she could hear the seas booming in long breakers on the shores below. Starting down a winding footpath, Jessica crouched low to make her body a smaller target for the buffeting winds. Gripping tufts of grass, she cautiously descended the steep incline.

The ocean side of Skyhead was cold and wet. When the path angled sharply, Jessica's boots slipped out from under her. She slid a dozen feet, shale rattling, until she managed to throw both arms around a boulder and stop her fall.

The wind blew her hair into a tangle and her silk scarf flapped like a piece of torn sail. At the base of the cliff, with hard-packed sand under her feet, she began to run, keeping well clear of the powerful waves crashing and sucking at the shore.

Scrambling over clusters of rock wigged with seaweed, she ran until her sides were hot with pain, until her breath came faster than the pound of her heart. Only then did she slow down, half-walking and half-running toward her goal, the snug and hidden beach where she had so often picnicked and swum with Andrew and the dogs—Angel's Cove.

One road led from the bluffs to these beaches, a

worn cart-trail, starting from the Ballytone Road and curving down the sea side of Skyhead.

At the junction of the beach and cart-road, Jessica stopped to catch her breath, the cold air searing her lungs.

But she would be safe at Angel's Cove. And the embrace of the rocks would shield her from the winds. At dawn she would climb the cliff and make her way to Miss Charity or Father Malachy.

The sea winds changed direction. Jessica listened intently, raising her eyes to the crests of Skyhead. Above the crash of wave and wind, she thought she had heard the sound of a car—a mechanical, throbbing beat somewhere above her on the cart-road. She couldn't be sure because when the winds changed again, the vague rhythmic vibrations were lost in the heavier crash of the waves.

She held her breath, listening with her imagination and will, as much as with her eyes. But she heard nothing then except the water and the winds against the granite cliffs. Tightening her scarf, she ran on toward Angel's Cove, dodging the curling waves that were aimed like frothing scythes at her ankles.

And then from above and behind her, lights flickered on the beach, gleaming like bright fires in the waves. Turning, Jessica saw the headlights of a car bouncing down the cart-trail from the Ballytone road.

Ignoring the pain in her side and the winds stinging her cheeks, Jessica ran even faster, knowing she had been trapped and realizing that her only chance of escape was to find natural hand-holds and to claw her way back up the face of the raw cliff.

She risked a glance over her shoulder. The headlights had winked out, but she could still hear the car grinding behind her like a sullen dog. Suddenly, that muted sound crescendoed into a heavy roar directly behind her on the beach itself. At the same instant the glare of the headlights exploded around her, pinning the girl in a circle of relentless illumination.

Risking another desperate glance, Jessica saw the sedan bearing down on her, Aunt Maud and Uncle Eric's faces shimmering and ghost-like behind the windshield.

Then Jessica paid the extravagant price for that glimpse of danger—her flying feet collided with a piece of driftwood half buried in the sand. She cried out and fell sprawling headlong to the damp beach. The impact knocked the breath from her body, and created a sickening vibration in her ears. She was barely conscious of the icy waves surging over her out-flung arms.

Footsteps sounded and they were beside her, turning her body with strong hands onto a woolen car rug.

"You shouldn't have put us to this trouble, princess." Eric's voice was edged with sarcasm. "Your Aunt Maud might just catch a cold."

They bundled the girl in the heavy rug, imprisoning her arms and legs. When she recovered her breath and tried to scream, it was too late; a fold of the blanket was tight across her face, covering her mouth and eyes.

Jessica was aware of being lifted and laid flat in the rear of the car. She heard the doors slam, felt the wheels backing and turning, then felt the damp wind on her face as the sedan rushed along the beach toward the cart-road.

Chapter Twenty-Two ────────────

"There's no way we can keep the wheels on this goddamn deal now." Saxe's voice was tight with frustration. "What the hell's your plan? Keep her locked up till she's twenty-one?"

Eric said, "We're in no danger, Tony, providing we keep our heads and resist your temptation to panic."

"I wish to Christ you'd spell it out," Benny Stiff said. "I came into this deal for some quick, safe loot. Now I got a murder staring me in the face. I didn't mean to kill that old bastard, I just wanted to—"

Eric interrupted him. "Of course you meant to kill him, Benny. As my mentor, Ira Washburn, often said, there are surprisingly few true accidents in life."

The three men were in the library, early sunshine splashing the glowing carpets, and gleaming on the burnished brass that framed the fireplace.

"That's worth remembering," Eric went on, "particularly when trying to portray Hamlet. There you have a man who sets out to kill one person and winds up 'accidentally' killing five. Still, if the player understands the dreadful compulsion behind these seemingly accidental—"

"Oh, for God's sakes!" Tony Saxe said. "What the hell's that got to do with anything? We're sitting here with a feisty kid locked up upstairs, ready to blow the whistle the minute she gets a chance, a whistle that could put ropes around our necks. And how long is that hayseed cop from Ballytone going to live with our story about the old gardener?"

Eric buffed his nails on his lapels. "Not to worry, Tony..."

He had called Constable Patrick Riley earlier, advising him in mournful tones of the heart attack that had stricken Capability Brown. The constable had arrived shortly with what passed for the village ambulance, a panel truck with a stretcher, an oxygen tank, blankets, and a pair of local lads in white jackets.

Eric had been at his theatrically most convincing, as the old man's body was carried to the hospital truck.

"He complained of a pain in his left arm only yesterday," he had said.

The young constable had nodded sagely, his face fresh and red in the brisk dawn winds. "Aye, there's your coronary."

"I told him I didn't want him to do any more work until he saw Dr. Cook."

With a sigh, Benny Stiff had added, "He came into my room just to chat. We'd got pretty friendly.

225

Without no warning at all, he just toppled over. Hit his head on that stone floor."

Constable Riley had written down these details in a black notebook. "The little lass, Miss Jessica, she'll be heartbroken. They were close, you know, old Brown and the girl."

"Yes," Eric had touched a handkerchief to his eye. "She's in her room now, not up to seeing anyone . . ."

"Well, Mr. Brown's heart never failed him when the country called," Constable Riley said. "He'll be missed in Ballytone and beyond."

Eric smiled at Tony Saxe and Benny now and sipped coffee from his Lenox cup, admiring the gold rim afire with sunlight. Then he said crisply, "We're not home free, of course, but we have nothing to fear if we keep our heads. Constable Riley will never doubt our story because he's been programmed for centuries to respect the gentry. We're in the big house on the hill, in a nation of fools and peasants. We can intimidate them with our fine cars and starched shirts as easily as if we had guns at their heads."

"You're going shut-eye," Benny Stiff said. "I don't want to bet this neck, which is the only one I've got, on that kind of bull. I killed that nosey old geek. I say I didn't mean to, you say I did. Which don't make no difference. That kid upstairs saw me hit him and knows what happened."

Eric shrugged, a gesture dismissing Benny's concerns. "Back in Camden, you and Tony were quick to suggest that I didn't want this deal badly enough. That I wouldn't, in effect, 'go all out.' Well, let me remind you, I paid my dues. We're in this together now. Up to our necks, to use the figure that seems to haunt you. But take old Eric's word for it. If you do exactly what I tell you, we'll be on a flight back to the States in a few days, with Swiss bank accounts and wads of money in our pockets."

Tony Saxe seemed reassured by Eric's confidence. "Okay, you're calling the shots," he said. "So, what do we do now?"

"Good. You and Benny go down to the Hannibal and explain the new schedule to Ethelroyd. Tell him I want him here about noon, bank notes in hand. That should give me plenty of time to convince little Miss Crystal Head that..."

A ghastly scream from the rear of the house fell across his words, splintering his sentence with the force of a falling cleaver.

"Christ! That's Maud!" Eric said.

The three men ran from the library through the great hall and down a long corridor into the kitchen, where they found Maud hurrying up from the wine cellar, two bottles clutched to her breast and an expression of mindless terror straining her pale features.

"Good God, Maud, what is it?"

"There was something down there. It brushed against my arms and face. I'd bent over to pick up a bottle. You would have wine with lunch, damn you, Eric. And I almost fainted when it touched me. It was dreadful. I knew I was awake, I knew I wasn't dreaming—" She shuddered, an involuntary spasm that shook her body, and the next words came so intensely and rapidly that they were barely audible.

"It was like the time in that closet and that bitch

227

Coralee lying about it and the smell of dust and perfume choking me, those silk ballgowns and nobody heard me."

"Now, Maud..."

"Don't 'now Maud' me, Eric. I could have died down there. It started growling. Then I realized it was that damned dog Fluter you ruined everything trying to poison. I screamed and screamed and he ran up these stairs and out the back door. I was down there in the darkness because I couldn't find the light switch. My heart nearly burst and you had to have your damned proper lunch, the fine gentleman of Easter Hill. Of course, nothing's too good for—"

"That's enough, Maud."

"—old Eric with his phony club ties and—"

"Shut up now," Eric said, staring over his shoulder at the corridor leading up to the great hall. "Just stuff it! We've got callers."

They all heard the chimes and their eyes turned to the directory panel in the service pantry.

One arrow in a row of indicators had lighted, swinging upright to point to the words: Main Entrance.

"Now everybody, relax," Eric said. "It's business as usual here. Remember, we're naturally sad about the gardener but my niece can't see anyone, *anyone at all*, understand?"

Composing himself, Eric walked to the hall and swung open the double doors which gave on views of terraced gardens and a circular driveway, views broken now by the purposeful figure of Miss Charity Bostwick.

"I stopped by to see Jessica, Mr. Griffith."

"Oh, yes. You are—? I'm sorry."

"I'm Charity Bostwick, a friend of the family."

"Of course. You've given the child riding lessons, I believe. But I'm afraid Jessica can't see anyone now. I presume you've heard the unhappy news about our gardener."

"Yes, that's why I came by. I thought it might help Jessica."

"That's good of you. It's the sort of neighborly gesture one doesn't find too often in this busy, modern world. However, this isn't the best time for it. My niece cried herself to sleep, waked with a touch of fever. Her aunt's with her now."

"Have you sent for Dr. Cook?"

Eric smiled and said untruthfully, "But, of course. He'll be here any minute."

"Mr. Griffith, I don't see the harm in letting me talk to Jessica."

"She's mentioned how fond she is of you, but I think just now quiet and rest are the best therapy."

"Supposing we let Jessica decide that. Would you just tell her I'm here?"

"Of course, Miss Bostwick. I'll leave it to her . . ."

Eric went up the broad curving stairway and walked along the corridor to the Clock Suite where he inspected himself in a clouded mirror set in the upper panels of a Winchester highboy. Smoothing down his thin blond hair, he bared his lips and inspected his teeth with a critical eye, after which he adjusted the knot of his wool knit tie, whistled softly for a moment or so, and then returned to the hall, his expression suggesting kindly concern.

"I'm terribly sorry, Miss Bostwick. Jessica asked me to tell you she's pleased you came by. But she'd rather not see anyone but family just yet."

Charity Bostwick would have loved to be incisive and candid with this foppish Yank, telling him exactly what she thought of his bogus suede elbow patches, carefully waved blond hair, and supercilious smiles. But if something was wrong here, and Miss Charity's suspicions were sharpening quickly, it wouldn't do to let this improbable gentleman know she was on to him.

With an effort, she smiled. "If there's any way at all I can help, Mr. Griffith, I'd be grateful if you rang me up."

"How generous of you."

"Thank you."

Eric stood watching Miss Bostwick's trim, athletic figure descending the garden steps to her sports car. Rocking on his heels, he hooked a thumb in his vest pocket and waved to her with his other hand, complacently aware of the picture he must present to this village matron, every inch the benevolent squire standing tall and virile in the high arched doorways of Easter Hill.

Chapter Twenty-Three ————————

The lights and shadows in her mind had grown so insistent and demanding, so frightening in their implications, that Jessica's awareness of the actual world around her had become tentative and fragile. An evanescent view of the future, details blurred and inexact but implicit in horror, so commanded her energy and attention that she was hardly conscious of the bolts being drawn in the locked door of her bedroom. When her consciousness surfaced to reality, she saw her Uncle Eric looming above her, tucking a key into his vest pocket.

Holding up a packet of letters and a folder, he smiled at her and said, "Time to talk. To let you know we're aware of your strange gifts, Jessica. Courtesy of this explicit correspondence between Dr. Homewood and the late Andrew Dalworth."

The sound of those cherished names, plus the

abrasive exploitation of her privacy, altered the fabric of the images obscuring her awareness of physical surroundings.

She got off the bed and stood and faced her uncle, vivid contempt in her eyes.

"Those letters don't belong to you," she said. "But I'm not surprised you've read them."

Eric sighed. "You're being unfair, Jessica. Maud and I have only your best interests at heart. Our one thought has been to help. We aren't rich, Jessica. You probably can't understand what that means. Since you were a mere child, you've been surrounded and protected by luxury. But had you trusted us, had you been responsive to your family ties, we would have been your friends. We would have helped you. Even as Maud and I—"

Eric's voice had become quiet and thoughtful, touched with resignation. Raising his eyes to the ceiling as if for approval, he went on, "—even as Maud and I helped your dear mother and father when they were in need of—"

"I don't believe any of this," Jessica said sharply, and now there was a deeper tone in her voice.

"It's sad to find such cynicism in one so young."

"Please stop it! You must think I'm a thorough fool. There was not even a postcard from you when Andrew was alive. You've lied to me from the start. I treasured the locket Aunt Maud gave to me until the morning that Mr. Flynn and I cleaned it with silver polish and found the tiny initials on the inside. They weren't my mother's at all."

"Your father probably bought it second-hand which explains why—"

232

"Stop wasting your breath, Uncle Eric. I know you poisoned Fluter. And I saw with my own eyes what happened to Mr. Brown. You're a pack of thieves and murderers and if it's the last thing I do—"

Eric grabbed her by the shoulders and shook her with ruthless strength. "Don't ever threaten me, young lady, or it *will* be the last thing you do. Have you thought how ridiculous your accusations will sound? As far as that old fool, Brown, is concerned, would a jury take your word against mine and Constable Riley's?" Eric released her and looked appraisingly at her slim, budding body.

"Jessica, you're at the age where your hormones and emotions are in a state of riot. The line between fantasy and reality is blurred, which explains your erratic behavior. Fleeing from the house without rhyme or reason, running to a beach where you could have caught your death of cold—fearsome things—" He sighed. "Faithful retainers, the victims of foul play? Beloved pet mysteriously poisoned? No." He shook his head. "It simply won't wash, Jessica. Maud and I brought you back here to protect you, and we've shut you up to prevent you from harming yourself..."

"That's not the truth and you know it!"

"And in return—" Eric went on as smoothly, "—and in return, Jessica, all we want is a small favor."

Jessica stared directly into his eyes. "I will do nothing for you."

"I urge you to reconsider," Eric said. "I might not ask so nicely a second time."

With apparent amiability, Eric said, "I like your spirit, because it suggests an emotional tension that suits my purpose."

As he saw her sharpening awareness, Eric nodded in gratification. "Let me refresh you with a paragraph from one of the doctor's letters."

Opening the leather file, he removed a page and unfolded it, a faint but sensual smile touching his lips.

"'Jessica's skills'," he said, reading aloud, "'that is, her processes of precognition, would escalate at a powerful rate in proportion to the profundity of her emotional states.'"

Eric glanced at Jessica and said, "This was written by Dr. Homewood when you were nine. To translate his medical gibberish into plain English, it simply means that the more terrified you are, the better qualified you'll be to help us."

Eric walked to the large bay window and looked down at the stables. With his back to Jessica, he said thoughtfully, "For some reason, our new groom, Benny Stiff—" He turned and smiled at Jessica. "For some odd reason, he's taken a fancy to you—" He jingled the key to her room.

Noting the repugnance in her expression, Eric shrugged. "It's just something to keep in mind."

In a level voice, Jessica said, "I don't even know the words to describe you."

Eric removed a cigarette lighter from his vest pocket, snapped the wheel and stared at the spurting flame.

"Another thought—so many unfortunate accidents occur around these lovely, isolated country homes. Wouldn't it be a shame, Jessica, if some careless person—a tramp or gypsy perhaps—accidentally started a fire in the stables?"

Jessica drew a quick breath, the sound sharp in the straining silence.

"Wouldn't that be dreadful, Jessica?"

Jessica shook her head slowly, eyes narrowing to pinpoints of light.

"You know how horses panic in fire," Eric said. "If the stalls are locked, they often break their legs trying to kick their way out. The screams of horses trapped that way sound almost human. And even if they are lucky enough to have someone around to lead them out, they're likely to bolt right back to the false security of the blazing stables. It's happened time after time."

Eric snapped his lighter shut, dropped it into his vest pocket. "I trust you'll be sensible, Jessica."

"That's only a word, Uncle Eric. It doesn't mean the same to everybody."

"Don't play games with me, Jessica. I'll tell you what I want and there'll be no damned discussion about it."

He dropped the folder on her bed and pointed to it. "There's the information you need, the names of the entries in the Grand National. You tell me the win, place, and show horses, understand? Use tea leaves, Ouija boards, or those precognitions your bloody Dr. Homewood is so awed by, I don't give a damn. *Just tell me the winners, how they'll come in.*"

"I can do that, Uncle Eric," she said quietly, and he was too agitated by the implications of that simple statement to hear a different tone in her voice, see a look in her eye, older than her years, close to ancient mockeries. "But people don't always know what they want, Uncle Eric," the girl went on. "They choose without light and make mistakes."

"I don't need any talk of your bloody lights and colors, Jessica. I've told you what I want. So what is it *you* want? *Think hard, girl.* Do you *want* me to give the key to your room to Benny Stiff? Do you *want* to see a fire in the stable and hear your horse scream? If that's what you *want*, I'll sure as hell give it to you!"

"I *know* what I want," Jessica said, shrugging and turning from him, a perverse smile touching her lips. In her mind there was a shimmer of radiance and through it the child saw the hill and river, Julian's metaphor of time and fate, with currents taking away the headstrong and unwary while she watched . . . "Leave me now, please, and I will do your work."

"You can, Jessica?" His voice was trembling. *"You will?"*

"Yes, I'll give you what you say you want, what you're asking for . . ."

Eric locked the door behind him when he left the room, holding the key tight like a talisman in his fist as he hurried down the stairs. He needed a drink now, a moment alone to savor his triumph.

In her bedroom, Jessica stood perfectly still as the figures of unrealized time began forming in her consciousness, streaking like quicksilver along the neurons of her mind.

After a moment, she picked up the manila envelope which Eric had dropped on the coverlet of her bed.

Chapter Twenty-Four ———————————

A concerned and thoughtful Charity Bostwick sat with a cup of tea in Father Malachy's parlor.

"I'm worried sick about Jessie," she said to the old priest.

"But it's her own aunt and uncle you're speaking of, Charity. Don't be rash in your judgments."

"Father Malachy, if you'd been there, you wouldn't be taking this so calmly. Mr. Griffith *pretended* to ask Jessica if she'd care to see me. I watched him. He turned *right* at the top of the stairs. The child's bedroom is left, in the opposite direction. He lied to me."

"We'd best go easy with such reckonings..."

"Oh, my foot, Father! Do you believe that story they told Constable Riley about Mr. Brown? Before I came here, I went to see Kevin O'Dell. The poor lad told me that Brown never had a moment's heart trouble in his life."

"Death can come like a thief in the night, Charity."

Yet, despite the old man's disclaimers and attempts to remain calm and judicious, Charity Bostwick saw that he was just as troubled as she was.

The unsettling phone call had come in early that morning, prodding him from sleep, the strident male voice speaking of signs and portents, of lights in the sky that matched those in the caller's mind, and a wild sea eagle that had settled at midnight on the roof of the cottage . . .

"You're not as serene as you're pretending, Father. I've called Mr. Ryan in Dublin, but the poor man's been taken to the hospital with influenza. And why do you think they whisked the child off to London in such a rush?"

The caller that morning had said his name was Mallory, Liam Mallory. Obviously unused to telephones, he had shouted and roared into the mouthpiece, numbing the priest's eardrums. Mallory and his wife were traveling by bus down to Athlone where they could borrow a pony and trap to cover the final miles to Ballytone.

What had chilled Father Malachy were old Liam Mallory's words foretelling the evil, shimmering and darkling, that menaced the child Jessica.

"There are forces gathering around her and she has need of our help, Father, need of the power of the elements, the strength of archangels. She is young in her gifts, she has yet to believe in the wisdom of her powers. She needs us and we are too far away. Her enemies are crowding around her . . ."

At that moment, a static drummed along the

wires, splintering the old man's words and the line went dead.

As the priest thought of these things and prayed for guidance, Charity Bostwick lit a cigarette with an impatient gesture, "You can't sit there and tell me you *believe* that Andrew's loyal servants were, in fact, no more than common thieves. And if Jessica could stand straight at Andrew's grave, do you suppose she'd take to her bed at poor Mr. Brown's death? I don't *believe* that child is sick. I think they're lying to all of us."

Remembering the fervor in old Mallory's voice— the words charged with the savage beliefs of Ireland, and truth and history and superstition so impenetrably twined together in them that no human mind or fingers could unsort or unravel it—preferring a fool who believed, to a scholar blinded by arrogance, Father Malachy put his pipe aside and said, "Charity, what do you think we should do in this matter?"

"The first thing I intend to do is make a call, Father. May I use the rectory phone? It's an overseas call to Dr. Julian in California. I'll check with the operator for time and charges."

"Never mind the charges, my dear. Surely we're doing the Lord's work now."

Dr. Julian Homewood let himself into his apartment the evening of that same day and dropped his briefcase into a chair before pouring himself a club soda with lime. At the open doors of his terrace, he looked across the lights of Palo Alto, the Stanford campus dusky and beige in the soft twilight, the stucco facades of old California styles blending effortlessly with the glass and brick masses of modern architecture.

He had given a late lecture to a group of FBI agents from the Bay area, outlining the possibilities of precognition as a tool in criminal investigations, relating this to the research presently underway in Russia and the U.S. in the field of global target identification through clairvoyant techniques. It was one of a series he had given to CIA case officers, including Simon Cutter, the week before in Washington, but Julian knew that today his efforts had been mechanical because he had been preoccupied by an earlier telephone call from Charity Bostwick in Ballytone.

Miss Bostwick's call had wakened him at three in the morning. He had immediately placed a call to Easter Hill; it was almost noon then in Ballytone.

A woman had answered, identifying herself as Maud Griffith. "This is a pleasure, Dr. Homewood. Jessica has told us so many nice things about you."

Julian had attempted to form a picture of the woman from her voice. She seemed to be trying to project a simple warmth and friendliness. And yet a thread of over-stimulated enthusiasm in her tone troubled him.

When he asked to speak to Jessica, Maud Griffith said, "But she's out riding, Doctor."

"I'd been told she was ill."

There had been the slightest pause. Then Maud Griffith said, "You've heard some village gossip, Doctor. She was in bed with the sniffles this morning but she had no temperature so we let her out into the sunshine with Windkin. Is there any message?"

240

Puzzled, he replaced the phone after giving Mrs. Griffith numbers where Jessica could reach him, this apartment and his office at Stanford.

Pacing now, he checked his watch. That had been almost eighteen hours ago. And not a word from Jessica.

Julian's sense of dislocation was not a new sensation. He had been plagued by this strange alienation ever since he had arrived in California. At faculty parties, he had found himself wondering what he was doing in this land of distances and mountains that took your breath away with their ungiving size. And why had he felt estranged from the California girls with their surfing and skiing talents, manes of blond hair, long, tanned legs, and eyes electric-bright with health and vitality as they chatted about their work and danced in discos and drove to the university in their bug-like sports cars.

It wasn't the presence of nothing, he found distressful here. It was the absence of something. And he hadn't realized what that something was until he had re-read that morning the poem that Jessica had written for him in her suite in London.

Of course, Julian had always known that Jessica loved him. As he loved her. But as dear friends, an older brother enjoying a sister's company, a teacher with a favorite student, an affectionate cousin who remembered birthdays...

They had shared many pleasures, the times at Easter Hill, the friendship with Andrew Dalworth, but more importantly, they had shared the exploration of her mental processes, examining the gifts of clairvoyance that were the essence of Jessica Mallory.

241

Julian had known these things and was grateful for them. But now he felt frustrated and helpless because he had never seen the coming years as Jessica had, or the future she had perceived in her last poem from London.

The poem was untitled. The words formed in Julian's memory as he looked out across the darkened campus:

> My heart is like a rough blue diamond,
> Brightest facets hidden,
> Secret brilliance
> Waiting to feel the sudden,
>   sharp silver hammer of my lover.
>
> For him I shall become a small
>   and perfect gemstone,
> With the shards of childhood
>   lying around me.
>
> He is a master.
> I shall know his touch.

Making an inevitable decision, he dialed his secretary and told her to book a flight for him to Shannon. He had showered and changed when the phone rang and his secretary was back on the line.

"I've tried everything, Doctor. Pan Am, Icelandic, KLM, even an Air Force circling up from Algiers. But it's the week of the Grand National in England and everything is booked solid..."

Julian then dialed another number and within minutes—courtesy of a private, unlisted number—spoke directly to a ranking CIA officer in Langley, Virginia.

When Dr. Homewood explained his problem, Simon Cutter said, "No sweat, Doctor. A chauffeur will pick you up in about twenty minutes. You can connect with our shuttle out of San Francisco for Alaska. Courier plane will take you to Reykjavik and on down to Prestwick. An Army jet will be standing by for Shannon. You'll be at Mach II all the way, so you'll beat commercial flights by about six hours."

Julian Homewood checked his currency and passport, strapped up his shoulder bag and within the hour was in a jet aircraft looking down thirty-five thousand feet at the choppy blue and white waters of the Pacific.

Chapter Twenty-Five ───────────

Seated on the curved cushions in her bay window, Jessica tried to isolate the emphemeral conviction that Dr. Julian was aware of her problems. But the effort was frustrated by stronger impressions, concepts of childhood, and the verbal metaphor of gemstone.

And her concentration was further splintered by the noises that she had been hearing that after-noon—heavy footsteps in the hallways and the sounds of furniture being lifted and carried down the stairs.

Standing close to her bedroom windows, she had seen the shining hood of a moving van parked at a side entrance.

She was distracted then by refractions from the curved panes, and when she stared down at the lawns and stables, Jessica saw yellow flecks glowing like fireflies in the velvet shadows. Jessica's heartbeat quickened. She realized, as the lights spurted again from a boxwood hedge, that it was Kevin O'Dell in the shrubbery signalling to her with matches. Four flashes, the same code they had used as children.

Taking her flashlight from the closet, she swept the beam of her torch across the windows—four rapid slashes—but just as she flicked off the switch, a lock clicked, the door of her room swung open and Uncle Eric snapped on the overhead lights. "What the hell's going on here?"

He was in a foul mood. The business arrangements with Ethelroyd had been abrasive, difficult and eventually a source of rancor and humiliation. Ethelroyd was gone now, on his way north to the border, objects of art from Easter Hill crated or wrapped snugly in thick quiltings in his vans. But the fat man had enraged Eric by referring to the things he had bought as "poor darling bastards—no baptismal certificates, no pedigrees, sent off into the world without bills of sale, proof of provenance, not even customs' attestations." And Ethelroyd had concluded this needling harangue with, "Ah, but the precious foundlings will find proper homes in England..."

"What's that you're hiding behind your back?" Eric demanded.

"A flashlight," answered Jessica promptly. "The lamps were flickering."

"Well, there's nothing wrong with them now." Eric hiccuped and felt an abrasive rasp of whiskey in his throat. "Did you do the work I told you to? Have you forgot what I said about that damned horse of yours?"

Jessica looked at him steadily and picked up the slim manila envelope from the bay window seat.

"I've done what you asked. I've seen the finish line." She extended the envelope to him, still staring impassively into his eyes.

"We'll just take a look." Eric's hands trembled as he opened the envelope and studied the entry sheets. If she were right, this was too bloody good to be true, he thought, hearing his quickening breathing as he studied her picks. The odds-on favorites, the newspaper picks, weren't in it at all; Etoile Rouge, Daedalus and Kerry Dancer, the Muirhead entry, all out of the money.

The girl had picked Sterling Choice, currently at fifty-five to one, to win it, Overlord at fifty-to-one to place, and Primrose to show, at twenty-five- to thirty-to-one. Not *one* of these entries had been touted to so much as *show* by the handicappers Eric had studied in newspapers from Manchester, Liverpool, Dublin and London.

"How do you know this?" he demanded, staring across the form sheets at Jessica. His voice had become noticeably hoarse. "What exactly did you see, girl? And don't lie to me. Everything I've got in the world depends on this. Are you sure, Jessica? *Are you sure*!?"

"I saw as much as I needed to know," Jessica said evenly. "When the field takes the canal jump on the second lap of the course, Sterling Choice will be leading by three lengths under a hand ride. Overlord's rider has gone to the bat but isn't gaining. Primrose, the only mare who'll finish the race, is the show horse. She'll be trailing Overlord by seven lengths."

Eric sat down slowly on the edge of the bed, feeling suddenly drained of strength. Yet he thought, with a touch of wonder, it was an exhilarating feeling, the sweet exhaustion of victory.

"There can't be any mistake, Jessica," he said softly. "This means so much to your Uncle Eric."

"I saw them finish. There's no mistake."

And Eric Griffith believed her. But that very confidence and faith in the girl—in some sad fashion—curdled and dissolved his optimism, his anticipation of winning, replacing them with the familiar bewildering and angering self-pity. It didn't have to be just one good afternoon at a track, he thought. It could be hundreds. And to think beyond tracks and horses, toward other contests even more profitable and fateful. It could be the start of something so heady he could feel it spurring the exultant stroke of his heart. If all of life, of knowledge, was so easy for her, why not ever for Boniface?

But again came the defeating realization that there were only starts for him, never finishes. College had been a time of mystery and initiation but where had it led? What had Ira Washburn's false promises amounted to? The times of challenge always withered and dried away for him...

Eric felt a painful dryness in his throat. He needed a whiskey to exorcise this draining self-pity, this invasion of weakening memories that stemmed in equal parts from the fat man's contempt and the conviction of being homeless and unwanted in a home that should have been his...

Stirred by resentment, he reminded himself that self-pity was the crutch, anger the club.

"By God, Jessica, you'll regret it if you've lied to me!" he said, and walked from her room, closing the door and locking it with a click of finality.

When the sound of his footsteps faded, Jessica snapped out the overhead lights, switched on her torch and swung its beams in four quick slashes across the gleaming night-dark window panes.

Eric worked for twenty minutes in Dalworth's study, the Tiffany desk lamp highlighting the figures scribbled rapidly on a paper. The same light found motes in the heavy air and shone in splintered patterns from the gun cabinet. A wind was rising and a rustling sound could be heard through the house, as stiff salt breezes came down the Connemara coast.

Calculations completed, Eric walked into the library where Tony Saxe and Benny Stiff were playing gin rummy at a chess table.

Eric placed sheets of paper in front of each man, then opened the envelope he had received from Ethelroyd and counted out three stacks of British currency, each totaling twelve thousand pounds.

"We will each wager ten thousand pounds in England this weekend," Eric said, "with Betting Commissioners in three separate cities. Benny, you'll take Liverpool, Tony, you'll cover Manchester, Maud and I will be at the Cumberland in London.

"Should the worst occur, if little Miss Crystal's predictions aren't accurate, we'll at least have two thousand pounds each to take us back to the States in luxury."

"But there's no parimutuel betting in England," Benny said.

"I'm aware of that. What's your point?"

"An obvious one. They don't cut up the pie according to the handle that's bet. The odds you get from a Commissioner don't change no matter how much action there is. So why go running around England like jack rabbits?"

"Simply this. The long shots we're betting on aren't touted by any of the top handicappers. And the amounts we're betting could cause gossip."

"Good thinking," Tony Saxe said. "So that leaves just one other thing."

Benny Stiff shook his head slowly. "No—*two* things."

"Very well," Eric said. "Let's take them in order. Tony?"

Saxe glanced at the sheet of paper Eric had given him, checking the three names—Sterling Choice, Overlord, and Primrose. At last he said, "Supposing there's a violation, a flag up after the first results? She only saw the finish, you say. We don't know about a jock caught with phony weights, saliva tests, or some owner screaming foul to a judge."

"I was coming to that. We'll split our bets between the number one and number two horse, Sterling Choice and Overlord. If they foul each other, their position at the finish will simply be reversed. We'll collect either way." Eric looked appraisingly at Benny Stiff. "What's on *your* mind?"

Benny stared at the backs of his hands. "I said it before, it's like back in Camden. You're thinking about the pay-off, not what you got to do to earn it."

"I'm way ahead of you, Benny."

"You better be, because it's as plain as a fly in an ice-cube that just winning that loot doesn't solve our problems. There's still one left and you better know what one I'm talking about."

"I told you, I'm ahead of you." Eric paced the floor, hands clasped behind his back, his eyes gazing at the dark, inlaid ceiling. "In another context, I told you that we were fortunate to be operating in such a simple and credulous country."

Turning, he smiled at them. "It seems there has been a recent curse on Easter Hill. The good people around here believe that in the depths of their souls. The death of the master, Andrew Dalworth, followed into that silent world by his faithful retainer, Mr. Brown. A distraught girl wandering the beaches like a demented thing. And when that same poor child goes riding at dawn, along the treacherous crags of that big cliff up there—well, if anything happens to her—" Eric shrugged and sat down at the chess table. "Well, her death will be laid to the damnable curse that's settled on this house."

He picked up a deck of cards, shuffled them, and dealt out three hands of gin rummy.

"Any other problems, Benny?"

"Not a one," Benny Stiff said, taking up his cards.

A light thump sounded on the roof directly above Jessica's head. As she unlatched the bay windows, thunder swelling around her, another thump sounded on her terrace. Hoisting himself over the sill into her room, Kevin O'Dell's face was hard with anxiety.

Jessica pulled the draperies behind him and snapped on her bedside lamp. Kevin took her shoulders and stared into her face. "Jessica, what in the name of God's going on here?"

"Kevin, keep your voice *down*. *Please*. There's no time to explain." She spoke in an urgent whisper.

"Just listen to me. They murdered Mr. Brown. I saw it happen. You must go to Constable Riley and—"

"I could call him from the stables."

"No, Kevin, no! Get away from Easter Hill. Go quickly, for God's sake."

Kevin gripped her hands. "I can't leave you like this, Jessica. Come with me!"

"Go, I tell you! *Please*! I can't reach the big oak from the roof. If you stay, we're both lost."

Kevin hesitated for an instant, a last tense appeal into her eyes, but seeing the unwavering determination in her expression, he nodded abruptly and touched his hand to her cheek before turning swiftly to the windows.

Jessica closed them behind him, hearing his boots in the heavy ivy, and then his footsteps running lightly above her on the mansard roof.

She murmured a prayer for him as a bolt of lightning struck the horizons beyond Skyhead, garish yellow flares illuminating the black clouds, heavy and roiling with the winds coming in from the sea.

The storms swept north of Ballytone, bending underbrush flat and raking the coarse grass with hail. Liam Mallory looked at the heavens and drew a cross in the air with his gnarled hand, a token of gratitude for this turbulent weather. He had prayed to the gods for it and they had answered him surely.

He was traveling in the county of Mayo with his wife, Corinne, in a four-wheeled pony trap down a rutted road toward the village of Ballytone. He clucked softly to the stout trotting pony who had begun to shy at the cracks of lightning and the thunder rolling down the hillsides.

"The child is in mortal peril," Liam said to his wife, who huddled close to him. "I must stop and pray to the gods for her."

"Why speak of gods? There is only one God, Liam," Corinne Mallory said, and tightened her grip on the wooden rosary looped around her waist.

"Whichever god answers me is the god I'm praying to, woman."

"But there are miles between us and the poor one."

"Aye, I know that well. But the face of evil is clear in my mind, clear enough to thwart, if my gods will it."

She knew he wanted only her silence now. "Aye," she said and watched with resigned eyes as he reined the pony to a stop, climbed from the trap, and stamped across the mud-slick road, his tall, dark frame merging and disappearing into a grove of black aspens.

Liam Mallory knelt and struck the bole of a tree with his thorn-stick and turned his face to the torn skies, a man eight decades and five years beyond the warmth of the cradle hewn by his great-grandfather. The ancient Irishman knelt in the storming weather and prayed to his gods to succor and preserve an innocent child in mortal danger that night.

His prayers were long because his gods were many. A powerful tenet of his myriad faiths held that good and evil, light and darkness, forever waged an equal battle for the souls of man, a conflict undecided until that human prize expired and its soul went to the victor's domicile—the darkness of hell or the lights of heaven.

And to fight and triumph against that always

menacing darkness, a man needed all the gods he could summon. The one created in candlelight, incense, and the priest's chalice at consecration—old Liam prayed first to that God, the dignified Lord who lived behind the Tabernacle's golden doors in all the churches and cathedrals of Ireland. And he prayed to that God's mother, and to all His saints.

But while praying to the traditional Deity and His company, old Liam also pleaded with older gods, the terrible and primitive minions and familiars of all the gods of life—the zephyrs and cooling winds, the raging fires, and clear, still waters, and he begged help and vengeance from other servants of light, the wise and holy Druids who permeated and protected all the valleys and forests of this great green island.

"Never for me, Hyperion and Caveran. Never for us, the Brothers of the Red Branch. It is not that I seek help for ourselves, for such as us have been blessed with your strength—"

His old woman called to him from the cart, her voice wavering in the winds. "Come, Liam. Your endurance is not endless." She knew better than most the ordeal her husband was undergoing, knew that the powers he asked for taxed his human strength.

"Quiet, woman," Liam cried and pounded his staff on the ground. "The girl and I, O Brothers, need your help, draw on your strength as a shield and rod against the evil that threatens her."

The old man's rugged face was coated by a flare of lightning, his next words lost in a drumbeat of thunder. "... her needs now, O Brothers, and the powers that I transfer to her ..."

And with the next roll of thunder, the old man felt

253

a surge of rushing energy within him and, knowing from whence it came, smiled in strained triumph and began a litany of prayers for Jessica Mallory.

When he gasped out the last of these entreaties, Mallory pointed his thorn-stick at the heavens, swinging it toward the jagged lightning above the far-distant mass of land called Skyhead.

He held that pose until his arm trembled with fatigue, then he cursed the evil threatening the girl, and called out her name, his voice ringing above the crash of the elements. Then he shuddered convulsively and fell forward, his body crashing like a tree to the floor of the forest.

Later, Corinne Mallory helped her husband to his feet and guided him back to the pony-trap. Taking the reins in her own hands, her husband's head resting on her shoulder, she set the pony trotting once again along the road to Ballytone.

Chapter Twenty-Six ─────────────────────

When the pain struck her shoulder, Maud Griffith was walking along the corridor to Jessica's bedroom. The ornate gold candelabrum she carried sent leaping lights and shadows in front of her, the reflections glowing on the chinoiserie wallpapers and rich carpets.

The electrical storm had knocked out the power at Easter Hill only minutes before. Benny had tried to activate a generator in the cellar but reported that the auxiliary power source had also been shorted by the lightning marching brilliantly from Skyhead down to Easter Hill and on toward Ballytone.

As the needlepoint of pain pierced the flesh below her collarbone, Maud gasped involuntarily. Her straining nerves were dangerously close to the breaking point. Her high heel caught on a fringe of carpet and she lost her balance, stumbling against the wall. The impact caused a spray of hot, beaded candlewax to fall across the backs of her hands. She cursed softly but violently, a mindless fear in her voice.

Placing the candelabrum on a hall table, Maud brushed the hardening wax from her hands, trying to fight back a rising panic. She felt close to tears, frightened by the surrounding darkness and the feeling that came with pain—a terror brought on by her body's weakness. The smothering blackness in the old house caused the memory of her dreadful dreams to resurface, the cage of musty garments, the sound of her pleading screams, the suffocating fear of impending death.

That presence seemed closer to her now than ever before, persistent and attendant, a spectral finger touching her shoulder with a streak of pain.

There would be no sympathy from Eric. He was furious enough without the burden of her concerns.

Picking up the candles, she walked on to Jessica's room and unlocked the door. "Come with me, dear," she said, raising the candles to illuminate the room.

Jessica turned from the windows and looked steadily at her aunt, her eyes gleaming with opaque fire. "Do you think it's wise to give me orders?"

"Please, Jessica." Maud was suddenly alarmed by the intensity in the girl's expression. But this was nonsense, she thought. She was just a child. How could she harm them?... Maud forced herself to meet Jessica's stare directly. "It's your Uncle Eric. He wants to talk to you. Do come along."

"Yes, and I want to talk to him," Jessica said.

They walked to the head of the stairs, Maud

holding the candelabrum in one hand, the other firmly on Jessica's arm.

Lighted candles stood in holders in the great hall. The yellow flickering illumination fell in shadowed beams into the open doors of the dining room and library.

Maud ushered Jessica into the library. Eric stood at the fireplace, a strange and disturbing smile on his lips.

Jessica's heart lurched when she saw the crumpled figure on the hearthstone, Kevin O'Dell, his face battered and swollen, a trickle of blood running from his parted lips. Kevin's eyes were closed and she could hear his labored breathing above the crackle of the logs.

Eric said pleasantly, "Your conspirator doesn't look quite so formidable now, does he, my dear?"

With easy strength, Jessica pulled herself from Maud and ran to Kevin's side, kneeling and taking his bruised head in her lap.

"It seems he had a little accident, Jessica," Eric's voice sounded strangely muted and distant to her, as if he were speaking from the far end of a tunnel. "Took a nasty fall climbing down from the roof."

"You are lying! He's been struck and beaten, just like Mr. Brown was!"

Eric shrugged and said, "You may be right at that. But we need a simpler story for your yokel Constable."

Footsteps sounded in the great hall. Tony Saxe and Benny came into the library, dressed for travel, Saxe in a top coat and hat, Benny wearing a leather jacket and driving gloves.

"Get-away day," Saxe said to Eric. "But we still got a loose end." With a nod at Kevin's unconscious figure, he said, "We better find out just what the little bitch told him."

Jessica's eyes swept across all of them, an arc of flashing contempt. "You are all brutes and murderers and thieves!"

Eric said, "That may be true but it's beside the point, which is: Did you spill all that to your playmate here?"

"Get out of my home!" Jessica suddenly shouted the words at him.

Eric glanced at Tony Saxe. "Maybe that's all we'll get for an answer."

"Now hold it," Benny said. "I ain't collecting any more scalps unless there's a damn good reason to. Maybe lover boy climbed up to her room for the usual reasons. He sure as hell knew the way."

"We can't take a chance on it," Saxe said. "If that was his only game, he wouldn't have put up the fight he did. So no more talk. Come on, Benny. O'Dell rides with us part of the way..."

"No, you can't move him! I won't let you!" Jessica said, in a deep, quiet voice.

"Be sensible, dear," Maud said, and pulled Jessica to her feet, locking her arms behind her in a grip that forced a cry of pain past the girl's lips.

As she struggled, helpless for an instant, Saxe and Benny Stiff picked up Kevin O'Dell and carried him from the library.

Familiar, brilliant lights began exploding with painful clarity inside Jessica's head. Without being aware of it, she had undergone a radical revision of temperament in only a few brief and bitter days, a

258

subtle metamorphosis of character since the ugly reality of Eric and Maud Griffith had poisoned her life. But even as she felt the sadistic strength in her aunt's hands, Jessica was aware of another shift in her own being, a physical change as significant as the alterations in her mental attitudes. A power was flowing through her slender arms and legs, a transcendant energy that seemed to take its own source from the elements of sea and wind and fields beyond Easter Hill.

In a strange fury, in a rage that was in league with the storms outside and inside her, Jessica cried out, *"You will all die for the evil you have done! You are doomed and terrible! You won't profit a farthing from your schemes!"*

"Shut up, you little fool," Maud said, tightening her grip so that Jessica flinched and arched her back against the pain.

"Those men will die—"

"Shut up, I tell you!" Maud cried. "Shut *up*, Jessica!"

"—in pain and fire," Jessica said, the pictures blazingly clear in her mind, terrible and final—a kaleidoscope of leaping flames, patterns glowing like neon, and other colors that were smooth and pale, a curve of white-hot ivory arching above the picture like a poised scimitar.

Jessica heard the front door slam and felt a stinging pain as Eric slapped her across the face. The lights in her mind splintered and receded and Jessica stared with growing anger at her uncle.

"Frankly, I don't believe you," Eric said. "You're just trying to frighten your Aunt Maud..."

From the driveway, they heard the sound of an

engine starting up, then a staccato noise as the car headed out the curving driveway.

Eric regarded Jessica with narrowing eyes. "But since you're so free with your malicious information, supposing you tell us *how* they're going to die."

"Benny Stiff dies in a cage of steel and fire—"

The change in Jessica's voice had become so pronounced by now, low and rolling and defiant, that Eric felt a stir of fear.

"I don't want to hear any more of this," Maud said shrilly, a tic pulling rhythmically at the corner of her mouth. She tightened her grip on Jessica's wrist, determined to silence her. But the girl wheeled, breaking the grip with a burst of numbing strength, hurling her aside with an almost effortless swing of her arm. The older woman staggered back, her face drained of color, collapsing into a couch as her knees struck the edge of a coffee table.

Jessica drew a deep breath, her presence filling the room, the luminous glow in her eyes matching the pictures in her mind.

"And Mr. Saxe can't escape," she said, and her voice was so vibrant that Eric could feel it shaking the floors of the old library. "None of you can escape... after Mr. Saxe breathes his last on the tusks of an elephant!"

This sudden, improbable announcement galvanized Eric to action. He always looked for the coward's advantage, to attack from behind or from shadows, striking then without mercy, for something in him quailed at the thought of an adversary striking back at him.

And when Maud gasped in terror and the child

turned swiftly to her, Eric whipped off his ascot scarf and slipped it powerfully about her throat, tightening it until Jessica's face flushed and she sagged against him, inert and unconscious after a helpless struggle....

Eric said to Maud, "She was obviously bluffing, the business about the elephant's tusk. If she'd come up with something reasonable, I might have gone after them and warned them."

He looked down at Jessica's slack body, face and hands white against the floor.

"We'll just make bloody sure she doesn't hurt anybody with these temper fits." Caution stirred in him as he remembered his first sudden fear of the child. There was something here he didn't understand, but he was cunning enough to respect it. "And get one other thing into your silly head," he said to Maud. "Don't listen to her anymore. Don't even talk to her. For some damned reason, she seems to get to you..."

Later that evening, Father Malachy left his parish rectory and crossed a walk to the ivy-dark church whose doors had not been locked shut for more than two centuries. Kneeling in a rear pew, the priest made the Sign of the Cross on his lips and began a prayer for the repose of the soul of Capability Brown.

Vigil lights glowed near the altar. There was the scent of incense on the cold air.

Old Brown had fought for his country, the priest was thinking, not intoxicated with the heavy anodyne of flags and martial music but in fields and woods and back streets, hunted like an animal by

261

Ireland's enemies, and now he was gone. God rest his soul.

A draft of cold air stirred about his head. His housekeeper's slippered footsteps sounded on the stone aisle. The old woman leaned forward to whisper in his ear.

"Dear, merciful Christ!" Father Malachy said, and repeated the Sign of the Cross on the breast of his black cassock.

"Do come quickly, Father," his housekeeper said. "It's a scene from Hell itself..."

Chapter Twenty-Seven ——————————

Eric Griffith descended to the great hall and walked into the library. Maud sat on the arm of a chair, massaging the worrisome pain in her shoulder.

Eric surveyed with satisfaction his flickering image in the brass facings that framed the fireplace. Another loose end neatly tied up, he thought, and smiled at the play on words. Two pairs of Maud's nylons and a swatch of adhesive tape had done the trick, and there would be no more threats or dangerous behavior from milady, Jessica, who now lay trussed up in her bedroom behind a securely locked door.

"I'm worried, Eric."

"What about? I can't see a cloud on the horizon." He glanced at his watch. "Saxe and Benny are just about airborne by now. One last detail and we'll be on our way, Maud—" His voice sharpened. "—with an honest-to-god shot at the jackpot."

"That's not what I'm talking about." She looked at him resentfully, wincing as she touched the flesh below her collarbone. "Ever since the lights went out, I've had a terrible pain like a needle in my shoulder."

Eric made an effort to mask his exasperation. It was just like her to pick a time like this for one of her neurotic attacks.

"I suggest you get hold of yourself, Maudie."

"Stop using that tone. I'm not some kind of hypochondriac freak."

"But you're always worked up about something. Now it's your shoulder."

"I'm worried sick, damn it!"

"Ah-ha! Now you've put your finger on it. You're not worried because you're *sick*. You're sick because you're worried."

A clap of thunder sounded and Maud started nervously. The window panes trembled, creating a singing hum on the air. A gust of wind from the fireplace caused the lighted candles to flicker erratically, sending shadows leaping about the tiered room.

"God, I've come to hate this place!" Maud said.

"Steady, old girl. We're almost home free. The first thing in London, we'll get you to a doctor—not just the hotel chap; I'll call a specialist. Meanwhile, I've got a job for you.

"I want you to write a cheerful note to Jessica. We'll both sign it. Tell her how much we've liked being here—" Pacing, Eric composed his thoughts. "Tell her how much we enjoyed meeting her friends, Miss Bostwick and old Ryan. Say we're taking the early flight from Shannon to London and will be at the Cumberland. Didn't want to disturb her at such an ungodly hour and so forth.

"Assure her that we're eager to have her visit us in the States the first chance she gets. Then close with love and best wishes for health and happiness from her auntie and uncle."

Eric made a drink and raised the glass to Maud. "You see, it is absolutely *essential* that the authorities conclude that the child took her last ride up the cliffs *after* you and I left for Shannon Airport."

"Eric, will you really help me find a specialist in London?"

"You have my word on it."

Eric left the library and went into the drawing room off the great hall. This elegant room faced the driveway and park. Candles created cones of warm light in the corners, providing a feeling of sanctuary against the storm still battering the trees and walls of the mansion.

Eric drank several whiskeys. The dark thought of what lay ahead blurred by the liquor, he slumped into his chair, his head lolling back against the leather cushion.

His thoughts were slow and drowsy. The sequence of events was inevitable. He enjoyed seeing them parade in measured cadences through his lulled consciousness.

There would be a funeral mass, of course, here where she had lived most of her life, lamentation for the soul borne to her final resting place in the cemetery. He would be there, of course, the devoted uncle, eyes flushed with tears, steadying himself with

265

a hand on old Ryan's arm. Whispers around them . . . "He's an American, her uncle is. They were very close."

And then as the seasons wheeled, Boniface might stay on here, somewhere in the neighborhood, a snug home with a view of the sea perhaps, servants, and enough land for a few good horses. There was salmon fishing. He had never tried that and he imagined he would fancy it. And riding on frosty mornings, the horse's hooves like iron on the hard ground, the village lads would greet him with quick smiles. . . .

The empty glass slipped from his fingers and dropped with a muffled thump onto the carpeting.

Maud sat at the desk in Andrew Dalworth's private study. Attempting without success to ignore the storm sounding around the house, she completed the letter Eric had requested her to write to Jessica, signing it—"with all love, Auntie Maud," leaving room for Eric's signature under hers.

It was then that the phone on Dalworth's desk rang shrilly, like a file rasping across her straining nerves.

Clearing her throat, she picked up the receiver and said as casually as she could manage, "Yes? This is Easter Hill . . ."

A voice she had heard before but was at a loss to place said, "To whom would I be speaking?"

"Mrs. Eric Griffith."

"Mrs. Griffith, there's been an accident in—"

"Who is this?" Maud said sharply.

"Begging your pardon, madam, this is Constable Riley calling from Ballytone. If you recall, we had the opportunity to meet on another occasion."

"What's happened? What are you trying to tell me?"

"I'm sorry, Mrs. Griffith, but I have quite shocking news. An elderly couple was driving a pony trap up the high street this evening. A black convertible passed them at high speed, causing the horse to rear, and something must have happened to the—"

"Can't you speak up? Was someone hurt?" Maud demanded.

"It's queer, the old couple escaped without a scratch, but—May I ask you, are you seated, ma'am?"

"Yes." Maud whispered.

Listening, she sank slowly into the deep chair behind Dalworth's desk.

Jessica lay on the bed in her room in the darkness, tightly drawn loops of nylon binding her wrists and ankles. Her eyes were closed and she was staring at an inner vision, dappled in brilliant lights and threaded with shifting, monstrous shadows. What she saw was so potentially senseless and violent that the vistas brought a sting of tears to her eyes.

She heard quick footsteps outside her door. Then the knob turned back and forth, desperately but futilely.

Standing outside Jessica's room, Maud twisted the handle of the door helplessly, a sob sounding in her throat. The upper floors of Easter Hill were dark with shadows. Only a shifting illumination from the candelabra in the great hall penetrated the gloom of the staircase.

Maud turned and ran toward that uncertain light, the slim silver scissors she had taken from Dalworth's desk gripped in her hand.

Descending the stairs, she crossed the hall quickly, silently. In the drawing room, she cautiously approached Eric's sleeping figure, listening to heavy breathing that caused a rhythmic bubble of saliva to rise and break on his lips.

Moving his arm gingerly, Maud went through the pockets of his jacket, finding coins, a cigarette lighter, a roll of peppermints. She moved around the chair and checked his vest pockets, watching his flushed features and lidded eyes for any response to her searching fingers.

Maud found what she was looking for, the key to Jessica's room, in his lapel pocket behind a display handkerchief. Fishing it out, she rose and tiptoed swiftly from the salon, her heart pounding like some wild animal caged behind her ribs. With a heavy candlestick, Maud went quickly up the stairs, the soft light from the candle revealing the pallor that had spread in her cheeks since she had first heard the sound of Constable Riley's voice.

Unlocking the door to her niece's room, Maud placed the candlestick on a bureau from where its flame enclosed the bound child in a cone of light. Maud sat beside Jessica on the bed and used the scissors to cut away the swatch of adhesive tape across her lips.

"I've been your friend, I haven't hurt you," Maud said, her voice strained. She was trembling so that the scissors almost slipped from her fingers. Placing them on the bedside table, she brushed a strand of hair from Jessica's forehead. "You must help me!

For God's sake, please! All my life I've been afraid of dying."

Maud laughed softly, a fragile sound which echoed the terror glittering in her eyes. "It's not knowing *when* it will happen, that's what terrifies me. I don't care *how much* time I've got left. But I've got to know *when*. Please tell me, Jessica."

Maud knelt on the floor, her hands locked in front of her. "Please help me . . . I want to know where I'll be when it happens, what I'll be doing. I can't bear to be taken by surprise . . ."

Jessica said quietly, "I'm sorry, Aunt Maud."

"Don't say that! You said *they* were going to die. You knew exactly how it would happen."

"I know what will happen to people if they won't stop what they're doing or change their courses—and *you won't change* . . ."

"I don't believe you! Why are you lying to me? *I've got to know.*"

A hinge creaked behind them and the door was shoved open unexpectedly. "All right, Maud. Get on your feet." The words were slurred, and Eric swayed as he entered the room, a hand reaching for support to the carved bedstead.

His eyes narrowed as he stared at Maud, still kneeling beside Jessica, an expression of shock and fear on her face.

"Supposing you tell me what kind of deal you're trying to cook up with the little princess here."

"Eric, I've talked to Constable Riley in Ballytone. He—"

"What a busy lady you are, Maud. Picking my pockets for the key, sneaking up here to conspire with Jessica the minute my back was turned. Why,

Maud? *Why*? What were you hoping to find out?"

"Goddammit, didn't you hear me?" Maud said, screaming the words at him. "Constable Riley telephoned while you were dead drunk, lost to the world. They aren't on their way to England, Eric. They aren't on their way anywhere. They're lying dead right now in Ballytone."

"What . . . what're you saying? Who're you talking about?" Eric's expression was baffled, his voice stuttering in confusion. "Not to England—what in hell do you mean, Maud?"

"I mean *they're all dead*, Eric. *That's* what I mean! Tony Saxe, Benny Stiff, and that kid they took with them, they were all killed in a freak car crash down in the village."

Jessica closed her eyes and said, "Not Kevin," in a soft, ambiguous whisper.

"Yes, all of them," Maud said. "And Tony and Benny Stiff died exactly as she said they would. Benny died in flames, trapped in the car when it flipped over and the gas tank exploded. But Tony Saxe was thrown out right in front of the Hannibal Arms. He went right through the plate glass window—" Maud laughed shakily and pointed at Jessica. "That's right, Eric. *Just like she told us!* Tony Saxe landed on that big elephant tusk right at the end of the bar. Just as Jessica predicted, that's how Tony died . . . gored to death by the tusk of an elephant."

The full impact was cushioned for Eric by the liquor he had absorbed. Narcotized by strong spirits, he was aware most forcefully of only one thing. That was the fact that *here* was indisputable truth that his niece could, in fact, foretell the future. With that realization, he could feel the surge of adrenalin charging through his body.

"Good God, Maud! Don't you see what this means? No, no, you don't," he said, the words running together with his excitement. "It means that the horses she gave us for the Grand National are good as gold!"

Suddenly Eric struck his forehead with the palm of his hand. "Oh, my God! What happened to the money? What happened to all our *money*, Maud?"

"I was too frightened to think about that."

"Jesus Christ! That's the first thing you should have asked the Constable about... *the money*. It's more important than ever now, because now we don't have to split it three ways."

As the flash-point of his anger subsided, Eric realized it had been therapeutic. It had burned away the whiskey fumes crowding his mind. Clear-headed and alert, he said, "Put that tape back on her mouth and get downstairs. We've got work to do."

After he had gone, Maud turned and stared at Jessica.

"Why won't you help me? Why should I be so frightened of death? Can't you even tell me *that*?"

In the new deep tones that so terrified Maud, Jessica said: "If you fear the question, then you must fear the answer. *I will tell you only this: As long as Uncle Eric lives, you shall live longer still.*"

"You can't leave it like that!" Maud said, trembling with excitement. "You must tell me—*how long he will live ...*"

"I will give you this knowledge," Jessica said. "His death will dissolve your every fear, give you the freedom you so long for."

Maud looked intently at her, feeling a numbing chill as she noticed the strange, knowing smile curving the girl's lips. Then she felt faint, her knees trembling with fatigue.

Dreading the next answer, she said, "You know that I'm terrified, Jessica. And now even Eric is afraid. He's pretending... but he is afraid. You know something else we don't. I can tell from your eyes. *You're not afraid, are you? You're not afraid, damn you!*"

"Only for you," Jessica said in tones that broke the last straining links of Maud's control.

"Oh, dear God!" Maud said in a ragged voice. She grabbed the candlestick and ran from the room, hurrying unsteadily through the shadows to the staircase.

Thunder broke above Easter Hill. A flaring bolt of lightning flooded the gardens with brightness, shimmering on brass weather-vanes and the wet panes of the house, falling in erratic patterns through the draperies of Jessica's bedroom. The spreading radiance traced glowing streaks along the silver scissors that lay close to Jessica on the night table.

Chapter Twenty-Eight ——————

When Maud ran into the library, she saw that Eric was in the adjacent study at Dalworth's desk, speaking into the telephone. Holding the candlestick high to guide her, she hurried to join him, seeing then the patronizing smile which usually accompanied his adoption of a successful charade.

"Please be good enough to tell Constable Riley I am most grateful," he was saying. "My wife and I are leaving within an hour for Shannon. We'll stop at your office on the way to collect our money. And, of course—" Eric smiled across the phone at Maud. "—we'll leave something tangible as a gesture of our appreciation."

After a pause, he added, "No, I don't have an address in the States for them. Mr. Saxe and Mr. Stiff were casual acquaintances, you understand. I suggest you contact the American Embassy in

Dublin for that information."

Replacing the receiver, Eric said, "Benny Stiff's pounds quite literally went up in smoke, but Tony's wallet and its contents are intact and in good hands. That was Riley's clerk I just spoke with. He bought my explanation without a quibble. I told the good man that Tony Saxe was acting as our agent, carrying a large sum of our cash to purchase certain real estate in England. I added, of course, that I had Mr. Saxe's fully legal receipt for said monies, which we'll just make out and sign before we leave for the village."

"Eric, forget the money. We can't—"

"Are you out of your mind? Maud, have you any concept of what twenty thousand pounds pays off on a fifty-to-one shot? We're talking about a million pounds, Maud. Nothing else matters now."

"Damn you, listen to me!"

"Maud, I'm warning you . . . I'm almost out of patience."

"I talked to Jessica. She said she isn't—"

"You idiot! I told you not to listen to her!"

Maud slammed her open hand down on the desk top. The sound was startlingly loud, echoing away to the corners of the murky room. "Shut *up*, Eric! Try to understand what I'm telling you. The child has changed before our eyes. She's strong, so strong I'm afraid to touch her. *She must know everything!* She told me she isn't frightened about what will happen to her tonight. She insists she has *no reason to be*. For God's sake, don't you understand what that means?"

"I'll tell you what it means. It means she's a fool and you're a bigger fool."

Eric signed his name to the bottom of the letter Maud had written to Jessica. Folding it into a neat square, he printed Jessica's name on it in block capitals. Tucking it into his shirt pocket, he unlocked the gun cabinet with a key he had commandeered from old Flynn, and chose a small calibre Belgian handgun with silver filigree and inlaid ivory handgrips. Opening a drawer inside the cabinet, he selected a clip of appropriate ammunition and inserted it into the butt of the gun.

"Eric, *please*. Let's clear out now . . ."

"You're more than a fool, Maud. You're gutless."

"We still have time—"

Eric closed the door of the gun cabinet and locked it. When he turned the automatic in his hand, he swung it around to point it at a spot just above the third button of her light gray jacket. She looked uneasily at the gun barrel and then put a hand to her throat.

"Eric, please . . ." Her voice was almost lost in a sudden break of thunder. "Just listen to me."

"No, goddamn it, you listen to *me*, Maud! This is my chance, the only one I've ever had and nothing's going to stop me now. With you or without you, I'm going for it. You've let that little bitch upstairs talk you into a galloping case of nerves. She's in her bedroom, trussed up like the Christmas goose, can't move hand or foot. Our job now is to jam her into boots and riding clothes, lead her and her horse up the hills to the cliff."

Eric turned the gun away from Maud, glanced at the play of candlelight along the barrel. "Imagine how Windkin will take off when I fire a few rounds from this beauty around its hooves."

They stared at one another through the flaring candlelight and then Eric said matter-of-factly, "Well, luv. What's it going to be? In or out? Play the cards I've dealt and we'll be home free in a suite in London tomorrow morning, on the phone to room service for a hot breakfast and then off to see a Harley Street specialist."

Maud nodded slowly. In a weary voice she said, "I'll help you, Eric, but for God's sake, let's get it over with."

She turned quickly then, holding the candlestick and glowing taper above her head. Eric followed her from the study into the library which was full of erratic shadows, some sent leaping by draft-stirred candles, others from the lightning that flashed through the heavy trees.

Eric pressed the sides of Jessica's note, crimping them so that the letter would stand upright like a small tent. When they went through the arches of the library into the great hall, Eric strode to the table beside the main entrance, placing the letter prominently on the silver tray set out for calling cards.

Standing in the gloom beyond the circle of Maud's candle, Eric wondered who would be the first to see the letter—the Constable perhaps, or the Bostwick woman, or Mr. Ryan; and who would put through the distressful telephone call to the child's uncle and aunt at the Cumberland Hotel....

The house was fittingly silent at the moment, Eric thought, the stillness marred only by the sounds of the storm and the tapping of Maud's high heels across the parquet floor.

As Eric turned, his mood poignant and reflective, Maud began screaming, the sounds beating like frantic flails against the carved walls and ceilings.

Eric wheeled around and saw Jessica Mallory standing motionless on the top landing of the great stairs, her face pale above her twill jacket, her dark hair brushed back, and the silken tips falling to her shoulders. There was a calm but almost hypnotic expression on her face. Her eyes were luminous and foreboding. The spectral concentration in her manner, a blend of energy and resignation to her visions, caused Eric's breath to become suddenly ragged.

He braced himself but took an involuntary step backwards as Jessica started down the long stairs, placing each foot down neatly and precisely, as formally as a young lady descending to join her partner at a hunt ball.

With an effort, he cried out, "Talk now, Maud, and talk plain and fast. What are you and this little bitch up to?"

"God, don't blame me, Eric. I didn't free her!"

"Stop lying to me! Or you'll take the same goddamn ride she's heading for!"

Jessica continued down the stairs, stopping on the last step of the staircase, her eyes almost level with theirs.

"No, I'm not going riding tonight, Uncle Eric. I'm leaving you now. They're waiting for me," she said.

Eric smiled at her but there was no humor in his eyes or on his lips. His expression was ugly and bitter, the menace emphasized by the false smile. "Do you honestly think, Miss Crystal, that I'm going to step aside and let you walk out of here?"

"I'm not concerned or worried about anything you can say or do, Uncle Eric."

"I told you! I *told* you, Eric!"

"Damn it, Maud, shut up *now*." Eric said. With the unpleasant smile flaring like a rictus on his face, he took the small automatic from his pocket and said to Jessica, "Just focus your attention on this gun then."

To his dismay, Eric heard a new and tentative tone in his voice, the gun gave him no sense of assurance, no familiar swell of authority or power. It would be different, he knew, if there was fear in those eyes, if she were begging and pleading with him to spare her life—but no, she had stepped down to the parquet floor and was walking without haste to the double doors as if she were not even aware of the steel threat in his hands, the muzzle pointed squarely at her slim spine.

"Stop, Jessica."

She turned her back on them and pulled open the double doors that opened on the terraces and park of the estate. A gusting wind blew her hair out behind her and caused Maud's candle to gutter and smoke, creating grotesque shadows on the walls and ceilings and up the empty, shining staircase.

"But I can damned well stop *you*!" Eric said, and trained the gun squarely and inexorably on her slender figure.

"No, Eric! Don't!" Maud's voice was a hoarse cry and the light from her candle glinted on the desperate tension in her eyes. With her free hand, she pointed insistently through the huge open doors.

Flashes of light streaked the darkness, yellow lances boring into the curtaining rain. "It's too late, Eric!" she cried as the first cars of a small convoy turned off the Ballytone road into the driveway of Easter Hill.

Jessica started down the broad steps to the lower terraces, and Eric, features working emotionally, steadied his hands, slowly increasing the pressure on the trigger.

Maud shouted at him again, a wordless cry of anger, and threw the heavy candlestick and flaming taper into his face.

The brass base struck his shoulder and jarred him off balance, and his two shots, shatteringly loud in the confines of the hall, went through the open doors and spent themselves harmlessly in the crowns of distant trees.

The burning candle had struck Eric's cheek. Arms flailing, he fell sprawling to the floor, the gun clattering from his hands. Scrambling to his feet, he reached for the automatic, his thoughts chaotic with panic and rage, unable to absorb the shocking fact that he'd lost, that he would never stand with cheering crowds and watch his horses charging on to victory. No winners' circle, no smiling bank tellers, no silver trophies for Eric Boniface Mallory—not now or ever...

Slamming the big doors shut, he saw in the instant before they closed that several cars had pulled into the circular driveway where Jessica waited for them near the bronze sundial on the flagged terrace.

Eric sagged against the doors, his breathing shallow in the sudden silence.

Yes, Boniface had lost but it wasn't, in truth, his fault. Everything he had wanted and worked for lay smashed in pieces around him, and there would soon be an even greater price to pay, the vulgar curiosity of jurymen, the humiliating contempt of a judge.

If only Maud hadn't lied to him and betrayed him. Boniface had had the brains and nerve, the style and the imagination, to conceive and bring this off, the flash of courage in a pinch, yes, and the grace to savor the rewards.

She had been on the little bitch's side all along, the two of them against Boniface.

With a smile in his voice, he called out, "Maud?"

He saw that the library was dark, and knew that Maud had pinched out the candles. Moving cautiously, he slipped through the arched doorway, freezing when he heard the delicate sound of glass breaking, falling in a tinkling cadence to the floor.

Not a window, he thought, the sound was too fragile. He knew then where she was—in the study adjoining the library. And he knew what she had shattered.

Crouching, Eric ran forward and dropped behind a fan-backed chair. He needed illumination now, to tell him where she was hiding. Raising his gun, he fired twice into the embers of the fireplace, the bullets slamming into the smouldering logs and bringing them alive, creating spurting bursts of flames in whose spreading glow he saw Maud's dark figure run through the door from Dalworth's study into the library.

Eric swung the gun and fired two shots at her. A scream burst from Maud's lips. When she dropped from sight, he stood and walked deliberately toward the illumination thrown up by the glowing logs, so thoroughly avenged, so sensuously elated that he never even heard the next shot that sounded, and hardly felt the bullet that ripped into his body and sent him spinning to the carpeted floor.

With an hysterical moan, Maud stepped from behind draperies and ran through the dark library, stopping only to fling the ornate dueling pistol aside and to stare for an instant in horror at her husband's carved and motionless features.

And then, heart pounding like a frantic drum, Maud ran on into the great hall and with clawing fingers unbolted the doors and flung them open, flinching as the wind and rain stung her face.

She saw cars parked on the gravel crescent, lights spearing the darkness, men and women climbing from them and running toward Jessica. A white bandage caught the light and she saw Kevin O'Dell with the others—The Irish groom, she thought, with another stab of betrayal. They had lied about that to her, O'Dell was all right, and Jessica had known it. On one car a blue light flashed and Maud saw there were officers standing near it in wet black slickers, carrying rifles.

Maud started down the rain-slick steps, calling plaintively to Jessica. "Please, please, help me! *Jessica*! Tell them it's not time for me to die—"

Maud cried out to Jessica again, screaming the words now, begging her to listen, but the scene was suddenly like a nightmare, a dreadful, paralyzing dream filled with stark, uncaring people—no matter how much you begged them for help or pleaded for mercy, no kind hand reached out to unlock that terrible door...

Her sandal slipped, her ankle turned, and she fell to her hands and knees, gasping at the impact of the cold, stone steps. Pain streaked through her bruised hands. As tears started in her eyes, she saw that one of the figures below had turned a powerful flashlight on her, and all of them were waving and gesturing. She could see mouths opening and closing in white faces, but their words were lost in the winds.

Then Maud realized that they were not pointing to her at all, but toward something behind her in the darkness. When she turned and looked up the steps, Eric stood there in the double doors of the mansion, a dark wetness gleaming against his white shirt, his face twisted with agony, and his arm extended toward her, the candlelight in the hall reflecting in the wet pavement and on the silver filigree of the gun.

But after an instant that seemed stretched to an eternity, Eric Griffith staggered and fell forward to his knees, the hand holding the gun dropping slowly an inch at a time toward the ground. He was staring at her, she saw, his eyes bright points of malice in his white face.

After a straining instant, he shook his head wearily. When his eyelids began to close, Maud laughed with relief, the sound mingling with the driving rain, because she remembered then what Jessica had prophesized—*had promised her*—that Eric would die before her—and Maud's laughter was an astonished accompaniment to the unfolding of that prophecy.

And what was the rest of it?...that he would somehow give her a release.

It was all coming true, she thought, as Eric fell forward on the wetly shining terrace, his gun-hand slamming against the flagstones in what seemed like a last gesture of frustration and defiance, the long fingers clenching in a gesture of fierce rigor mortis.

Maud heard the crack of the gun through a rill of thunder, but it wasn't until she felt the wet stones against her cheek that she realized she had been shot, and she knew that because she was surprised in a hurt and childish fashion by the intensity of the pain.

As she began to lose consciousness, she lay very still, watching the blood from her wound mingle with the rain water on the steps of Easter Hill. Maud tried to laugh but that hurt too much. She pressed her lips tightly together and let the laughter surface only in her mind where it seemed to circle with the sound of excited, springtime birds.

What amused Maud so strangely in her last moments of awareness—Constable Riley was beside her then, hand gentle on her shoulder, she was aware of that, too—was the superb irony of Jessica's second prediction, the prediction that Eric would somehow bring her freedom from the fear of death, which he had done (oh, yes—oh, yes) by freeing her from life itself....

Jessica stood alone, the flash of visions still gleaming in her eyes, her face illuminated by the sinister play of lightning above the trees. She stared back at the gray facade of Easter Hill and at the slack figures of Maud and Eric Griffith sprawled on the terrace below it.

Jessica's lips began to move slowly as she said a fated farewell to the innocent child she had once been. And then she found herself speaking aloud, her eyes shining, her voice soft and clear.

Collect our moments,
heaven's melding fire.
The time is ours.

I am what I am.
We have chosen...

DISPOSABLE PEOPLE
By Marshall Goldberg, M.D.
(Author of Critial List)
and Kenneth Kay

PRICE: $2.25 BT51574
CATEGORY: Novel (Original)

The ultimate thriller, in which today's medical and political morality determines for millions—who shall live and who shall die!

A disease more horrifying than the Black Plague rages out of control. In a mighty effort to contain it, Dr. Noah Blanchard is assigned by the President to head the Epidemic Task Force. When the hard choices have to be made, doctors and politicians are forced into a sinister plot to choose the "Disposable People."

DEATH OF A SCAVENGER
By Keith Spore

PRICE: $2.25   BT51465
CATEGORY: Mystery (Original)

Dr. Hugo Enclave takes on only the most clever
and cunning crimes, and is intrigued by those
considered unsolvable by the police. Enclave set
out to unravel the tangled threads surrounding the
death of Harland Rockmore, an investigator for a
law firm, whose body was found near his boss's
home after a scavenger hunt. Enclave moves
through a torturous labyrinth of murder, mayhem
and mystery to uncover a conspiracy aimed at
the White House itself!

THE CLAIRVOYANT
By Hans Holzer

PRICE: $2.25 T51573
CATEGORY: Novel (Hardcover publisher:
Mason/Charter 1976)

The story of a beautiful young Viennese girl whose
gift of prophecy took her from the mountains of
Austria to the glittering drawing rooms of Beverly
Hills. She began to exhibit psychic powers at the
age of four. Terrified of their daughter's "gift," her
parents sent her to a remote school. As she moved
from school to school and then from man to man,
she used her psychic abilities to climb to perilous
heights of fame and success!

Author of the best-selling
Murder In Amityville

SEND TO: **TOWER PUBLICATIONS**
P.O. BOX 270
NORWALK, CONN. 06852

PLEASE SEND ME THE FOLLOWING TITLES:

Quantity	Book Number	Price

**IN THE EVENT THAT WE ARE OUT OF STOCK
ON ANY OF YOUR SELECTIONS, PLEASE LIST
ALTERNATE TITLES BELOW:**

Postage/Handling

I enclose...

FOR U.S. ORDERS, add 50c for the first book and 10c for each additional book to cover cost of postage and handling. Buy five or more copies and we will pay for shipping. Sorry, no C.O.D.'s.

FOR ORDERS SENT OUTSIDE THE U.S.A., add $1.00 for the first book and 25c for each additional book. PAY BY foreign draft or money order drawn on a U.S. bank, payable in U.S. ($) dollars.

☐ **PLEASE SEND ME A FREE CATALOG.**

NAME_____

(Please print)

ADDRESS_____

CITY_____**STATE**_____**ZIP**_____

Allow Four Weeks for Delivery